RIGHT PLACE WRONG TIME

TOM WARD

Published by Compass-Publishing UK 2022
ISBN 978-1-913713-96-6

Cover photo by © Colin Hyslop Photography

Designed by The Book Refinery Ltd
www.thebookrefinery.com

A CIP catalogue record for this book is available from the British Library.

For Freya & Cairo. The best grandchildren a grandfather could wish for. I love you both, dearly.

1

Benny Fox isn't exactly what you'd call conventional. He has his own understanding of what's right and what's wrong and not everyone would agree with him.

Benny is a thief. Let's start there. To be specific, he is a modern version of an old-fashioned cat burglar. He has been for over thirty years, and he's never been caught. Not once. He's never been questioned by the police so I would say, by definition, that means he's good at what he does.

I say Benny isn't conventional and here's the reason.

He would think nothing of stealing every penny he could from a Post Office or a Building Society or anywhere else that carried a lot of cash. In fact, he has done so on numerous occasions.

The same man, however, would spend half the day tracking down the lady or man who's purse or wallet he'd found in the street, just to make sure they were safely returned.

Benny would tell us it was okay to take from institutions, but he wouldn't dream of taking a penny from an ordinary Joe. The irony in that was lost on him.

Another irony lost on Benny was that in the purse or wallet scenario, he would never consider handing either into a police station. You could say he is something of an enigma.

"They're all corrupt, and they can't be trusted." That's what he would tell you.

For a man in his early fifties, he is wearing exceptionally well. He keeps himself in good shape, running or swimming most days. He eats well, doesn't drink or smoke or do drugs and as a consequence he is as fit, if not fitter, than most men in their forties or even thirties.

Benny lives on the other side of the River Kelvin from the Botanic Gardens in a red sandstone on Glasgow's Kelvin Drive. The turreted swollen bay window provides a corner aspect that looks down on to the entrance to the Kelvin Walkway and further on to Hyndland, Hillhead and the rest of the ever-sprawling West End. It's amazing how far the 'West End' stretches these days, depending on what estate agent you speak with.

He purposely keeps himself to himself and doesn't mix with his neighbours. It's not that he is anti-social. He is very much the opposite and enjoys a wide and varied circle of friends who he meets with regularly. He simply wants to maintain a level of detachment between his neighbours and his personal life.

Benny is a widower with one adult daughter, Stacey, and two grandsons who live in Surrey. They moved there eight years ago when his son in law, Gary, secured a senior management job with an international pharmaceutical company. Despite the miles, they've always kept in regular contact thanks to Skype and Facetime. More recently, it's Teams and Zoom.

It was only three years previous that Benny's wife Emma was tragically taken from him in the most needless and senseless way imaginable. It was the very epitome of being in the wrong place at the wrong time. She had stepped out of a corner shop, walked no more than twenty yards and realised she had come away without the very thing she had gone in for. She turned and made her way back towards the shop.

What happened next could be described as fortunate or unfortunate. It was a matter of perspective.

She died instantly, according to the first responders. As she reached the front door of the shop, an HGV truck left the road and took her with it as it smashed through the front of the building. It came to rest almost twenty feet inside the store with a trail of carnage and destruction in its wake.

Three people, including Emma, died and a further five people sustained injuries ranging from minor to critical.

Later, that statistic changed from three dead and five injured to four dead and four injured.

There were several eyewitness accounts that provided varying versions of what happened. There were however, two standout points on which no one disagreed.

Emma Fox never saw the truck as it came from behind. One moment she was there, the next, she wasn't. Small mercies.

The other undisputed point was that the driver had been texting at the time, and that was the only reason he crashed. An investigation was undertaken by specialists from Police Scotland Roads Policing Unit which confirmed this conclusively. There were no other vehicles involved, no change in road conditions, no adverse weather. Nothing. A stupid driver, a mobile phone, a fully laden 42-tonne truck and four dead bodies.

The driver had been a full-time employee of a well-known national logistics company for six years. There was no question of it being anything other than what it was. The outcome was that the families would receive significant compensation and the driver would get a nine-year prison sentence.

The logistics company settled out of court with the families each receiving six-figure sums.

The media reported it such, that suggested the bigger the restitution figure, the more acceptable it somehow was for having lost a loved one.

To date, Benny hadn't spent a penny of that money. This wasn't a decision based on morals or ethics or principles. Popular fiction might refer to it as 'blood money'. It was nothing to do with any of this. Quite simply, he didn't need it. He was self-sufficient from his nefarious activities. That money, and a lot more besides, was secured away for his daughter and grandsons.

It was a beautiful morning, seasonally untypical for the time of year. It was October, nearer the end of autumn than the start and the pace towards winter was gaining momentum. The very best of summer seemed such a long time past and the first sign it was over was the disappearance of the migratory birds. Benny noticed things like that. Next came the drop in temperatures, the change of foliage colour and more recently the shorter days and longer nights.

A subsequence of colder days is that the air doesn't hold as much water. A consequence of that, is that the sky can take on the bluest of azure-like blue. That was how the sky looked today.

Benny locked his front door and came down the stairway, taking the steps two at a time. His block was fortunate enough to have the original Art Nouveau tiles all the way up each floor and not just on the main landing. Overall, the whole building was an impressive piece of architecture, and the location was sought after.

Quietly closing the main door behind him, he looked up and down the street before moving on down the steps. The only movement he saw was the postman delivering letters a few doors along. There was nothing sinister or clandestine at play. Checking out the street was for no reason other than habit. He wasn't hiding from anyone.

Benny didn't have a car and he took the bus or the subway most places. Of the people that knew him, most assumed he couldn't drive. That wasn't the case, he could. He just chose not to have a car. What he did have, was a motorbike. A Diablo Black Kawasaki Z1000SX, to be precise.

He never kept it at his home. If there was no public transport and he did need to use it, he was careful to park a few streets away on the other side of the River Kelvin. He would use the Ha'penny Bridge to cross, cut through the woods to the Kelvin Walkway and follow the path to his own street. All in, it was a three-minute walk.

The bike, along with many other things that he never kept at his home, was kept at a rented secure storage unit that was specifically designed for motorbikes. The aluminium 5-bar plated flooring and the fold-down heavy-duty bike ramp came as standard. His particular unit could have facilitated another ten bikes if needed. The cost of the larger unit wasn't an issue, and he wanted the extra space.

He chose the storage facility mainly because it had 24-hour access and it was located within an 8-minute walk from the nearest SPT Subway station at Kinning Park. From there, six stops clockwise on the Outer Circle line would see him at Hillhead, the closest station to his home. At approximately a mile and a half, he could walk between them in 21 minutes. If running, he could do it in under 15.

Although it was a sunny morning, it was autumnal sunshine. Easy to be fooled if only looking out from the warmth of a cosy lounge. Not quite cold enough to see condensation on your breath, but it was close enough.

Benny was prepared with his Ted Baker flat cap, black leather gloves, a three-quarter length black cashmere coat and a scarf.

Walking at a brisk pace, he would be at his meeting with time to spare. He was meeting a lifelong friend, Jack Buchanan, in the upstairs bar of the 'Chip'. Before taking early retirement, Jack had spent most of his adult life as a Glasgow based journalist for one of Britain's biggest newspaper groups. For the majority of his career, he was a Senior Crime Reporter. At his peak, there would not be a big-named criminal, a senior police figure or a Glasgow barrister that Jack wasn't on first name terms with. He got on with everyone and that's what made him good at his job. That, and the fact that his features were always objective and unbiased. He reported the truth as he saw it, without embellishment and without prejudice.

Latterly, he saw the direction his industry was moving in, decided it wasn't for him and reckoned it was time to hang up his guns. He still maintains you have to, “Invest shoe-leather and look people in the eye if you want the real story. No short-cuts.”

As a consequence of that career, Jack is still very much a man-about-town which is one of the reasons he is Benny’s go-to guy for information on anything he needs. He got over the moral dilemma of providing information for a thief, many years earlier. Jack said there was underhand corruption in every walk of life in the world around him these days. He would say morals and principles all went out the window a long time ago. He made his peace with the fact that men like Benny Fox were, in his opinion, ‘honest crooks’.

“Wouldn’t hurt a soul and wouldn’t take a penny from an ordinary man or woman.” That’s what Jack would say about his friend.

Although Benny didn’t drink, his friends did, and the Ubiquitous Chip in Ashton Lane was their local.

As he walked down Byres Road, approaching Ashton Lane, his senses would have told him where he was, even if he was blindfolded. First, came the unique smell that you only get in subways, as he walked past the open doors of Hillhead station. A few yards further, turning into Ashton Lane, was the unmistakeable feel of old-fashioned cobbles under his feet. Add to this, the combined smells of the spices from the Indian restaurant that was there and the burning peat smell from the open fire, upstairs in the Chip. It was all very familiar to Benny and gave him a real sense of belonging.

Upon entering the bar, his first observation was that there were only a handful of people in. That was good. The less people the better. It was understandable for lunchtime on a

Wednesday. He recognised some of them, giving them a polite nod and smile. They were sitting in their usual seats, some sitting alone reading a newspaper or a book, others deep in conversation. The people that he didn't recognise were most likely just passing through.

He saw Jack sitting at one of the tables that had some privacy to it. It wasn't the biggest of places, but they would be able to speak without being overheard.

He was more than half-way through his Chateauneuf de pap. Benny knew that's what it was. It was all Jack ever drank.

Jack gave Benny a smile as he approached the table. As he was taking off his coat, hat, gloves etc, the barman, Gavin, called over. "Alright Benny? How's things?" It was only conversation. Busy polishing glasses, he wasn't looking for an answer, but he got one just the same.

"I'm fine Gavin, thank you. If you have a minute, I'll have a fresh orange and lemonade and another red wine for Jack please."

"Sure thing. Just grab a seat and I'll bring them over."

Jack was sitting with his back to the wall. As Benny sat opposite him, it resulted in them both being partly screened from the rest of the bar. Benny took the opportunity to discreetly take an envelope from his coat pocket and pass it to his friend. Jack slipped it into his own pocket without opening it.

Benny said quietly, "There's £1,500 there."

Jack's eyes widened slightly, "£1,500? That's a lot. Are you sure?"

"I am. That information you gave me was spot-on. It's just how it is. I appreciate it and fair's fair."

Jack raised his glass a few inches and tipped it towards Benny in a salutary toast. "Cheers mate."

As he swallowed the last of his wine and set his glass on the table, the timing was good. Gavin appeared at Benny's side with a replacement and the fresh orange and lemonade. "I'll just put these on your bill, and you can square me up when you're ready?"

It was a question, but it sounded like a statement. He returned to the bar and went about his business without waiting for an answer.

"That's good that everything worked out as planned. If you liked that, you're going to love this," said Jack as he discreetly passed a small USB memory stick across the table.

Benny still referred to them as 'thumb drive's'.

He held it in his closed hand for a few moments as if using body warmth to heat it. He waited until he was certain no one was taking any notice, before he slipped it into his pocket.

He wasn't entirely sure where Jack got his information from, but for all the time he had known him, it had always been accurate and precise.

He never asked and Jack never volunteered it. The detachment that created, suited them both.

"All of the detail is there but as a broad outline, it's a cash job in the city centre. You'll need to get in and out at least twice. One to see what safe they use and the other for the job itself, assuming it's not something too high-tech. It's a lot of money so it stands to reason they will have a big safe or vault of some sort."

Benny nodded as he considered this. He was good with most older safes, but modern ultra-high tech or purpose-built strongrooms were too much. In those situations, he would simply walk away. In most cases, the owner had no idea that he had even been in the room.

Jack continued, "You know these pay-day lender type places? The modern pawn shop / buy your stuff for cash and sell it on, set-ups? Over 90% of what they transact is in cash. It would frighten you, the amount of money they carry on-site. One chain that has over a dozen stores in the west of Scotland alone, holds all the money in one place and it is taken to and from there using a cash-in-transit security van. Throughout the month the security company they use, uses smaller vehicles, but once a month they use a big truck. As far as I know, the bigger truck is the cash coming in and it's the same time every month. Always on a Thursday in the last week of the month – which is twenty-two days from today."

"Why would you not vary the drop times?" Benny thought to himself, but never asked.

"When you say city centre, where is it exactly?"

"It's one of the roads that runs from the City Chambers side of George Square, down to Argyll Street. You've probably walked past it a dozen times and never took any notice. It has one of those huge sets of black wrought iron gates set right into building. The gates give access to underground parking and some deliveries. They're usually closed and the building patrons with access are provided with key fobs. When it arrives and someone opens the gates, the security truck can only reverse part-way in because of its size and the guys have to make the deliveries on foot using wheeled strong-boxes and a service lift. It's all on the drive."

They moved the conversation on to more normal, everyday things and had another couple of drinks over the next hour or so. When they were finished, Benny insisted on settling up the bill although most of it was for Jack's wine. He included a decent tip for Gavin which was appreciated.

After putting on his coat etc, they said their goodbyes and Benny walked back around the corner on to Byres Road and into the subway station. That smell again. He was sure it was mostly from the train brake pads.

He had a ZoneCard that was more than adequate to get him around. He swiped that, got through the barrier and made his way down the stairs to the platform. The trains run every four minutes at peak times so he wouldn't have long to wait. As he came off the last step, he could already hear it approaching and he felt the swoosh of the air that was being pushed up the tunnel. It arrived at the platform ten seconds later.

The train wasn't busy, and he stepped through the nearest set of sliding doors, finding plenty of vacant seats. It took him twelve minutes to reach his destination and another eight minutes to walk to his secure unit.

He unlocked it, entered and closed the door, locking it behind him. This was a normal thing for Benny to do. It's highly unlikely that anyone would ever come to his unit, let alone walk in without knocking first. That aside though, he never took any risks that he didn't have to, and the door was locked.

He had a small desk with a laptop on it. Although there was no internet connection in the unit, the laptop had come with a portable 4G wireless router that you simply plugged into one of the ports on the side. A 'dongle' was what his grandson had called it. Benny had never used it. It was still in the packaging. The technological differences between his equipment in the unit and the equipment in his home, were chalk and cheese. That was by design and not a result of an accident. At home he had the latest technology. His laptop and smartphone were both top end products, fully enabled with Bluetooth and Wi-Fi. Here in the unit, it was the complete opposite. He had a laptop that had never been online other than when it was purchased and that was only for the IT guy to load on the software packages. He had an old pay-as-you-go flip phone that should've been in a museum. It had no online connectivity at all. It could make calls and texts. Nothing else. When it was manufactured, it was cutting edge. You could make calls, text and play Snake on it. The phone was specifically chosen due to how easy the SIM card and battery could be removed and replaced.

Benny was very aware of how intrusive modern society was, whether you wanted it or not. Today, like all other days he visited the unit, he never carried his own mobile phone with him. That was left at home. He knew very well that his movements could be traced should anyone with the ability and capability feel inclined to do so. People like the police for example. He couldn't stop them, but he could minimise the opportunities they had to do so.

Likewise, with the small flip phone, he always kept the SIM card out whether it was here in the unit, or he was moving around, and he had to take it with him, which was very rarely.

Having booted up the laptop, he put the thumb drive in, accessed the only folder that was on it, slowly and meticulously going through each of the files, absorbing the content. All in all, it had taken him forty minutes. By the time he was finished, he knew the payday lender offices would be his next job.

With the thumb drive removed and put safely back in his pocket, he wiped the laptop history, powered it down and unplugged it. He put the lights off, secured the unit and made his way back to the station. Instead of heading home, he had a stop to make first. Benny held a number of safety deposit boxes with a private, independent firm in the city's southside. Having used public transport to make the trip across the river many times before, he knew the train times inside out. He took the subway to St Enoch's, walked to Central Station, took the Cathcart Circle line to Pollokshields East Station and walked to the deposit box office.

He could have taken a box with any bank in the city centre. It would have been considerably more convenient, but he just felt the independent firm had a bit more privacy to it.

Accessing his box, he took out £1,500 cash to replace the money he had taken from his home for Jack and put the thumb drive in. He made the same trip in reverse and continued the journey which saw him back at his home in just over ninety minutes in total.

He sorted himself some tea and a sandwich. When he was finished, Benny made himself comfortable on the sofa with his feet up and his eyes closed. A routine he was very familiar with, was now in motion. It was how every job began. Meet Jack and get the info. Get a verbal 'high-overview' from him. In his own space, somewhere private, read through the information from the paperwork he provided (or these days, the USB drive). Commit it all to memory then go home, lay down, close his eyes, and walk it through his mind, step by step, like watching a movie.

In this latter stage, he found it worked better if he created the right conditions before he began. In the same way a masseuse would prepare her massage parlour with the correct feng shui, the zen-like tranquil music and just the right amount of incense or the clairvoyants might set out their room for the occasion, by using just enough of the colour purple, choosing the correct crystals and the selecting the most appropriate tarot cards.

Benny's version was a lot easier. He would close all the internal doors of his home to reduce outside noise, draw the shades, turn off the tv or radio if they were on and ensure his mobile phone was on silent. On the sofa with his feet up and a cushion under his head, he came as close to meditation as he was capable of.

For some, it might seem like a lot of fuss for nothing, but not for Benny. In his mind's eye, he could almost smell and touch the cold stone of the buildings and the black metal of the big heavy gates. He could see the people walking past the building, going about their everyday business. He could hear the traffic passing, cars, vans, buses, taxis. Daytime life.

He could also see the same scene but played out from an entirely different perspective.

This time it was around 03.45 am when the city was at its most still and took on a whole other dynamic. Unless it was 24-hour businesses, the late-night people would have gone home, and the early morning people weren't out yet.

Between the thumb drive files and his own knowledge of the city centre, a city he knew intimately, he built up a composite in his mind. He knew what information he had and more importantly, what he didn't have. From this, he was able to determine what was important, what wasn't and what he would need next.

By the time he was finished he had a plan for the next day, and he knew where he would need to start. He didn't need to write any of it down. Benny Fox was eidetic and saw mental images with the same clarity that other people saw photographs.

To be more precise, it was a combination of being eidetic and having an element of photographic memory.

For the rest of the evening, he put in a 6-mile run, had a light supper and as was often the case, went to bed around 10.30 pm. He would read for an hour or so before turning the lamp off.

Four and a half hours later, as he was sinking deeper into a dreamless sleep, a Black V-Class Mercedes was rolling up the on-ramp to the Glasgow-bound motorway, on the other side of the city. The driver was up front, two men sat behind him, and their extremely valuable cargo was in the back. They were very careful to drive within the speed limits and observe all the road signs and traffic lights.

The last thing they wanted was to be pulled over by the police but in the unlikely event that they were, all three were armed with VP9 9mm handguns and the two men behind the driver had SP5K semiautomatics. None of the three would hesitate to use them. Not for a second.

The weapons were all Heckler & Koch. The three men in dark clothing were big fans of the arms manufacturer from Oberndorf in South-West Germany.

2

Kyle Stack is eight years old. He is the middle child of three with an older sister and a younger brother. He is quiet, shy and politely spoken, always mindful to say please and thank you and never to refer to his elders by their first name unless they said it was okay to do so. It was always Mr This or Mrs That.

With Donald and Marion Stack being his parents, and Frederick Stack being his grandfather, Kyle would want for nothing in his life.

Except for tonight.

Tonight, Kyle wanted his mum and dad. He desperately wanted them. He wanted his brother and sister. He wanted to go home.

What he didn't want was to be here, wherever here was. Sitting in a car with a hood pulled down over his head and his hands tied together. Sitting in his Spider-man emblazoned pyjamas wet through with his own urine so badly, that it had soaked one leg all the way down, not stopping until it reached his Marvel Avengers slipper. That had been brought on when one of the men who took him, decided it was okay to slap him across his face so hard that it knocked him clean across the seating of the car, smacking him into the side window. Kyle had never been slapped before, not once in his life. The initial shock had registered a split-second before the inevitable pain that followed. Then came the burning sting that would last half the night. The welts on the child's face would last at least three times that long. The slap was to stop him from crying. An oxymoron right there, if ever there was one.

He didn't understand what was happening, who the men were or why they had taken him from his bed. He didn't understand why his mum and dad hadn't stopped them from coming into the house or how they got in as the door was locked. It was always locked at night when he went to bed. Wasn't it?

What young Kyle couldn't know was that the house was locked up like it always was, and the alarm was set, like it always was. Donald Stack did this every night as a matter of course as he was usually the last person to bed.

Around 02.00 am in the early hours of Thursday morning when the Stack household was still, two men in dark clothing had stealthily approached the property by way of a rehearsed plan they had gone over many times. The third man in dark clothing, sat in the V-Class, 100 yards along the quiet country road awaiting the signal to bring the car to the Stack driveway.

Using an unsophisticated tool, they easily and quietly unlocked the front door. They wouldn't need the cutters they had brought in case there was a chain. The Stacks were sure that there would be no need for a chain as the Banham Mortice Deadlock that came as standard with the door would suffice, as they had a state-of-the-art alarm system.

Unfortunately, for the Stacks, the two men in dark clothing had brought a very sophisticated state-of-the-art piece of kit of their own. They had ninety seconds in which to disarm the alarm system. They did it in less than forty.

With the layout of the house imprinted on their mind, they made their way straight up the stairs to the top landing. Expensive and professionally built, there were no creaks or squeaks.

They knew where all the doors were, where they led and where everyone slept. They were here for one reason only. To get Kyle Stack, the 8-year-old boy with the blonde hair and the piercing blue eyes.

His sister was too old for their purposes in the same way his brother was too young. They would be left behind.

The instruction was clear. In and out undetected and leave everyone else unhurt.

However, there was a contingency plan. There was always a contingency plan. If the parents wake up and become aware of their presence, shoot the mother if there is no other choice but not the father. He must live.

The only reason he must live, is because Frederick Stack is the paternal grandfather.

One of the men took up a position at the top of the stairs where he could see all the bedroom doors. His SP5K was loaded and primed for use. The other man quietly opened the door to Kyle's bedroom. There was a soft-tone nightlight plugged in to a wall socket and it gave off the right balance of light. Not too bright that it would keep you awake but not too dark that it was a waste of time. Kyle was starfished across the bed, partly wrapped under the duvet but mostly outside of it. He was too young to snore in the way adults do, but his breathing was making the almost cute wheezing sound that only comes from contented children who are fast asleep.

The room itself was not much different from that of most other boys his age. Clothing, toys, books, computer console with different games scattered around it. On the bedside table, there was a lamp, a digital clock and a half-drank glass of milk.

At the side of the bed was Kyle's slippers. The man glanced at the array of cartoon characters on them. He had seen some of them before, but with the exception of the huge green angry man, he couldn't have named any of the others if his life depended on it.

He had the foresight to pick them up and push one deep into each of his front pockets. He knew the child would need something for his feet. These would do.

In one sweeping movement he clamped one hand tightly over the boy's mouth and nose while scooping him up from the bed with his free arm. At less than four stone in weight, the resistance was almost non-existent. Kyle came off the bed as easily as a pile of laundry. He tried to scream but so tight was the hand over his mouth, nothing came out. It wouldn't take long for the fear of what was happening to be replaced by a worse fear of not being able to breath.

As he stepped out of the bedroom door, his fellow child-snatcher gave two clicks on his walkie-talkie.

That was the signal for the V-Class to start moving.

The first man went downstairs with Kyle wriggling under his arm, almost as quietly as he had come up. The second man silently closed Kyle's room door and followed. At the bottom of the stairs, he paused to strategically place an envelope on the hall table. He had brought it with him in his inside pocket. It was pre-typed and sealed. He didn't know what was in it, but he could guess. It was addressed to Mr & Mrs Donald Stack.

They stepped outside the house just as the car was quietly reversing into the monoblocked driveway with all the lights off. The first man carrying Kyle moved in through the open side sliding door. The second man closed the house door as quietly as he had closed the bedroom door. He followed them into the car. The driver pressed a power button that closed the sliding door before slowly rolling out of the Stack's driveway, switching his lights on and disappearing into the night.

It was only when the sliding door was closed and they were moving, the hand was removed from Kyle's face, and he could breathe again.

Like someone who was drowning then breaking the surface of the water for the first time, he swallowed in huge gulps of air, in and out, over and over. For a time coming down the stairs, he thought he might die. Only 8-years old but nonetheless, that's what he thought.

It was now that he started crying and shouting for his parents. That's when one of the men hit him the hardest of slaps with an un-gloved hand that was almost as big as the boy's face. It was the man who didn't have the Marvel slippers in his pockets.

The man with the slippers, spoke to his colleague in a language that Kyle couldn't understand. Without replying, the other man moved forward through the seats and sat behind the driver.

The man with the slippers took them out of his pockets and put them onto the boy's feet. That's when he noticed the boy was wetting himself. There was no point in telling him to stop because he knew it was involuntary, and it was not something he would be able to control.

He produced plastic ties from his pocket and bound the boy's hands together, then pulled a hood over his head. Driving through one of the sleepy villages that was dotted along this road, there was enough ambient streetlight coming in through the windows to see what he was doing. The last thing he saw before the hood went on was the terrified look on the child's face as tears streamed down his cheeks.

Speaking English this time, he said to Kyle in a low voice, "Do not cry. Do not cry or call out or cause any trouble. If you do, you will get another slap but this time it will be harder. It will be a lot worse." He then moved through the seats and sat beside his colleagues.

As they continued driving, Kyle did cry but it was not loud. Not loud enough to warrant another slap. Eventually it became a constant whimper. He was still and compliant. That was all his captors were concerned about.

An hour later, just as Benny was turning over in his bed, the dark V-Class was navigating the streets of Glasgow's Merchant City. Five more minutes would see them at their destination.

The Freeman Building mirrored many others in the area that were built through the nineteenth century. Although there are numerous features that give them their individual identities, the basic fundamentals are the same. The ground-floor would be given over to retail outlets, restaurants and occasionally, bars. The street they are on would determine how salubrious the outlets are. Rents charged in one street could easily be more than double that charged for the same floor space, two streets away.

It was the same with the space above the street. Typically, the buildings would have three floors above the ground level but again, the address itself would determine what percentage of those floors was given over to retail, hospitality, offices or living accommodation.

The Freeman Building was somewhere in the middle. It was a G1 postcode, but it wasn't Ingram Street. The building was listed as 92% occupied. The mix of businesses within it was consistent with those immediately around it.

The V-Class was heading for the 8% that wasn't occupied.

The three men in the car were Russian. The driver was Oleksander Kulik. Olek to his friends. The man who thinks it's okay to hurt children was Pavlo Volkova and the third, the man with the slippers, was Fedir Moroz.

They were part of an Eastern European criminal organisation based in Glasgow. The three shared a three-bedroom flat with three others, in Govanhill on the south side of the city. The man they worked for didn't live in Govanhill. That man was Yegor Omelchenko, and he lived on an idyllic tree-lined road in Strathblane in a magnificent big house that cost the better part of £1.2 million. Dropping the children at Glasgow's finest private school in his Bentley Continental GTC before going to the golf course or waving his beautiful young wife off in her Range Rover Autobiography as she headed to the country club to play tennis with her millionaire friends, his life was in a different stratosphere from life in Govanhill and he was the epitome of success and respectability.

Except, he wasn't.

He was a Russian thug, up to his waist in the cesspit of misery that was the very worst of Glasgow's criminal underworld. Having arrived in Scotland in 2006, he now ran an operation that netted him tens of millions every year.

Some would argue that there are criminals and there are 'criminals'. At one end of the spectrum there are hard gangsters like the London East End twins, Ronnie and Reggie Kray, for example. Criminals nonetheless but they are revered in some circles because they would wear their heart on their sleeve and call a spade a spade.

At the other end of the spectrum there were people like Yegor Omelchenko.

Until now, his speciality had been people trafficking. Invariably, it was young girls who would be put to work as prostitutes or sold. You could be forgiven for thinking people can't be sold, not in the first world, in the twenty first century. You would be wrong. It happens far more often and much closer to home than you could imagine. They would be sold on to other criminal gangs, sold on to 'grooms' for sham marriages with the sole purpose of obtaining a passport or sold into modern day slavery. They were simply seen as part of a supply chain. A commodity with a value. Nothing more.

Against a background of abject poverty in their villages or towns across Eastern Europe, young girls were lured by the promise of a better life and well-paid jobs and coming here was an easy decision for them. It was only after arriving and finding there was no way back, that the reality emerged but by then it was too late.

Yegor had forged a working relationship with a sizeable Asian crime gang and to date, it had proved very lucrative for both parties. The Russians would supply the girls and the Asians would provide the accommodation which included, among other places, Govanhill, Glasgow.

Of late however, their operation was increasingly coming under the scrutiny of the authorities. Yegor felt this would be a good time to sever ties with the Asians and change direction.

Social acceptance was hugely important to Yegor. It was all about image and respectability. For that reason, he did not have bodyguards or travel with a driver. In many other countries he would never consider this, but he was in Scotland. Very few people here, if any at all, went about their business with a bodyguard in tow. He had observed this in the early days but didn't give it too much thought. It wasn't relevant then as he had no significant wealth, and he didn't have children. Today, he had both.

It was on one of the days he had dropped his children off at their school and was sitting in his car waiting for the car in front to move off, he was looking around him. A thought came to him from nowhere. That's when he knew what his change of direction would be.

Yegor realised that many of the parents were incredibly wealthy. It didn't come to him like some unexpected revelation. It stood to reason. The school had an elitist reputation. It's just that he had never thought about it before.

He knew some of them personally, recognising them from the golf club or the country club where his wife played tennis and his children learned horse-riding. He recognised others from the business section of the newspapers.

That was when Yegor Omelchenko decided he would stop human trafficking and start kidnapping children.

The V-Class turned left into a deserted one-way street and immediately indicated right, to drive through an opening between two buildings that gave on to a small service area at the back. The space occasionally doubled up as a car park after businesses were closed. It could accommodate six or seven vehicles at a squeeze. At this hour, there were two cars parked there. Olek, the driver recognised both. The owners also worked for Yegor.

When they stopped, Pavlo used his walkie talkie to speak with someone inside the building. This time he spoke English and the conversation was short. He was first out of the car and by the time he reached a featureless heavy metal-plated door, it was unlocked and opened from the inside.

As he went in, Olek waited outside to lock up the car when they were finished. Fedir went to the back and helped Kyle out through the open side door. Unable to see where he was going because of the hood, he relied on Fedir to guide him. He wasn't making any sound now, but Fedir could feel him shaking as he had his hand on the boy's upper arm. It was either the cold, fear or a combination of both. He walked Kyle up a flight of stairs as he heard Olek close and lock the big door before following behind him.

Kyle Stack had been the third child to be taken from their home and brought to this place in the last thirty-six hours. Fedir knew the procedure well. At the end of a short corridor, there was a room where Pavlo had joined the other Russians. Two men and a woman. Just before he reached it, Fedir stopped at a door on his left that had a key in the lock. He turned it, unlocking the door and took Kyle in, closing it behind him.

There were two signs of life in the room. One was building materials from a job that looked like it had been partially completed before the work was abruptly stopped. A paddle mixer stood in a 40 litre, two-handled tub that was half full of rock-hard plaster. The mixer and the hard plaster were fused together, and it would take a lot of patient and careful chipping to separate them without causing any damage. It was still plugged into the wall. It's like someone was mixing plaster one minute, then they simply switched it off and walked away never to return. It had a Mary Celeste feel to it.

The other sign of life was another two children, each on a blow-up mattress on the floor.

The room had no windows and was illuminated by a single bare bulb hanging from the ceiling. It was low wattage and created an insipid gloom that gave Fedir a pallid complexion. Not that any of the children would have noticed. Like Kyle, the other two had hoods over their heads. They had been instructed to keep the hoods on at all times unless told to take them off. That would only be to eat or use the toilet, in which case the person tasked with guarding them would wear a mask of their own.

There were another two mattresses on the floor, next to the first two. Kyle was told to sit on one, which he did, clumsily. The other two children were listening but didn't say a word. They had also experienced Pavlo's viciousness and short fuse. Even though they were only 8-years old, that was old enough to know they did not want a repeat of it.

As well as the criminal activity, Yegor had many legitimate businesses that were far reaching and profitable in their own right. Wherever possible, there was a deliberate disconnect between him and those businesses. This was done for two reasons. Firstly, it would make it difficult for the authorities to tie him directly to them, in the event of an investigation, for any reason. Secondly, it meant the income streams they generated would not be at risk if it all went wrong for him and the Proceeds of Crime Act had to be initiated. He never really considered this as something that would happen to him, but he also appreciated that one can never be too careful.

Of all the people who worked for him, his most trusted was Artem. He was his general. The man with unswerving loyalty who could be relied on to get things done. Artem had been with Yegor since the very beginning and rose through the ranks as the organisation went from strength to strength.

Between Yegor and Artem, they identified four targets that had two factors in common. One was that the child would be 8-years old or within six months either side, give or take. The reasoning was, they would be most compliant at this age. Both men were parents and knew this from personal experience. If the child was older, they may already be developing attitude issues and if they were younger, it could bring physical complications. That is, they may need more mothering or not fully grasp the gravity of what was happening to them. Either would be problematic.

The other factor they had in common was that each family would have the wealth to meet a ransom demand of £10 million for the safe return of their child.

3

Benny woke just before 08.00 am on Thursday morning, showered, dressed and was sitting having some breakfast by 08.30 am.

His plan for today was to take a discrete 'walkaround' of the building with the payday lender offices in it. This would allow him to subtly check street level entrances, exits, locks, alarm systems, cameras both on the building and on adjacent buildings. Benny was well versed in undertaking this sort of surveillance. He was tuned in to just how commonplace cameras were these days. The most obvious was usually the CCTV camera high up on the side of buildings or stand-alone metal poles. Some looked like cameras. Others looked like dark blue goldfish-bowls. The less obvious were bus lane cameras, ATM cameras, 24-hour public transport and taxi dash-cam cameras, automatic number plate recognition traffic cameras. They were everywhere. The list went on and on.

This was the reason he didn't park his motorbike at home and was happy to let people think he didn't drive. He knew that all available and relevant footage would be reviewed as a matter of course after each job he did. Assuming the police checked out all the traffic within a reasonable radius, maybe three or four streets back, in all directions, they would have seen his bike along with any other traffic on the road at that time.

To address this, Benny would change his bike every eighteen months or so and would only buy common models. The bike equivalent of the Ford Focus or the Vauxhall Corsa. He would always buy private using false credentials that couldn't be traced back to him and as a secondary precaution he would check out big city dealers like Victor Devine or Mickey Oates before a job, look for a used bike the same model and colour as his own and take a note of the number plates. Using a trusted contact, he had a few sets of plates made up and replaced his own for the one night. Any police follow up that noted the bike from the footage could only trace it back to the dealer, find it hadn't turned a wheel and they would run into a dead end. The enquiry into the bike simply ran out of steam. In reality, it never got that far. Benny was always careful to park up near the job but only in a place that his previous recce had confirmed as a blind spot. Blending in was good but not being seen at all, was better.

The false number plates were kept in the unit along with all his other tools and equipment. Unlike the phone and laptop, some of this was as modern and high tech as money could buy. It's the reason he wanted a unit that had more space than was needed for one bike. It also served as his small office and his storeroom.

Before undertaking the recce, he needed to go to the unit. He needed appropriate clothing and he had a phone call to make.

Although the storage company had dozens of units on the site, it was unusual to see anyone else there when he was using it. Today was no different. He let himself in but this time he didn't lock the door behind him. He got his flip phone and put the battery in but left the SIM card out. There was over 50% battery life. That was more than enough. It would only be switched on for a few minutes to make his call then it would be switched off again.

He put the phone and SIM into his jacket pocket, left the unit and locked up behind him. The storage facility was on an industrial area in Kinning Park, sandwiched between the M8 motorway and Paisley Road West. Benny knew the area inside out. He took a few lefts and rights, zig zagging between the businesses and workshops, only using the streets where he knew there were no cameras. He was heading for a specific spot where he knew there were no windows overlooking it and it was closed off to traffic.

He got there in less than five minutes. Not far, but far enough that he was satisfied his phone couldn't be linked to the unit if anyone ever had any need to track it. Even with the age of the phone, he was sure it could still be tracked. It had a SIM card therefore it must have the capability.

He sat on one of the concrete blocks that was there. He would assemble his phone, use it, then disassemble it when he was finished.

Benny had thought many times that a lot of what he did seemed like overkill and was not necessary. Over-the-top things like this, to make one phone call, or the rigmarole with the bike or the safety deposit boxes.

Each time he thought this however, he reminded himself that he has been doing this for over thirty years and has never been approached by the police, let alone arrested.

Better to be safe than sorry. There was no doubt what he was doing was for the best.

Jack answered on the third ring. He recognised the number.

"Morning Benny, how are you?"

"I'm doing fine Jack. Everything's tickety-boo. I just wanted to check something with you."

"Fire away."

"On the thumb drive you gave me, there was a blueprint page for the building. Plans of the layout. Do you know where it originated and how old it is?"

"I do. It came from architect drawings. A company up Park Circus way. They were commissioned to design a new outlay for a small section of the building. I think the work ground to a halt as there were some concerns about structural issues and they couldn't get agreement on who was liable for the costs to put them right. They would be about two years old. Does it cause you a problem?"

"It might. The drawings would lay out how the building would look after completion of the work. If it wasn't completed, it's not accurately going to reflect how the place looks now. I don't think it's a big issue though. The construction work is on the opposite end from the payday lender and it's one floor above. I only ask because it looks like the most accessible part to get in. It will be fine though. I'll just keep it in mind when I am going to give the place the once-over."

"Are you sure you're okay with it?"

Benny said he was. They ended the call, and he disassembled the phone then made his way back, using the route he had come.

When he re-entered his unit, he locked the door behind him this time.

He put the kettle on for a cup of green tea. He had been drinking a lot of it lately. He then set about getting the panniers and top box on to the bike. When he was done, it had the full tourer look about it. It was the practicality he was concerned with. He needed the space to get his equipment in and leave room for the leathers and helmet which would also need to go in when he parked it up later tonight. He was planning on visiting the payday lenders at 03.45 am. The quietest time of the night.

After finishing his tea, he spent the next hour laying out everything he would need. It was like preparing for two weeks in the sun, but in reverse. Most people lay out everything they want to take or think they'll need, then systematically start removing items one at a time until they get the weight down to an acceptable level for their baggage allowance.

Benny started with what he absolutely needed then systematically added the 'might come in handy' things until he was at capacity of what he could carry with him without compromising the stealth.

Before he handled any of the equipment he would be taking, he wore his gloves. This was to ensure there were no fingerprints on anything as he was always aware that there may come a time when he has to discard everything for a quick getaway.

They weren't the gloves you would pick up in your local Sports or DIY store. These were thin, ultra-high dexterity gloves. Anatomically designed and years of use, gave them an almost made-to-measure feel. They were like a second skin.

He laid out the clothing that he would wear. There were three layers. At the bottom was a black, all in one, spandex unitard. Very strong material but incredibly flexible. It was one piece from the neck to the ankles and wrists. To accompany this, he had a black full spandex mask hood with two eye holes and a mouth opening. It wouldn't look out of place in a backstreet sex shop in Amsterdam's Canal Stratt district. Add to these, the climbing and mountaineering harness, the gloves and a pair of Cobra climbing shoes and he was ready to go. The elastic inserts and pre-tensioning of the shoes meant there was no need for laces.

The layer above this was a non-descript hooded sports sweatshirt and bottoms combination that gave the appearance of someone out jogging. The clothing wouldn't draw a second look from anyone unless they saw the climbing shoes and realised them for what they were. Jogging at nearly 04.00 am, might raise eyebrows but then it was a city, and cities – even Glasgow – were renowned for having their share of weirdos and eccentrics.

The top and final layer would be his leathers for the bike.

Satisfied that he was ready, he moved on to the equipment. First up was his backpack to carry everything. Black, of course. In the early days he would leave everything in the pack after he had completed a job. As he got older – and wiser – he became ever more careful up to the point where he now bordered on paranoia, albeit, justified.

These days, after a job, he removed everything from the pack one item at a time and cleaned it down with anti-bacterial wipes. This was to remove any trace material that might be carried from one job to the next and tie both jobs to the same thief. It also reduced the likelihood of trace DNA should he ever need to run, leaving the equipment behind.

After the backpack came the night vision goggles. This was a pack in its own right. It came complete with the head mount assembly, the spare lithium battery, the neck cord, the sacrificial filter etc. Next was his Mag-Lite Mini LED torch with spare batteries. These were followed up with the climbing gear. The rope, hook eyes, folding grappling hook etc. He knew the folding hook could take his weight. He had used it before.

He finished off the inventory with a small 'miscellaneous' pack that he knew from experience carried things that might be required. These would include small pliers, screwdrivers, adhesive tape, cutters, a knife etc.

All that was left to do now was to get changed into the clothes he would wear this afternoon when surveilling the target area in preparation for tonight. Being mindful of the number of cameras that he would inevitably be caught on, he never wore the clothes he had left home in. Whatever outfit he wore for a job was either on him or in the unit. The only exception to this was the occasional trip to the coin-operated launderette.

The look he preferred was 'easily forgettable casual'. To this end he wore non-descript trainers, jeans, a plain polo shirt, a cotton weave short parka with a faux fur trim lined hood and a non-branded baseball / golf cap. He favoured this style of cap because the peak was slightly longer than other caps and covered a lot of his face. He accessorised these with a pair of thick square large frame glasses. Not that anyone would know, apart from the wearer, but the glass was non-prescription. It was only for effect.

After changing his clothes, he locked up the unit and made his way the subway station. He didn't use his ZoneCard on this trip. He paid cash for a day ticket and took the train to St Enoch's.

Exiting St Enoch's Square, he turned right into Argyll Street and casually moved with the flow of pedestrians who were mostly shoppers, head down and purposely ensuring he didn't make eye contact with anyone.

Just over five minutes saw him where he needed to be. With an air of nonchalance, he ambled along, looking to the world as if he had no interest in anything around him, whilst in reality he was taking in everything. Thirty minutes later, he had all he needed and was taking the escalator back down to the subway in St Enoch's Square.

After changing back into his own clothes in the unit, he locked up and made his way home, picking up something for his dinner on the way.

It was already dark when Benny left his home again, later that evening. He would not be returning until the next day. Because it was a flat, it afforded him the privacy he needed. No one would know if he was in or out. He had checked the weather and although it would be cold, it wasn't frost which was good news. There would be clouds but no rain which was also good news. The clouds brought the added bonus of no moonlight.

Arriving at the unit, the first thing he did was change into his leathers and got the bike out. It still had the legal number plates on, which was what he wanted. He drove half a mile or so then pulled into the kerb on a quiet stretch of road. Lifting the bike seat, he produced his flip phone and battery from his pocket. The SIM card wasn't required. Under the seat of the bike were two USB ports. He inserted the battery, plugged in the phone charger, checked it was doing its job then set off again. He drove a further five miles in the opposite direction from the city to a petrol garage where he filled the tank to the top. He paid cash and left. He drove around until he was satisfied that the phone would be fully charged.

After returning to the unit, he changed back out of the leathers and swapped over the plates for the ringers.

As well as everything else in the unit, Benny had installed a three-seater sofa which took up almost all of one wall. He couldn't envisage a time when there would ever be anyone in there to sit on it, apart from himself. That wasn't why he bought it though. He bought it because it was long enough and comfortable enough for him to sleep on. He had a pillow and a duvet folded away behind it, for the occasion. The only time he needed to sleep on it, was before a job. A night like tonight.

He had a small battery-operated DAB radio that he sometimes listened to, to pass the time, or a small selection of books. He liked the Lee Childs Jack Reacher series, but he struggled with the character now that he had seen a couple of the books made into films. Up until that point, Jack Reacher had been a 6' 6" tank of a man. With Tom Cruise at 5' 7" playing the lead role, it didn't quite work for Benny anymore.

He put the lights out, except for a small nightlight that was, coincidentally, similar to the one in Kyle Stack's bedroom. Without windows, the place would otherwise be pitch black. Black to the point where it would be easy to be disorientated. It was 10.45 pm and he had set a small wind-up alarm clock for 02.30 am.

Having dozed more than slept, Benny was awake before the alarm went off. After sorting a cup of tea, he double-checked his inventory before getting dressed. At 03.10 am on Friday morning he quietly folded down the bike ramp and rolled the big Z1000 down into the yard. Everything he needed was packed into the side panniers and the top box.

With no big revs, the bike was quiet. He made his way out of the industrial area using Portman Street and turned right onto Paisley Road West, making sure not to drift over the line into the bus lane.

With the lights in his favour, he rolled through Paisley Road Toll at just under 30 MPH. Understandably, given the hour, the roads were deserted apart from the very occasional car or taxi. As he was approaching the old red sandstone Kingston Halls building on his left, he could see the lights ahead changing to green. On the opposite side of the road, coming in his direction, was a police car rolling to a halt, indicating to turn right across his path, into Springfield Quay.

"Probably heading down to the waterfront car park by The Harvester, for a sleep," Benny thought to himself. Cynical as ever.

Without turning his head in their direction, he had a sideways glance from the corner of his eye, as he passed them. The two officers in the car were deep in conversation about something or other. Neither took the slightest interest in him as he rode past.

Benny carried on to the West Street junction, took a left and followed the road round to the right onto Clyde Place. By the time he turned onto the King George V bridge, the flow of traffic into the city centre was already looking busier. Still a million miles from the nose-to-tail daytime flow, but it wasn't deserted anymore.

He knew exactly where he was going, having used the spot before. It was a back street, two streets away from the job. He knew there were no cameras. Because the road was split in half with bollards, there were virtually no ground-floor businesses which meant very few people at the busiest of times. There were traffic restrictions but at this hour, he knew there would be zero chance of anyone enforcing them. The little backstreet near the back of The Corinthian Club had a few blind spots. Benny parked up the bike in one of them, stowed his leathers and helmet, did his changing routine and within minutes, he was a jogger taking advantage of the sleeping city to get his exercise in. He tightened up his backpack, put the hood up on his jogging top and set off.

The layout of the majority of the city centre is grid like. Laid out in squares or rectangles, framed with four streets, one on each side. Merchant City was no different. Benny was heading for a specific block in one of those rectangles. The blueprints that Jack had given him had showed an elevation, an end-elevation and a plan.

It was called the Freeman Building.

4

Just as Donald Stack was usually the last one to bed, his wife Marion was usually first up. It was 06.00 am on Thursday morning, just under twenty-two hours before Benny Fox was making his way to the Freeman Building. A school-day. As was her normal routine, she would come downstairs, unset the house alarm system and put the kettle on, taking advantage of twenty or thirty minutes of 'me time' before waking her children and her husband. As she stepped off the bottom stair into the hallway, she noticed the upstanding letter on her table.

Unaware of the puzzled furrow lines that had formed on her forehead as she walked towards it, she was equally unaware that the usual soft beeping of the alarm countdown wasn't there. It would normally give her the prerequisite time to unset the system before coming to life and doing its thing. This morning there was nothing.

Marion picked up the letter still trying to work out where it came from. She knew it hadn't been there the night before. She walked into the lounge and sat on the sofa, looking at it as she did so. No stamp. Mr & Mrs Donald Stack. Typed, not handwritten. Typed directly onto the envelope, not onto an adhesive label that had been placed onto the envelope later. In the same way some people claim to know that someone is watching them, although they can't see anyone, Marion Stack instinctively knew something was wrong. A sense. A feeling. Whatever it was, she knew something wasn't right. She slid her finger under the flap and in an upward sawing motion, opened it. There was one sheet of plain A4 paper, with typed writing on one side. It was folded over in three so it would fit into the envelope.

Mr and Mrs Stack. By now you may or may not know, I have taken your son Kyle…

It was as far as she got. Dropping the letter to the floor, she scrambled to her feet, calling out for her husband as she did so. "Donald. Donald!"

She was taking the stairs two at a time. She lost her footing once. "They've taken Kyle!"

Her voice was faltering. Donald was coming out of the bedroom door just as Marion reached the top landing. "What do you mean? Who's taken Kyle? What are you talking about?" His panic levels hadn't reached the same height as that of his wife. Not yet, but he was getting there.

She barged past him, knocking him against the wall. The other children's doors were opening just as Marion burst into Kyle's bedroom.

Her cries would stay with the whole family for a long time to come. A sickening sound that none of them would want to hear again for as long as they lived. She pulled the duvet off the bed in the desperate hope that it was all a dream, and he would be there, tucked up as always. A dream, or even a sick joke. She would settle for that.

"I think we need to call the police. I don't think we have a choice. They have people who specialise in these things." Freddy Stack sat the letter on the lounge table as he stood looking at his son and daughter-in-law. The worry and concern were written all over his face. He loved his three grandchildren very much.

Donald said nothing. It was Marion who spoke, "No. You've read it. We've all read it, over and over. They specifically say if we go to the police, they will kill him." This brought the panic back. "Donald, tell him. Please. They'll kill our boy."

Donald put an arm around his wife's shoulder. It comforted her, but only slightly.

"Dad, nobody is going to the police. OK?"

"Okay, I'm just thinking they have specialists for this kind of thing, that's all. I'm only thinking of Kyle."

Donald knew his father meant well. They both did. It was 07.05 am and Freddy had come straight away. Neither Donald nor Marion had thought to call him. For the most part, the last hour was a blur. A roller-coaster of emotions from alarm and confusion to panic followed by hysteria, settling for the time being on anguish. Both parents were clearly, and understandably, distraught and really didn't know what to do for the best.

It was Freddy's granddaughter, Jayne, who had called him from the mobile phone she had received for her birthday. His was one of nine numbers that were stored in it. Both Jayne and the youngest sibling, Josh, were told there would be no school (or pre-school nursery in Josh's case) today, and their parents had asked them to go into the front room and put the tv on for a while. The front room was basically a second lounge, but smaller. It was the room where they would relax in the evenings after they had dinner and spend some family time before the children's bedtime. The bigger lounge, where the adults were sat, was more formal and was where the family would entertain guests or visitors.

Freddy had sorted Jayne and Josh some cereal after he arrived. He made tea for Marion and coffee for himself and his son. He knew that Jayne was aware someone had taken her brother. She was eleven and would ask you to speak to her 'as an adult if you don't mind'. "I'm not a child you know," she would say with ever increasing regularity. Even still, she was a child and couldn't be party to any of these discussions taking place in the other room.

Josh on the other hand was only four and as such hadn't really grasped the enormity of what was happening.

Donald picked the letter up again for the umpteenth time.

Mr and Mrs Stack. By now you may or may not know, I have taken your son Kyle. He is well and unhurt. How long this remains so is entirely in your hands. If you comply with my demands your son will be returned to you, unhurt, in less than 72-hours.

If you do not comply, he will die. If you contact the police, he will die. You will not tell me you are unable to raise the money, or you need more time. If you do, he will die. I will call Mr Stack's mobile phone once only. I will do this on Friday at 10.00 am. I will give you details of an overseas bank account, and you will transfer the sum of £10,000,000. When this is done, your son will be returned to you. If you do anything, other than meet my instructions, you will never see him again. If you do not answer or if I suspect anything is wrong, you will never hear from me again.

Despite the huge sum, paying the money was not an issue for Donald Stack. The family business was telecommunications and was valued in the hundreds of millions. The business had been started in the 1970's by his father and uncle. Freddy's brother, James, had never married or had any family of his own. Freddy, his wife Bridget and young Donald were James' family. When he died, James had left his share of the business to his brother and nephew, in equal amounts.

Bridget passed away seven years after James. Freddy missed her dearly. After all these years, he still missed her every day. Apart from the obvious hurt of losing his wife, what hurt just as badly was that she never got to see any of her three grandchildren. Freddy knew she would have loved them with all of her heart, as they would have with her.

Donald's biggest fear was that they paid the money as instructed and his son wasn't returned to them. For him, the money didn't matter. Only his son mattered. His mind was already moving to a dark place that he would never share with his wife, nor anyone else for that matter. Maybe Kyle had seen something he shouldn't have and now they don't want any witnesses left behind. What's to stop them from taking the money and killing him anyway? No loose ends. What if something had already gone wrong? He could be dead right now for all he knew.

"Are you alright Donald?" It was Freddy. It was a timely intervention and it brought Donald back into the here and now. No more thinking the worst. Just deal with the facts.

That's all that could be done. Anything less was a waste of time and helped no one. Least of all, Kyle.

"I'm fine Dad." He sat up and cleared his throat. "I think we're all agreed that we are not calling anyone. Unless I've missed anything, I think all that can be done right now is to make sure my phone stays switched on and fully charged in case they call before Friday. Dad, as CEO of the company and first Trustee on our holdings, this amount of money is going to need your signature as well as mine. Are you okay with that?"

There was no hesitation. Not in the slightest. Freddy said he would do whatever was needed. Anything. All the mattered was getting Kyle back.

Marion looked at him and started crying again. She knew before he spoke, that would be his reaction but when she heard his words out loud, it overwhelmed her, and she loved him all the more for it.

Eight hours after the Stacks had formed some semblance of a plan in their formal lounge, their son Kyle and the two other kidnapped children were having their hoods and wrist-ties removed. It was a lady who was wearing a hood of her own. She told them they should take turns going to the toilet if they needed. "Make sure you wash your hands when you finish as you have some food coming." It was the second time they had gone through this procedure today. When the hoods had first been removed, the children realised they knew each other from school. They were in the same form class. The only acknowledgement was by eye contact. They were too scared to speak. Earlier, around 10.00 am, the other Russian, the man, had gone to a local café / food take-away and picked up a selection of sandwiches, filled rolls and pastries with an assortment of water and soft drinks. He got enough for the three children, himself and his colleague. The other colleague had left around 06.00 am in one of the two cars that had been parked outside, when Kyle was brought in. Before this, the three who brought him, had also left. Olek and Fedir in the V-Class and Pavlo in the other car. There would be no trace of their presence in the service area before businesses started opening up for the day.

The Russian was coming back from the café / take-away at the same time Benny Fox, dressed in his 'easily forgettable casual' clothes was undertaking his discrete survey of the Freeman Building and the surrounding area. They could have passed within inches of each other, oblivious to just how intertwined their fates would become.

The small toilet was only accessible from the room where the children were being held. For the duration of their time here, they would not leave this room. Although it would have been frowned upon by some within the organisation, Pavlo for example, the woman in the hood had taken it upon herself to bring in colouring books, crayons and comic books for the children. A small part of this decision was borne from maternal instinct. The bigger part was common sense. As she saw it, they were less likely to be a problem if they could amuse themselves for a few hours. After they had had their fill of food and juice, the lady with the hood allowed them to remain as they were, reading and colouring-in for the next two hours.

The Stack family lived in a country house, just off the A72 Lanark Road. It was within walking distance of the nearest village, Rosebank, which lay about 8 miles south-east of the town of Hamilton.

Like the Stack's, two similar scenarios had already unfolded in Newton Mearns and Bearsden respectively. In both cases, a letter had been opened and it brought the world crashing down around another two families.

The Newton Mearns family, the Galbraith's, reacted in very much the same way as the Stack family. They had no reservations about paying the demand and they would not, under any circumstances, contact the police.

The Bearsden family, the Munro's, had taken a different view. More specifically, John Munro had taken a different view. The problem was the family set-up. When the couple had first met three years earlier, John Munro had a personal wealth and a business wealth that had a combined value in excess of £60 million. By comparison, his wife-to-be, Anne, had no money to speak of. What she did have was a 5-year-old son.

Young Clark was only in John Munro's life because it was a package deal. That's how he saw it. No Clark meant no Anne. John was infatuated with her and taking on a 5-year-old child was a very small price to pay in his opinion. That was then. Now, three years on, the infatuation was long gone. If John Munro had to be summed up in word, it would most likely be 'shallow'; or, 'vain'; or 'selfish'. The one-word adjectives could go on and on, none of them positive or flattering. It's not that he was a bad man, he wasn't. He just didn't care about anyone or anything as much as he cared about himself.

When Anne read the letter, she almost collapsed. When John read it, he was already resigned to not paying the ransom and was working out the best way to put that to his wife. He had started in much the same way Donald Stack had been thinking. "What if I pay it and we don't see him again?" "I" not "We." Although they were married, it was, in his eyes, very much his money.

He was contemplating contacting the police. Surely, they would advise the family not to pay. Wouldn't they?

Some might call it fatum - Latin for Fate. Others might call it Destinare - Latin for Destiny. In the end, it wouldn't matter.

Three families had already been drawn into a world they couldn't start to comprehend. Events unfolding in the most profound way imaginable. Unknown to them, they would be joined by a fourth.

As Thursday progressed, it saw a middle-aged thief laying down meticulous plans for his next job.

It saw two captors hidden away in a Glasgow city centre building with their three young captee's, invisible to a world going about its business, all around them.

It saw a man called John Munro set wheels in motion that would ultimately be his undoing and would see him going through a lengthy and very costly divorce. Against his wife's pleading and begging, he lifted the phone and called the police. It was not out of the slightest concern for his stepson. His only motivation was money and not having to pay a ransom.

As the day became night, it saw the children having colouring books and comics replaced with black-out hoods and wrist-ties, in sleeping bags, on airbeds on the floor of a strange place, crying themselves to sleep. Young enough to be crying for their mothers but old enough to know they had to do it quietly or the bad man will come back and hurt them again.

As Thursday became yesterday and the incessant tick tock of the clock saw midnight become 01.00 am, then 02.00 am, another family, who lived less than a mile from the Galbraith's, slept through a Déjà vu moment as two men in dark clothing entered their house, unset their 'state-of-the-art' alarm system and left with their 8-year-old daughter, leaving nothing behind but an empty bed and a pre-typed letter, just inside the front doorway.

Again, the hushed streets of Merchant City saw a black V-Class Mercedes pull into the service area behind the Freeman Building just as Benny Fox was changing into running gear and tightening his backpack, two streets away, in a deserted spot behind the Corinthian Club on Ingram Street.

By the time Thursday night had quietly slipped over into early Friday morning, lives and outcomes would be inextricably linked in a way that no one could have envisaged. Not in their wildest dreams. Or their worst nightmares.

5

As Benny jogged through the city centre, it was uneventful. This was partly due to the route he had taken, making sure to stick to the quieter roads and pedestrianised streets wherever possible. It was mostly due to the time. 03.20 am.

Having already done his homework, he knew exactly where he was going. This was only another recce to scope out the actual job. There was no pressure. If there was anything he didn't like or didn't sit right with him, he could simply turn and walk away. Or jog away.

He was heading for the front of the Freeman Building. His earlier observations told him that the best point of access was a passageway 60 yards or so, along the street from the big wrought iron gates. The passageway was very narrow and would have taken two adults walking side-by-side, at a push. It was actually very easy to miss. He hadn't gone into it during his walkaround, but from what he saw, it looked like it went right through the building, opening out onto the area at the back. If it didn't, his B-plan was to go one street over, to the street on the opposite side behind the building. He knew there was an opening there that vehicles drove through for servicing and emptying the bins etc. He didn't know armed Russians used it to deliver hooded, kidnapped children. Not yet.

As he got to the passageway, it was as he hoped and there would be no need for the B-plan. It cut right through the Freeman Building and opened out onto the service area at the back. It quickly crossed his mind that it would probably be used as a short-cut by locals to get from one street to the other, without going all the way around. At the end of the passageway, he looked around and saw three vehicles parked up. He recognised two as a Mercedes V-Class and a Skoda Octavia. He thought the third was a Volkswagen Golf, but in the darkness he wasn't sure. He removed the jogging top and bottoms, stowed these away, pulled on his mask and he instantly evaporated into the night. From this point everything would be silent, slow and methodical.

Benny sat on the ground with his back against the wall. It was part of his routine before every job. He called it 'Sensory Acclimation'. It would take four or five minutes at the most. Firstly, he regulated his breathing. Next, his eyes adjusted to the lack of lighting. His sense of smell became more acute and in tune with what was around him. It was unlikely to be of benefit to him tonight, but in another situation, a disagreeable smell for example, might suggest people coming from pubs or clubs, who found themselves caught short, use the place as a public toilet. An unpleasant thought, but it would mean he had to be on his guard for anyone appearing unexpectedly. The other sense that adjusted and acclimatised was his hearing. When he listened, really listened, the listening stopped and became hearing. His hearing became keener. From his sitting position he could hear traffic in all directions. Some near, some far. In the mid-distance he heard a dog bark. Very unusual for the city centre, let alone the hour. He thought he heard a voice one or two streets away. The farthest off sound he could hear was a train. Too early for commuters, he figured this to be the carriages being shunted between Polmadie Marshalling Yard and Glasgow Central. Maybe it was the Caledonian Sleeper on the move.

All in all, it put him more in touch with his surroundings.

He stood up, lifted his backpack and took a few steps to his left, hugging the wall as he did. His backpack was off and being carried by the straps in his right hand. The reason for hugging the wall was two-fold. The more obvious was that it kept him in the shadows, out of sight of any insomniac who may be awake at their window or anyone outside, even at this hour. Unlikely, but always better to be safe. The less obvious was that there may be motion-sensor wall lights for deliveries or any tenants in the surrounding blocks, arriving or leaving, late at night. Or early in the morning.

As he moved through the space keeping to the wall, there was no sign of anyone, and no lights came on. He was moving towards a featureless heavy metal-plated door that he had seen through the vehicle access opening when he was taking his walkaround, the afternoon before. He knew from the plans Jack had given him that the door was the exit from a set of concrete stairs that served as the fire escape for this end of the Freeman Building. There was a mirror-image of the stairway at the other end of the building.

He also knew fire safety regulations would dictate that there would need to be a lock (or locks) that could be opened from the outside. Experience told Benny these would most likely be one of four types. It would be a Cross Lock, a Pin Tumble Lock, a Dimple Lock or a Mortice Lock.

Regardless of the type, he would open it in a matter of seconds. As part of his kit, he had brought his fully charged electric power lock-pick gun in his backpack.

Fate or Destiny? As he was approaching the door and getting ready to retrieve the lock-pick gun from his backpack, he heard the faintest of sounds that was very much out of place. He stopped. Not moving a muscle, he held his breath in the knowledge that it helped him hear better. It was a 'plinking' sound. A metallic clicking and ticking. The sound drew his eyes to the V-Class. Benny set his backpack down and slowly moved towards it. It was coming from the engine compartment, down towards the chassis. He knew what it was. It was cooling metal contracting. He removed his glove from his right hand and carefully placed it on the bonnet. It was warm. This car had been driven not more than fifteen minutes ago. He quickly checked the other two cars. They were cold. He wiped the bonnets where his hand had been, to remove any possible prints.

His intention had been to unlock the ground-floor fire door, use the stairs and make his way up to the second floor where the construction work had stopped, anticipating this would be an empty space that he could use as a hub. From here, he would find a way to move through the building and down one floor, until he was at the offices of the payday lender.

Now with this new development, he wasn't so sure. He couldn't be sure, but it was a reasonable assumption that whoever came in the V-Class had gone in the same door. It was the only one here. It's human nature to be lazy. Most people would drive in and pull as near to the entrance as they could. Like this car here. Like all three cars.

He stepped towards the door and pressed his left ear against the vertical divide where the door meets the doorframe. He held his breath again.

He heard a man's voice. It was faint but it was there. At least one floor up, possibly two. The sound was muffled and inaudible but there was no mistaking it for what it was.

He was about to lift his head away from the door when he heard another sound that stopped him completely. He isn't a gambling man by any means, but if Benny Fox had £100 to bet, he would have put £99 on it being the sound of a crying child.

Standing motionless for almost a minute, Benny didn't hear the voices again. The crying had trailed off and now there was nothing. Retreating back to the darkest shadows he was once again rendered invisible. He took a few minutes to take stock of what was happening. He had heard a man's voice and he had heard a child crying. He was as certain of both as he could be. He considered his options, walking through them in his mind in the logical step-by-step manner that he was used to.

Leave now and forget about it? With even the most remote chance of there being a child in any form of distress, that was never going to happen.

Leave and make an anonymous call to the police? With Benny's cynical mistrust of the police, he pictured a scenario where they may – or may not – turn up, knock on the door, get no answer, and leave. He wasn't prepared to take the chance.

Having decided he wasn't leaving, he was, to state the obvious, staying. Staying meant getting into the building to check for himself. Going in through the emergency exit door was no longer a consideration so he would need to find another way.

One of Benny's hobbies, for obvious reasons, was Outdoor Climbing. Traditional climbing, Sport climbing and more recently, Bouldering. With or without ropes, he was very adept in all disciplines. Stepping back to look up at the rear of the building, he took in all of the protrusions, some being the accoutrements of modern living and others being the stone and concrete of the building itself. In Benny's mind, they may as well have been ladders.

Securing and tightening the clips of his backpack, he started his ascent with the stealth and agility of a circus performer. In less time than it would have taken him to unlock the door and walk up all the flights of stairs, he had reached the roof. He quickly made his way across it to the corner immediately above the 8% of the building that was unoccupied. It's from that end that he had heard the voices. The roof itself was a mix of slated, pitched and flat surfaces. There were aerials, heating and cooling vents and ducts. Even a satellite dish.

Carefully positioning himself on the front edge of the building, he leaned over and looked down. There were no lights on in any of the windows, from what he could see.

Unfolding his grappling hook, he secured it to one of the metal structures. Leaving most of the rope on the roof-side, he let out enough to see him down to the first floor and dropped it over the side of the building. He would not need any more than that. After connecting his locking carabiner to the belay hoop on his harness, he was ready to go. Checking there was no one in the street or in any of the windows in the building opposite, he started his rappel. Stopping at the third-floor windows, there was a tight ledge, a foothold, that he could stand on. He looked in and could see it was an office. Carefully moving along the ledge, the second and third windows also looked in onto offices.

He took up the tension on his rope and moved down the wall to the second floor. What he saw here did not instantly make sense. The window had the same ledge as those above. He moved along it to the second window, then further on, to the third. As far as he could see, what he was looking at was a room within a room. Using one of the tools he had brought from the roof, he quickly and quietly opened the sash window, sliding it upwards slowly, to avoid any unwanted squealing. Benny could see they were most likely the original windows which he presumed hadn't been replaced as the building was probably listed and getting planning consent was very often, more trouble than it was worth. Like the majority of similar buildings, the sash windows had secondary glazing on the inside. Curling his fingers into the side groove and applying a little pressure, the window slid open without any resistance. The opening wasn't very wide, but it was more than enough for him to slip through.

Once inside, he took a minute to adjust to the lighting. It was easier here as the room was flooded with outside street lighting spilling in through the uncovered windows. There were six in total, including the one he had just come in.

The space he was standing in was one big room. It looked like it was midway through some form of renovations. He put it at 60' long and 35' deep from the windows to the back wall, as a minimum. It looked like it been multiple rooms at one time, but the walls had been removed to make it one big space. Benny thought about Jack's blueprint. If that was the case, the plan had been to knock out all the old rooms, make one big empty space then build it back into separate rooms again but in different sizes and dimensions. It looks like they had managed to start work on two of those rooms. He had seen one from outside a few minutes ago. That's what he meant by a room within a room. There was a second room next to it, that he couldn't see from outside. They gave the outward appearance of two portacabins, standing side by side. He could see the near side of one and the back of both. There were no doors or windows from where he was standing. They were in the other walls that he couldn't see. The plasterboard sheets only lined one side of the stud partitions. That would be the inside of those rooms. Where he stood, these constructions were still partially in wooden frame form.

Benny could hear muffled voices through one of the walls. At least three adults. It sounded like two men and a woman. He couldn't make out what was being said. The closest he got was from a man. "Many sketch no set him" or "Men he sketch no set him." None of it made any sense to him but that's what it sounded like. He couldn't hear a child. Maybe there was no child and he had imagined it. But then, he hadn't imagined the man's voice. Maybe the child was in another part of the building.

He moved to what he now thought of as the back of the second room. There was no sound at all. Taking a small screwdriver from his belt, he gently pressed it against the plasterboard and slowly turned it clockwise in a corkscrew motion. The chalk easily gave way. Within moments he could feel the resistance pressure easing. He was almost through. He finished in slow motion. Removing the screwdriver, he put an eye to the tiny hole. There was some loose debris in the way. He gently blew it out. Putting his eye back to the hole, he could see there was a light on in there. It was gloomy but there was no mistaking it was an electric lightbulb. Using the screwdriver, he painstakingly made the hole bigger, but only a fraction at a time.

Eventually able to see in and down towards the floor, what he saw there made him gasp and momentarily pull away. His mind was still trying to comprehend the image as he moved back to the hole. There, on the floor were what looked like two children with blackout hoods over their heads, on mattresses on the floor. Surely, he was seeing things. He made the hole slightly bigger and looked in again. Bigger hole. Better aperture. Now there were three. Definitely children, and it looked like at least one of them had their hands tied together.

Benny stepped back and tried to make sense of it. Now, he had no choice, he would have to call the police. He thought about what that entailed on a practical level. It would mean going back out of the window, up to the roof, get his things together, cross the roof to the back of the building, climb back down the way he came up. That would only see him reach ground level. He had no phone. He would then need to put on the sportswear, run back to his motorbike which was two streets away, get the phone, assemble it and wait a minute for it to boot up and the signal to be established, get through to the police, explain what was going on. Maybe get passed through to someone else and explain to them what was going on – without telling them who he was or why he was there. Then there would be the inevitable time lag for someone to arrive, even if they took him seriously and were there within minutes. Then.......

Then what? He thought for a minute. Maybe there is no finesse, and they start banging on the doors. Maybe they break the door down. Maybe they don't take him seriously at all and all that happens is a cursory door-knock or a simple drive-by then they leave. What then? Who knows who has brought these children here in the first place? Whoever they are, it's reasonable to assume they have a backup plan or an escape route. The police come in the front door, and they slip out a back door? Why not? It's no more ridiculous than the very notion of what was three feet away on the other side of a plasterboard wall.

Benny knew right then that he wasn't calling the police. He would find a way to get them out, get them somewhere safe – one of the local 24-hour businesses for example - and the police could be called to sort things from there.

He looked back through the hole as if to confirm that he hadn't been seeing things and they really were there. They were.

It pained him to leave, even though it was only for a short time, but he knew he had no choice. He slipped back out the windows, closing both without locking the sash and made his way to the roof. Without close inspection, you would never know they had been opened.

Bringing up the rope, he stowed his equipment back into the relevant sections of his backpack ensuring he had left nothing behind. All that was left out was his lock-pick gun. He secured this to his belt and strapped on his backpack again. About fifteen feet across the flat roof from where he stood, there was a concrete structure with a featureless metal plated door in it. The door was the same as the one on the ground-floor he was planning on using to get in, earlier. He knew exactly what it was. It was the top of the concrete stairway that served as one of the building's two internal fire escapes. As he started moving towards it, he stopped. He heard voices. Men speaking to each other. At first, he thought it was at the front, down in the street. It took a moment to realise it was coming from the back. He quietly moved to the back roof-edge and carefully looked over. Four men were exiting the back of the building. They moved to the V-Class and the cars. Benny's eyes widened and his stomach took an involuntary lurch.

"What in the name of fuck...," he thought to himself. Two of the men were carrying what looked like semi-automatic machine guns, strapped over their shoulders.

As the door closed and the cars drove away, he remained rooted to the spot. This had just moved up to a whole new level. On one hand he just wanted to get away from here. The very same emotion however, removed any notion he may have had about leaving these children here.

He made his way back to the top fire escape door. Without any trouble he opened the three locks within seconds. A top, a middle and a bottom lock. He quietly opened the door. There was a dim stair light. He guessed it stayed on 24-hours a day. No point in trying to escape a fire only to find you have to look for a light switch. Before stepping through the door, a thought came to him. He pulled a 15 to 20-foot length of his climbing rope out of the backpack and cut it off with his knife. He fashioned one end into a specific type of knot that he could easily make bigger or smaller by simply sliding it up or down the length of rope. Like a Hangman's Noose.

As quietly as was possible he stepped into the stairway and took small-measured steps. On each floor landing, there was a door that opened out from a corridor that served the offices. At the second floor, he opened the corridor door and immediately saw the new plasterwork with two doors set in it, about ten feet apart. This had to be the other side of the portacabin type rooms he had seen earlier. From here he knew the nearest one, was the one with the children in it. It was reasonable to assume the other still had adults in it. Adults who may or may not have guns like their mates' downstairs. He shuddered at that thought. Benny stepped back through the door and moved up the stairway to the landing above. He thought it best to wait a while in the hope that whoever may be in there might try and catch some sleep.

In all, he waited almost half an hour. It felt like ten times that. Seconds had passed like minutes. Minutes had passed like hours.

The only positive thing he had so far were the handles on the doors of the two rooms.

He made his way back to the second-floor corridor door for a second time. Waiting within earshot for a few more minutes, there was no sound from either room. He was hoping for snoring from the farther door of the two. No such luck. Where there was a little luck though, was that the door handles were levers and not knobs. It's what he hoped for when he made the knot in his length of rope. He quietly slipped this over the handle of the adult's door and tightened it as much as he dared. He pulled the rope out to the stairs metal handrail until it was taut and tied it on. At the very least, it would be enough to slow someone down.

Moving to the children's door, he didn't need his lock-pick gun. The key was conveniently in the door. Not wanting to frighten the children any more than they already were, if that was possible, he rolled his mask up uniformly at the front, sides and back. The result was that it looked like a black bob hat.

Stepping inside the door and softly pushing it over behind him, the first thing he saw was that there were four children – not three.

He thought to himself, "Jesus Christ almighty. Who are these people?" The children were all hooded and they all had wrist-ties. Three were motionless. Probably asleep. The one on the right was awake. He could see the twitching inside the sleeping-bag and hear the breathing. Benny moved in, gauging what was close enough but not too close.

"Can you hear me?" he whispered. "If you can hear me, nod your head but don't make any sound at all." He saw the hood slightly moving in the affirmative.

"Listen to me. It's very, very important that you don't make a sound. Do you understand that?" Again, the hood moved a little as the head inside nodded.

"I'm a good man and I'm here to help you. I want to take your hood off but there might be bad people in the next room, and they can't know I'm here. Is it ok if I take your hood off?" Another nod.

Benny leaned forward and gently slid the hood up over the child's head. It was a girl who looked like she was seven years old, at the most. She was eight, the same as the others.

He saw her little face, red and swollen. Like she had been crying for days. Maybe she had, for all he knew. She sat upright on the mattress. As a father and a grandfather, confronted with this - he could have cried, himself. He didn't. He smiled. It took all he had, but he smiled the biggest, most beaming smile he could manage. "Hi, my name's JoJo." He had no idea where that came from, but he wasn't going to say "Hi, I'm Benny Fox the thief."

"What's your name?" he asked in a whisper.

"Fiona. Fiona Semple."

"Well, it's a pleasure to meet you Fiona Semple," he said as he extended his hand for a handshake. It was surreal in the extreme.

With her own hand, tiny by comparison, she took his. Instead of shaking it, she used it to pull herself up off the mattress and gave him the biggest and tightest of hugs. It's the last thing he was expecting. As he hugged her back, the lump in his throat was so big, he almost felt it constricting. This time he did cry. A little.

He was quickly and abruptly brought back into the moment.

Another voice whispered from the next bed. "Mr JoJo. My Name's Kyle sir. Kyle Stack. Can you take my hood off too, please?"

"And mine please." It was the third child along. Steven Galbraith.

Benny removed their hoods, cut the wrist-ties, held his finger to his lips and made the universally understood "Shhh" sound.

So far, so good. He knew the next move was without a doubt the riskiest. He had to wake the fourth child out of a sleep but ensure he never made a sound. He knew there was only one certain way to do this. He gathered the other three children nearer to him. After cutting off their wrist-ties, he'd explained what he was about to do. He said he would need to cover the other child's mouth for a moment until he realised, he wasn't one of the bad people. The apprehension was evident. The children were already thinking of their own experiences when they were abducted from their beds, but no one voiced an objection.

Benny saw it in their faces as he looked at each in turn and tried to reassure them. "It's only for a second until he wakes up. Is that okay?" They nodded. "Good. Now, I'll need your help too. As soon as he wakes up, I need him to see all of you at the same time. You need to let him know it's okay, but you can't make a sound. Can you do that?" They nodded as one.

Benny moved around the boy, got into position and in one movement he pulled the hood off with his left hand as he covered his mouth with his right. The child's eyes opened wide, but it all went a lot smoother than Benny thought it would. Clark Munro saw his friends kneeling around him, eyes wide, excitedly holding their own finger to their lips and shaking their heads. Kyle whispered, "It's okay Clark, it's okay. It's Mr JoJo. He's going to help us."

The boy looked back at Benny who put on his best smile again. He moved his hand away, fractionally, ready to clamp it back on if necessary. It wasn't. "Can you keep quiet Clark?" He had picked up on Kyle using the boy's name. Clark nodded and Benny removed his hand. He helped him up and cut his wrist-ties.

He brought the four of them in close and said, "We are going to leave here but we need to sneak as quite as mice. On our tiptoes. Can you do that?" They nodded.

Getting up from the sleeping-bags and the mattresses, Benny realised they were all in cartoon or fairy-tale themed pyjamas. One of them, Clark, was wearing a Star Wars dressing gown complete with the pockets and hood that were designed to give a Jedi appearance. He had been wearing it to bed when he was abducted.

Benny felt the lump in his throat again. As the three boys stood in their slippers, he realised the girl – Fiona – was in her bare feet.

"Where's your slippers?"

"In my bedroom," she replied, matter-of-factly.

He picked her up and clamped her on to his left hip, one leg at the front, the other at the back with her right arm up around the back of his neck. As they moved out to the stairs, he felt compelled to put his finger to his lips one last time. It was mimed. No sound this time. When they reached the rope, he gently lowered Fiona, got everyone under it and picked her up again. As they made their way up the stairs, they really were like mice. There was no sound at all. At the top, he grouped them outside the rooftop door, and quietly closed it over. No point in locking it. It was a push mechanism on the inside.

Still holding Fiona, he crouched down until he was eye-level with them and said, "I want you three to follow me. You need to stay right behind me. Really close. Understand?" They nodded.

As he moved over the rooftop, they couldn't have taken that last instruction any more literal. They were like magnets.

They got to the other fire escape, unlocked it and made their way down three floors to the ground-floor where it opened out of the Freeman Building onto the other end of the service area. The only sound he could hear was a car engine out on the street through the service area opening. It was in a hurry. Benny heard it going down the gears as it approached and realised it was slowing and coming in to where they were. He got the children huddled down, out of sight in the darkness, just as the headlights swept in. He was thinking it was moving fast given the limited space, just as the driver applied the brakes hard and it slid to a halt.

He saw it was the black Mercedes V-Class again.

As the doors opened and three men got out, he also saw two of them had machine guns strapped over their shoulders.

6

The three men disappeared in through the open door as Benny watched it close behind them, from the shadows. For the briefest of moments, he considered approaching the car to see if the driver had left the keys in it, but he dismissed the idea just as quickly. It would have been foolish and extremely dangerous on any given day, but with four children in tow, it was reckless.

He checked on his charges to make sure they were okay. They were.

He whispered, "Everybody, you're doing great. I just need you to sit down, keep staying still and keep being very quiet."

"Can we go soon Mr JoJo?" It was Kyle.

"In a few minutes son. Not just yet though." He turned his attention back to the fire escape door.

Benny was visualising the scene unfolding upstairs. The three of them appeared far too quickly after he had gotten the children out. It could have been that the people in the next room had realised what was happening and had raised the alarm. He didn't think so though. It was too soon. To get here as quick as they did, the V-Class would have needed to be sitting round the corner. Literally. No, they were already on their way here and coming at speed. Whatever was wrong, it was about to get a whole lot worse for them.

Very quickly, he considered his options. By now, they would realise the children are gone. A few minutes would pass while the captors tasked with taking care of them were berated for their stupidity. They can't just drive away so they stay and search. They will search the immediate area at the two rooms. Then what? Search the roof? Search out here, in the back service-area? Widen the parameter and start searching the streets immediately around the Freeman Building? It had only taken seconds, but Benny knew what he had to do. He also knew he had minutes in which to do it.

He got the children to their feet. No stealth or finesse this time. Fiona had been sitting on his backpack to keep her bare feet off the ground. He scooped her up with his left arm and grabbed the backpack with his right.

"Let's go," he said, as he set off with the children close at his heels. Along the building back wall, through the covered passageway out on to the front street, he turned, heading deeper into the Merchant City. He thought it unlikely the kidnappers would carry out a street-wide search on foot, so he stuck to the pedestrianised areas or streets he knew had bollards to cut off vehicular access.

It was barely 05.00 am yet, and thankfully, the streets were still deserted.

He was heading for the junction at Ingram Street and Candleriggs, at a pace slightly less than jogging. On at least three separate occasions, traffic passed him. Two cars and a delivery van. As far as he could tell, none of them took any interest in him or his small entourage. Maybe they did though, and they would call the police. That wouldn't necessarily be a bad thing, as long as he was able to get himself away. He couldn't imagine where he'd start, trying to explain his way out of this. He was very aware of the number of CCTV cameras in the area, and he made sure to keep his face down, the whole time.

By the time he reached the junction, he was listening hard but there were no high revs. No racing engines. The sound of either could have been the police or the V-Class. He got the children down as low and tight together as he could. There were a few cars parked in the nearest corner of the open-air car park. Between the public phone-box that was there, the parked cars, the trees, the small metal utility boxes on the pavement and the darkness, they should be hidden from the street, unless they were really unlucky.

"Can any of you remember the phone number for your house or your mum or dad's mobiles?" He looked at each child in turn. There was a no, a maybe, another no and a yes. The yes was Kyle Stack.

"I know my dad's mobile number."

"That's good Kyle. What's your dad's first name?"

"It's Donald sir. Donald Stack."

Bang. It hit Benny like a well-directed punch. It had been there to see the whole time. He had been so focussed on getting these children out of harm's way, he never made the connection. The Stack family own the Fachan Media Group and are one of the wealthiest families in the country. He had read a feature in one of the Sunday papers magazine sections, a couple of years ago. From memory, the father and uncle started the business and the name – Fachan – was something to do with a giant in Scottish folklore. The Stacks were giants in the telecoms business, that was for sure. It stood to reason their son would be a target for kidnappers. Benny guessed the other children came from similar backgrounds. Assuming they were, and the other families had a net worth anything like the Stack family, it would explain why the kidnappers openly carried automatic weapons. They must surely be serious players in the organised crime world. Somebody is going to be well-pissed when they learn the children are gone.

That wouldn't change anything in the immediate here and now he thought, but it might do later.

Again, he considered his options. Again, they were very limited. He could use the public phone-box in front of him, assuming it worked. As neither he nor the children had any money, he would need to go through a process of reversing the charges. At this hour, he knew it would not be a quick process and the idea of standing in a brightly lit glass box on a street corner held no appeal at all.

He could wait for a taxi, wave it down and pile the children into it. He knew with a degree of certainty that the driver would take one look, lock all the doors and drive straight to the nearest police station.

There was only one thing to do. He could see across the road that the Ramshorn Graveyard gates were closed and padlocked for the night. The old Ramshorn Church, now a theatre, had a small graveyard at the side and back. Choosing his moment when there was no traffic sound at all, Benny took his lock-pick gun ran across to the gate and quickly opened the padlock. After coming back for the children, they made their way through the gate, and he closed it behind him.

After stressing the importance of the children staying put for the next few minutes, he took a few pieces of equipment from his backpack. As he did so, he also took out his jogging bottoms and wrapped these around Fiona's feet to keep them warm.

Never losing sight of the graveyard gates, he moved diagonally along and across the street to a small shop that served hot and cold food, sit-in and to go. He had seen the alarm cover above the front door and knew that the system would be at least fifteen years old, probably more. Given the nature of the shop and its contents, he knew there would be no complex system at work in the background.

He went to work and quickly disabled the alarm. The system, based on surface mount magnetic reed switches, offered him no resistance at all. Similarly, with the door, he unlocked it in minutes and stepped inside. As expected, there was a PIR motion sensor, but his work outside had rendered it inoperable. Mindful that his mask was rolled up, he put his hand over his face and checked for CCTV cameras. There were none.

"Right Benny, last time. Here goes," he thought to himself.

Gently bringing the door to rest behind him, he checked up and down the street, ensuring it was clear. He ran back for the children, got them and his things, pulled the gate over and replaced the padlock, and hurried them to the shop. Once they were safely in, he closed the door and locked the latch. Moving them to a table and chairs that were out of sight of the windows he sat them down and moved through a door at the back. It took him less than a minute to find what he was looking for. A small office with a phone in it. There were no windows. He switched on a desk-lamp that he knew couldn't be seen from outside.

After checking the phone had a dial tone, he called for Kyle to come through. The other children stayed seated. As the child recalled his father's mobile phone number one digit at a time, Benny dialled it. It was answered quicker than he was expecting. Understandably, Donald Stack was finding it difficult to sleep and was wide awake. Out of consideration for his wife, his other two children and his father who was staying with them for the time-being, his phone was set to silent, and it vibrated instead of ringing, dancing across the coffee table where it lay.

"Donald Stack speaking." The voice that Benny heard wasn't the confident sound of one of the country's most dynamic entrepreneurs. It was the wearied voice of a man carrying an unbearable weight on his shoulders.

That was about to change.

Benny thought the only logical thing to do in a situation like this was to start at the end then come back to the beginning.

"Mr Stack, I have your son Kyle with me. He is safe, well and unharmed. He, along with three other children were held captive and I have managed to get them all out and away to safety. How long will it take you to drive to Glasgow's Merchant City?"

"Thirty minutes, maybe less." His voice had taken on a new level of energy and although his mind was racing, he didn't interrupt.

"Come straight away. I need you to come to the Ingram Street open-air car park, just opposite the Ramshorn Theatre. Do you know where that is?"

"Yes. I know where you are, that's just at the end of Candleriggs?"

"That's it."

"I'm on my way, right now."

Almost as an afterthought, Benny said, "Keep your phone connected and put it on speaker when you're in the car."

He could hear the scuffling and shuffling sounds as Donald Stack was moving around, getting his car key fob etc. It was the sounds you hear when you've been 'pocket-dialled'. He heard a woman's voice. He presumed it was Mrs Stack. He could hear Donald briefly explaining to her, what was going on. Another hurried conversation but he couldn't make out what was being said this time. Then there was a different conversation, this time with a man. It was Donald asking his father to stay with the kids. There was no explanation as to where he and Marion were going but that didn't matter. Whatever it was, Freddy knew it was important. Benny heard the house door close over, the car doors open and close, the engine starting and the sound of the mobile connecting to the in-car system.

Donald came back first, "Hello, are you still there?"

"I am. Give me one second."

This time it was Donald and Marion who were listening to a conversation at the other end of the phone.

"Kyle, your mum and dad are on the phone. Can you speak to them please? Here you go." He handed the phone to Kyle.

"Mum? Dad? Are you coming to get me?"

They both answered at the same time. The words were rushed. His mother's voice could be heard over his father's.

"We're coming son. We're coming right now." She was crying. Benny knew it was tears of relief.

"Are you okay Kyle?" Donald asked. Benny had already confirmed that he was, but it was human nature to ask, just the same.

"Yes. Mr JoJo saved us dad. He saved me and Fiona and Steven and Clark from the bad men. The lady wasn't bad. She got us comics and colouring-in books and crayons."

Benny asked for the phone back. Kyle handed it to him, said thank you, then went back to sit with his friends. That's how he saw them now. His friends.

Another afterthought. He called Kyle back. "Your friends Kyle. How do you know them?"

"They're at my school."

He turned his attention back to Mr & Mrs Stack. After confirming that the shop's number had come up on Donald's phone, Benny said he would hang up, asking Donald to call him back when he got here.

He went out to the front shop, looked around and saw there was a small selection of sweets behind the counter and juice in the fridge. He took some of each and brought them to the table, telling the children to help themselves. Although they were sitting in the dark, the streetlight coming in through the big plate-glass windows illuminated the room, more than adequately. As they were opening the sweets and juice, he noticed the Jedi Warrior - Clark – had a small pack of crayons in front of him on the table. Benny recalled what Kyle had told his father about the 'not bad' lady bringing in crayons for them. Already knowing the answer, he wanted to be sure. He asked Clark where he had got them. Clark said the lady had brought them and he had put them in his pocket when they were leaving. He asked if Clark would mind if he borrowed them. Clark said he didn't mind and slid them across the table. Using a finger and thumb on two corners, Benny carefully picked up the pack, took it behind the counter and slipped it into a clear food bag that he found there. He placed this into his backpack and zipped it up. Wearing gloves, he wasn't trying to avoid getting fingerprints on the pack when he picked it up by the corners. He was more concerned about inadvertently rubbing fingerprints off of it. Maybe something, maybe nothing, but it might be something the police could use later, in the inevitable investigation that would follow.

The next twenty minutes or so, passed without incident. From inside the shop, Benny saw an Audi SUV pull to a halt just as the shop phone started to ring. When he answered it, Donald Stack said they were at the junction. Benny asked him what he was driving, and Donald confirmed it was an Audi Q7. Benny asked him to look along the street and say if he could see the shop. Donald said he could, and Benny asked him to pull up outside of it. He suggested Mr & Mrs Stack stay inside the car and keep the engine running.

As the car pulled up outside, Benny got the children together and led them to the front door. The way the car was facing, the driver's side was nearest. Donald Stack had his window down. He desperately wanted to get out and come to his son. Both parents did. He knew however that this man dressed entirely in black from head to toe, whoever he was, had brought all of these children this far and he trusted him. He did as he was asked and stayed put. Benny held up one finger in front of the children and told them to wait for one moment as he put his head out and checked up and down the street. Satisfied it was safe, he stepped forward to the car, opened the back door and told the three boys to get in. Kyle was first, the back of this car was familiar territory for him. He scooted over and the other two followed. Fiona stayed where she was. He stepped back to the doorway, picked her up and carried her, putting her in the back with the others. Before he set her down, she gave him another tight hug and simply said, "Thank you Mr JoJo." As if on cue, all the children said thank you. Even Kyle managed to wriggle from his mum who was all but smothering him. Her tears were all over his face. Kyle told his mum it was 'gross' but inwardly he didn't mind at all.

Still really confused, with a million questions that would go unanswered, Donald Stack was clearly overwhelmed. He spoke to Benny through the open window.

"I will never be able to thank you enough for what you've done here. If there is ever anything that I can do for you, and I mean anything, please let me know. I will forever be in your debt. We both will." He extended his hand out of the car window. He knew it fell a mile short in expressing his gratitude to the man in front of him, but he did it, nonetheless. Benny took his hand in his own gloved hand and gave him a firm handshake.

"There are two things you can do, if you don't mind," said Benny.

"Of course, anything at all."

Benny took another look up and down the street. Still safe. "Firstly, you could see to it that these other children get home okay." Whether you call the police first or sort it yourself, I'll leave that up to your judgement. I'm sure you'll do whatever is for the best. Yours was the only phone number I had, thanks to Kyle. These children's parents won't know that they are safe yet. The quicker you can let them know, the better. I'd appreciate it. The girl, Fiona, has no shoes. You might need to carry her at some point. All I can tell you is that the connection between them appears to be Kyle's school. That's how they all know each other."

"No bother at all. I'd be more than happy to take care of that. I'll get on to it as soon as we start driving. You said there were two things?"

"Yes. You'll have to speak with the police at some point. That's clear. They are going to ask you about me. I would ask that you leave nothing out and tell them everything, exactly as it happened. Everything, that is, except a detailed description of me. Or my face, to be more specific. The black clothing is fine. I'll be on a million and one cameras by now. That's not an issue. For reasons of my own however, I'd rather stay off of their radar and the vaguer you are, would help me immensely."

"Well, that's not an issue at all. I was so engrossed in getting my son back, I never even looked at your face. Consider it done. And your name? Do I tell them it's Mr JoJo?"

"Yes, that's okay. It's actually John Johnstone."

Donald nodded, smiled and simply said, "Sure it is."

Benny smiled back, took a step away from the car and re-checked up and down the road. He looked in the back window, gave the children a wave and they all waved back. Without thinking, and for reasons he couldn't fully understand other than being a father and grandfather, he lifted his right hand to his lips and blew Fiona Semple a kiss. She smiled then blew him a kiss back and that small gesture made him smile.

Turning back to Donald Stack, the smile fell away. He nodded and said, "I think this would be a good time to go, Mr Stack."

Donald nodded in agreement, dropping the car gearstick into Drive and releasing the parking-brake. As he started to slowly roll away from the kerb, he said, "Take care of yourself John Johnstone and thank you. Again."

Benny watched the car pull onto the other side of the road and drive away. He knew he had done a good thing. The children were safe.

Stepping back to the shop to get his things and change into his jogging gear, he thought to himself, "I think this would be a good time for you to go too Benny boy."

7

Depending on the situation, Yegor was Artem's friend, or he was his boss. Today, he was most definitely his boss. A sequence of events had unfolded in less than 24 hours between Thursday morning and Friday morning and now, in the former storeroom that was one of a set of luxury offices, Artem was sure Yegor would order someone killed before the day was out.

They were in a building on Glasgow's Bath Street that backed on to Sauchiehall Lane. Through a combination of intimidation and the availability of ready cash - and an off-the-books deal, Yegor had acquired the four-storey building four years previously, for less than half its market value.

The ground floor was given over to a handful of small businesses, the first and second were converted into a hotel and the top floor was predominantly offices. That floor had spent decades as storage space and through neglect, had fallen into a state of serious disrepair. Now, after an extensive refurbishment, the same space offered prestige offices. 50% had long-lease tenants and the remaining 50% was used by Yegor Omelchenko from where he ran his sizeable portfolio of legitimate businesses. Apart from a select few, no one knew that two of the long-lease tenants were actually businesses, also owned by Yegor, but at arm's-length, to maintain a disconnect from his other enterprises.

As they were not averse to paying wages cash-in-hand or employing people who had a criminal record and as such, found it difficult securing any form of work, they garnered a lot of loyalty from the people who worked for them. It fostered a 'You scratch my back, I'll scratch yours', mentality.

It was through these legitimate businesses that a lot of their information came. One such, was a cleaning operation that catered for everything from industrial cleaning of business premises to residential properties. Moira, who's life at its lowest point, had bounced between prison and sleeping rough for years, was a case in point. Through social workers and a first-rate support mechanism investing the time and energy in her, she was able to get off the streets, into sheltered accommodation and get herself cleaned up. Through a friend who never gave up on her, she found herself sitting in borrowed clothes and borrowed make-up, at an interview for a full-time job with a manager of the cleaning company. Despite her past, she felt like she would be forever in his debt when he said yes, and she started work the following Monday morning.

Within a year, she had her own rented one-bedroom flat. Not much, but it was her own space, her own bed and her own food in the fridge.

Within two years, she had been promoted and had progressed to a rented two-bedroom flat.

Three and half years later, Moira had been promoted three times in total. She had a mortgaged two-bed semi, a small company car and was in a stable relationship. Life was good.

For her situation at least, social work said it was a textbook success story. She never lost sight of the fact that it was her own hard work and determination that brought her to where she was. That aside however, she would never forget the opportunity the company had given her, when most of the rest of society would have been content to write her off.

It was this loyalty that eventually brought her into the fold. Into the inner circle.

As a manager, Moira was no longer doing 'hands on' work, and spent most of her days undertaking administrative functions or overseeing rotas and making sure that the day's workload was adequately covered. A role that was very much part of her remit, was carrying out assessments on new contracts. She would visit the premises, photograph or video the layouts where appropriate, take measurements, make notes and hand everything back into the office for pricing and quotes to go out. In the last ten months she had carried out 94 such assessments across Central Scotland. Of these, 61 were industrial and 33 were residential. 12 of the 33 were on the 'Premier Clients' list. They were VIP's. Of the 12 Premier Client property owners, 4 of the families had 8-year-old children in the same class at the same top-end private school.

It was from Moira via Artem that the Russian snatch team had learned the layout of the houses, including the alarm systems and the door-locks.

From meticulous planning, to hand-picking the right people, to securing the space in the Freeman Building, to executing the plan and having all four children safely locked down, the whole exercise had gone like clockwork.

The spanner in the works came to light when they found out from one of the many police officers on their payroll, that a chortiv imbetsyl – a fucking imbecile – a Bearsden man called John Munro, had decided he was not going to comply despite a child's life being at stake, and had taken it upon himself to call the police. An investigation had commenced by Thursday evening.

Yegor and Artem had received the news of the investigation in the early hours of Friday morning, shortly after the fourth child – the girl – had been lifted from her home. They had discussed this and decided it may or may not affect things but as a precaution they should consider moving the children to a different location. It was a judgement call. Moving them ran the risk of the team being stopped by the police, but if they could clear the city without incident, they had a place which was remote and a couple of miles off the beaten track. That, however, was only until later in the morning when the forestry workers and the wind-farm workers started using the same roads after which, it wasn't remote in the slightest. It was why they had initially chosen the Freeman Building instead. 'Hidden in plain sight'. The alternative was to leave them where they were and hope the investigation didn't catch up with them before the money had been wired.

In the end, Yegor decided. Move them. With the sums of money involved, he wasn't prepared to take the chance.

Just over an hour after the three-man team had left the girl hooded and tied, with the other three children and their two jailers, Artem called them and told them to get back and collect them all and await further instruction on where to take them.

When they got there, the cupboard was bare, so to speak. Olek the driver had drawn the short straw and phoned Artem to say what had happened. As he did, he went to great lengths to make it crystal clear that it was the jailers who had let the children escape, not the kidnappers.

Artem knew from experience that Yegor would make no such distinction. Everyone would be blamed and would be held accountable. Unfortunately for Artem, there were no straws for him to draw, long or short. He alone would deliver the news. As he watched his boss take it in, trying to comprehend how five grown men and a woman could lose four 8-year-old children, the voice, the rage and the blood pressure were all going up in equal measure.

Artem could only listen without interruption. He was certain of one thing. Someone was going to die for this. Of that there was no doubt.

Detective Sergeant Jenny Mullen was well aware that questioning the ability of your peers within the Force was not viewed in a positive light. Nonetheless, she had asked to see her boss, Detective Chief Superintendent Richard Cook. Both officers worked in the Specialist Crime Division and were based at Police Scotland's HQ, the Clyde Gateway building in French Street, Glasgow.

The mid-day sunshine was mostly screened by the vertical blinds in DCS Cook's office, but there were isolated spots here and there where it managed to peek in, with the breeze from the partially open window gently moving the blinds, creating dancing shadows as they dappled the wall behind him.

DCS Cook was destined for great things within the Force after his part in recently steering one of the country's biggest surveillance operations to a hugely successful conclusion.

For all of that, he was a well-grounded professional and was not one given to egocentrism. Besides the fact that he was DS Mullen's boss, it was another reason why she was comfortable requesting the meeting with him, rather than another senior officer. He was objective and pragmatic. He didn't judge.

"Thank you for seeing me, sir, especially at such short notice. I know Friday is a particularly busy day for you."

"That's okay, DS Mullen. How is it I can help you?"

"It's the kidnapping case sir. Clark Munro. As you know, it was passed to me yesterday. I have a problem with the forwarding of information. The situation needs to be addressed but I don't want to rock the boat. These are my colleagues and I have to work with them. Plus, I don't think it's my place to try and sort it."

"And what is the problem, specifically?"

"It's the time it's taking for information to be forwarded. From the outset, as I understand it, the Stepfather – John Munro called in on Thursday morning. It took almost an hour before that was passed to us. In a case like this, time is everything and that's unacceptable."

"I'd agree with that."

"It gets worse. A lot worse. I've just learned that a delivery van driver called in around 05.00 am this morning saying that, in his words, "A man dressed in black from head to toe, is running along Candleriggs carrying a young girl, with three wee boys in pyjamas, running behind him." It turns out one of the boys, based on the driver's description, matches that of the boy Munro. I'm finding this out over seven hours after it was called in?"

DCS Cook was visualising the image in his head as DS Mullen carried on. "I've also just learned that the businessman Donald Stack called in just after 10.00 am this morning to say he needed to speak with someone about the abduction and subsequent safe return of his son. Granted, there isn't a direct link between both situations but to reference an abduction within twenty-four hours of the Munro abduction, it's not much of a stretch to assume the two things might be linked, sir."

"No. You're absolutely right, it's unacceptable. You can leave this with me, and it will be sorted. It's not good enough. Be rest assured, you don't need to concern yourself about any fallout as a result of this conversation either. It's slippage, and it will be me who is addressing it. I want things tightened up."

"Thank you, sir."

"As regards this latest development with Mr Stack. What's happening there?"

"He is expecting a call back. I'm going to do that now. If he's available, I'll drive out and see him. He lives up the Clyde Valley. Somewhere between Hamilton and Lanark."

"Good. Who is working with you?"

"No one yet sir. Because of the time lag in information being passed on, I'm only starting to get a clear picture now."

"Ok. I'd like you to take DC Hannah along with you. The experience will do her good."

"Very good, sir. Thank you for sorting this."

DCS Cook asked DS Mullen to keep him in the loop with the case as things developed. She said she would, and she left his office. After a phone call to Donald Stack, she found Audrey Hannah, and within twenty minutes they were in the car heading for the southbound M74.

Yegor sat down on the expensive green leather Tronso executive chair, behind the equally expensive Hampshire, a beautiful walnut twin pedestal desk. His voice had started to calm and Artem took this as a sign that it was okay for him to sit in the chair opposite.

"So, what do we know Artem? Facts, no guesses."

"We know the four children were lifted as instructed and brought to the Freeman Building as planned. The team executed the last handover as they were instructed to do. Fedir ensured the girl, the last of the four, was hooded and wrist-tied and relocked the door. I have spoken with him and there is no doubt about this. They left around 03.45 am, as they were supposed to. We have a three-man arrangement to take care of the children. Watchers. Two men and a woman. The watchers are instructed to rotate shifts so there are always two on-site. One of the men left with Fedir and his team at 03.45 am. After our discussion about the Munro man involving the police, I contacted Fedir and told him I wanted the team to get back and collect all four. When they arrived, approximately one hour later, the children were gone. Fedir said there had been a delay between them arriving and one of the watchers opening the door. They open it from the inside as an added level of security. Fedir asked what had taken so long and the watcher said he could not get the room door open. He had to cut his way out. Someone had tied it closed with rope. When he got upstairs, Fedir said the children were gone. They searched the building, the immediate area and widened the search to three or four streets in all directions. They found nothing."

Artem had seen the look on Yegor's face when he mentioned the door being opened from the inside as 'an added level of security'.

Yegor thought for a few moments then said, "So if I have this right, a person, or persons, unknown have made their way into the exact part of the exact building, at exactly the right time, between our team leaving then arriving again, using rope to lock our Watchers in and leave with four children, vanishing into thin air, and no one sees or hears a thing. Do I have that right?"

Artem saw the anger starting to flare up again. He knew he would need to choose his words carefully. He wasn't going to be a casualty of this fuck-up.

"You do Yegor. I am calling in all our contacts. There will be CCTV footage. We will get a copy of all of this. I do not think for a moment this was from within. No one would dare cross you, but I take nothing for granted. Every one of our people who has had any involvement, will be held accountable for their movements and actions until I am satisfied that they are to be trusted. I will deal with this myself. There will be no exceptions."

This seemed to relax Yegor, slightly. His head was nodding in agreement.

"If I may Yegor, do you still intend contacting the families this morning?"

"No. I fear that the children may have been reunited with their families and if they have, I am sure the police will be more involved now than they were before. Also, there would be no reason to pay any ransom now. Whoever took them from me. They will pay. They will pay with their lives."

"And the Watchers. What of them?"

"Kill them. Kill them all."

Artem did not question the warped logic in killing the third man. The one who wasn't even present. Yegor had instructed it, so today, all three would die.

8

Benny had made it back to his bike by 06.15 am. The streets were starting to show signs of life but were still relatively quiet. As far as he could tell, no one had given the jogger with the backpack a second look. It was still dark and would remain so until after 07.30 am. Still confident that the place he chose to park up was a blind spot, he changed into his leathers, without too much concern of anyone seeing him. He stowed everything into the panniers and top box before setting off.

Observing all the rules of the road, his main focus being on the speed limits, Benny rode through the city heading for the westbound M8. After joining, he stayed in the inside lane, riding until he came to the M8/M77 split. He took the M77 as far as the first exit, turned left onto Dumbreck Road, made a big anti-clockwise sweep through Pollokshields and was back at his unit before 07.00 am.

By 07.30 am, he had gone through his 'winding down' process as he always did in these situations. The number plates were changed, the clothes were changed, and the equipment was cleaned down and put away in its place. The ringer plates would be destroyed. He had two alternative sets that could be used for this bike. Leaving the unit just after 08.00 am, he made his way to Kinning Park subway station. After getting off at Hillhead, he picked up a newspaper and morning rolls on Byres Road and was home by 09.15 am. He didn't need the things from the newsagents. It was all for the neighbour's benefit. If anyone saw him coming in and was taking any interest, they would just think he had been out at the shop.

Benny called Jack Buchanan and asked if he was free for a catch-up today. It was code. Jack understood, said he was free, and they agreed to meet in the Chip at 12.30 pm. Benny used the time to sort some bacon and scrambled eggs. More famished than he thought he had been, he ended up having two of the morning rolls he had brought in.

Showered, shaved and dressed, he took the stairs up to the Chip two at a time, and entered the room on the stroke of 12.30. It was a déjà vu moment. Gavin behind the bar, a scattering of people, some regulars, some not, and Jack at the same table he had been at the time previous. Benny took his hat, gloves and coat off. With a fresh orange with lemonade and a Chateauneuf de pap ordered and brought to the table, Jack looked at him and asked in a low voice, "So, how did it go? Were the architect drawings okay or did you have a problem?"

"To say I had a problem is the understatement of the century, and it had absolutely nothing to do with the drawings."

The puzzled expression on Jack's face was clear. Benny started at the point where he left the unit around 03.00 am, finishing the story around the point where he changed back into his leathers and drove out of the city centre after 06.00 am.

It had taken fifteen minutes to take Jack through the story from start to finish, during which time he never interrupted. Not once.

When Benny was finished, Jack said, "That's the wildest thing I have ever heard, and believe me, I've heard a lot of fucked up shit in my time."

He ordered another round of drinks and asked Benny, "What now? Where do you go from here?"

"Nowhere, I guess. Forget the job, lie low and let it blow over. Realistically, it should be impossible for whoever these people are to trace any of this back to me. You know me better than anyone. I'm meticulous about this stuff and there is absolutely nothing to connect me to that place or those children."

"But?"

"But what?"

"I hear the words Benny, but your face is saying something else."

Jack really did know his friend better than anyone.

Benny nodded. "Donald Stack. He saw my face and that connects me to the children. Given that I got his son back I have no doubt he will do his best to keep his word. It's the police I'm thinking about. It depends on who is assigned the case. Some of them are really sharp and others are mediocre at best. With a case like this, I don't think it will be passed to a dud."

"Nor me."

"Then there's the machine guns. Jesus Christ Jack, who runs around Glasgow with machine guns? It's not Los Angeles or New York. I can't start to imagine who this would be."

"I could. I can think of a few outfits that wouldn't think twice about it. I guess it would depend on the worth of these children to them. Did Stack tell you how much the ransom was?"

"No, he didn't volunteer it and I didn't ask."

"Well, you can bet it was serious money. Think of a big number then multiply that by four, one for each child."

Marion Stack showed DS Mullen and DC Hannah into the formal lounge, explained that her husband would only be a few minutes and left to brew some fresh coffee.

As they waited, they couldn't help but be impressed by the view through the big picture window that looked on to the landscaped gardens and beyond.

DC Hannah thought it was more a vista than a view. The beautifully tended lawn and flower beds were in the near view, herbaceous borders and flowering shrubs were in the mid-view and what looked like fruit trees were farthest away where the garden ran down to meet the river. It was designed to draw the eye to the end as if looking down a foliage lined avenue.

It still looked great given the time of year, but it was easy to imagine it in its glory during the summer months.

Her thoughts were brought back into the room as Donald Stack came in. After introductions, the three of them took a seat.

"Detectives, thank you both for coming. As I was explaining when I'd called earlier, my son Kyle was abducted from this house between Wednesday night and Thursday morning. The house was locked up, the alarm system was set, and everyone was asleep. At some point, he was taken from right under our noses. No forced entry, no system malfunction with the alarm, and we never saw or heard a thing." More for his own benefit than the detectives, he then said, "The very thought of it will give me sleepless nights, for years to come."

He went on to explain what had happened and how his wife found the letter on the hallway table early on Thursday morning. He gave it to DS Mullen who quickly put on her gloves, read it then put it into an evidence bag. He said they took the threat seriously and did not call the police. There was some discussion around this but from Mr Stack's perspective, it was irrelevant. He would have paid the ransom and not involved the police. DS Mullen said she would arrange for someone to follow up today to check for fingerprints etc. Although it remained unspoken, none of the three of them held out much hope of it yielding anything worthwhile. Still, it was procedure, and it would be done. After Mrs Stack joined them, setting out coffees and a selection of biscuits, she sat next to her husband and the conversation carried on. DC Hannah was taking notes while DS Mullen did the talking. Mr Stack explained that he couldn't sleep that night and at best managed an hour or two, catnapping here and there. He was awake when his mobile phone vibrated at 05.15 am. The number that came up on the screen had an 0141 STD code. He knew it was a Glasgow number, but he didn't recognise it. It was a strange time to get a call, but with his son's situation, he had no hesitation in answering. He walked the detectives through the conversation, the drive into Glasgow, the subsequent call he made back to that number, the instruction to pull the car up outside the shop and the man dressed in black who brought their son and another three children out through the shop door, putting them all into the back of his car.

Four children. This was the first confirmation DS Mullen had that there were definitely four. The early morning call from the van driver had been accurate. Kyle Stack and Clark Munro, she knew about. She said she had no idea who the other two were, as yet.

"I can tell you that," said Donald Stack. "The boy's name is Steven Galbraith. The girl's name is Fiona Semple. They are all in the same class at my son's school. The man who had saved them – that's the only way I can describe it – told me this. He said his name is John Johnstone. As soon as we left him, I went to work on tracking down their families."

He explained that he had called his PA from the car, stressed the urgency hence calling her at home and so early in the morning, and told her what he needed. Between some contacts and a member of the school office staff, she was able to put him in touch with both families.

He contacted them, explained their children were safe, in much way Mr Johnstone had done, and took the children to their homes. He gave DS Mullen the names, addresses and phone numbers for the Semple's and the Galbraith's.

DC Mullen asked Kyle's parents if they would have any objection to her having a quick word with him. They said they didn't mind, and he was brought into the lounge. The other two children were in another room with their grandfather.

After five minutes or so, Kyle had filled in a few blanks. He told them how Mr JoJo used a rope to lock the bad people in, how they went up some stairs, over the roof, down some stairs, hid until the new bad people from the black car went inside, how they ran to the 'scary graveyard' then went in the shop until his mum and dad arrived.

When the detectives were satisfied that they had all the information that was available, they thanked Mr & Mrs Stack, thanked Kyle, went to the car and headed back to Glasgow.

After they had left, Marion asked her son if there was something else, he wanted to tell her about what had happened. Something that he knew but didn't say. His head went down slightly, and his face took on that look that sat somewhere between, 'guilty' and 'am I in trouble?' Marion knew her son the way only a mother does.

Donald hadn't seen it but felt it would be helpful to reinforce what his wife had just said.

"It's okay Kyle, it doesn't matter what it is, I promise you, you will not be in any trouble. It's just that it might be really important."

The boy thought for a moment then looked at each parent in turn. His head was still down.

Sheepishly, he said, "There was one thing, but I didn't want to tell the police lady in case Mr JoJo got in trouble."

Not knowing what was coming, Marion tensed slightly but smiled at Kyle. "It's okay son. What was it? You can tell us."

"It was in the shop before you and dad came. Mr JoJo gave us some sweets and juice, but I don't think he paid for them. He had no pockets to keep his money in."

At the same time DS Mullen and DC Hannah were pulling into the Clyde Gateway building car park on French Street, Artem was giving his instructions to Olek, the driver. The three Watchers were needed. They were to be picked up and taken to a warehouse behind the recycling works by the river, just off South Street in Glasgow. This was only one of many premises the Russians owned.

He had already given separate instructions to Pavlo and Fedir who would make their own way there before Olek arrived. By 04.00 pm, the Watchers would be dead and there would be no trace of them ever having been there.

The tentacles of Yegor's operation stretched far and wide. There were his legitimate businesses, his criminal connections and the people who were on his payroll. These ranged from police officers to councilmen, from the business community to pubs, clubs, restaurants, and taxi-drivers. In Glasgow, like most cities, money talked. Grease the right palms and you'll get anything you want.

Artem had put the wheels in motion after his meeting with his boss. He had already started receiving information. He was in his office, next door to Yegor's, on the top floor of the Bath Street building, reviewing some CCTV footage collected from the nearest camera to the front of the Freeman Building. The start of the coverage was based on the timings that Olek had given him, and he got his first glimpse of Benny Fox. A figure dressed in black from head to toe, carrying one child with another three, close behind, exits a passageway and moves on. The contact that supplied the CCTV footage had already spliced and edited it. He had joined together the pieces of footage from various cameras which meant Artem could watch it continuously. He watched the figure with the children, exit the passageway, and move away in the opposite direction to the camera. After he had taken some left and right turns, it became obvious to Artem that the man he was watching knew where the cameras were positioned and chose his route, accordingly, continually moving with his back to them. On the few occasions where there was no choice and he was moving towards them, he deliberately kept his head bent forward, face to the ground.

Artem spoke to the laptop screen, "Very clever, whoever you are. I think you may be a smart man. You should know, I am smarter."

"What did you make of the Stack's?" asked DS Mullen.

"I felt they were being as helpful as they could be. There's no doubt they want to see whoever orchestrated this, caught and imprisoned," she replied.

"Mr Stack. Was he holding anything back?"

It wasn't a test, but it felt like it. Audrey Hannah knew her reply would need to be measured. If she says yes, she will need to explain what she thought he was holding back. If she says no, and DS Mullen thinks he was, it runs the risk of bringing her ability into question. She opted for noncommittal. The middle-ground.

"I think he was holding something back, but I couldn't put my finger on what it was. I'd need to speak with him again."

"He was holding back. I specifically asked him about this John Johnstone character, and he went to great lengths to make it clear to us that he had no idea what he looked like. I hadn't asked for a description at that point. He volunteered that all on his own. When we review the CCTV footage that we have, if we're lucky, we might see how close they were to each other and whether Donald Stack was telling the truth or not."

Thanks to their discussion with Donald Stack, they knew where the handover had taken place and they had a time.

As well as 'Traffcom' - Traffic Management cameras - Glasgow City Council also controls PSCCTV – Public Space CCTV. In situations like this, Police Scotland is able to assume control of the PSCCTV or to access the archives. With the help of one of the technicians in the Gateway Building, they were soon able to see the Stack's Audi Q7 at the kerb outside a shop. They saw a man dressed in black from head to toe. Mr John Johnstone. The image did not show his face and the camera angle did not definitively confirm if the Stack's would have been in a position to describe him, or not. For now, the detectives would have to take his word for it.

DS Mullen asked the tech' to pause the frame. She had an idea. She asked him to slowly roll forward from the point Donald Stack drove away. The figure in black moved into the shop. For now, he would be JJ. They sped up the footage until they were an hour later. JJ never came back out. Not out the front door at least. She was certain he hadn't stayed in there for any length of time. She engaged another tech and asked them to look at all CCTV they had for that timeframe, in the streets that immediately adjoined the one the shop was on. She was thinking this JJ person might have slipped out a back door. While the second tech' went to work on that, she asked the first tech' to start working backwards from when the Audi had left.

It took them longer to review the footage, than it had taken Artem. They didn't have the luxury of watching a pre-spliced and edited version. They had to watch it frame by frame, camera by camera, all in reverse. Eventually, they arrived at the point where JJ and the children had emerged from the passageway. DC Hannah googled information on the location. It looked like the children had been held in the Freeman Building in Merchant City.

Artem's disadvantage was that he only had the file that was sent to him, to work with. Granted, he could get any footage he wanted, but that would take time, and his request would need to be specific.

The detectives could move forward, backward and sideways as and when it was required. Thanks to the resources and the work of both techs simultaneously, they had what the Russian had, but they had something more. The second tech' had reviewed all footage for the timeframe as instructed and concluded there was only one figure who appeared from a building, one street over, eight minutes after JJ had gone back into the shop. DS Mullen knew this was her man. He was dressed, not in black, but in running gear.

DC Hannah took the opportunity to join in with an observation of her own. The runner was wearing a black backpack. It looked like the same backpack their mysterious man in black had been carrying in his free hand when he was carrying the child.

"It is. Good work," said DS Mullen.

They were able to follow the footage forward until the runner disappeared in the area behind the Corinthian Club after which they never saw him again.

Back on the first tech's screen, they ran that footage backwards from the image of the passageway in the Freeman Building, until they saw their runner entering it. This was then wound backwards until they saw him emerge from the same area, where they had lost him, on the other screen. Between both screens and agreeing the man in black and the runner were one and the same, they had a full picture of him running into the first frame, through to handing over the children to Donald Stack, and running back to where he disappeared from view.

She left instruction for the techs to keep looking, widening the search and the timeframes and she went to see if her boss was available. He was.

As she sat in DCS Cook's office, she covered everything from when she was first assigned the case, to their earlier meeting about communication issues and the lack of joined-up thinking, to her visit to the Stack family and finally to what they had uncovered with the review of CCTV.

She explained that the runner had his hood up in every shot and that he never looked up once. There was nothing to identify him. As far as she could tell, he emerged from an area somewhere at the back of the Corinthian Club on Ingram Street before 03.30 am, ran to what she believed was the Freeman Building and disappeared into a passageway in the front of it. A man dressed in black emerged a short time later with four children. She is certain it was the same person. She walked DCS Cook through the CCTV to the shop; Donald Stack arriving then leaving with the children; The man entering the shop then reappearing elsewhere as the runner again and running back to the very same area where he had first been picked up on camera, after which they lost him. She told him the techs were continuing their review of the footage.

She finished the meeting by saying she was arranging for Scene Examiners to visit the homes of the four abducted children and the shop, then herself and DC Hannah would be heading back out, to the Freeman Building.

9

By mid-afternoon on the Friday, in the Chip, Benny was thinking about calling it a day and heading home. Jack suggested that he stay for a while as a few of their friends were coming straight from work for an hour or two, but Benny said he wouldn't. Saturday was their regular day, and he would see everyone then. He said there were things he wanted to take care of, then he would have an early night, given that he hadn't slept much at all on the Thursday night. Jack understood and didn't press him. As a parting shot, he asked Benny if he wanted him to look into things for him. "Make a few discrete enquiries here and there?" was how he put it.

"No thanks Jack. I appreciate it, but for now, I think it best if I just leave things and hopefully it will all blow over."

As he said the words, he wasn't entirely convinced. Neither was Jack.

Leaving his friend in the pub, he made his way into the City Centre. He had a couple of things he needed to pick up from the shops then he planned on having a Skype with his daughter and two grandsons later if they were at home. The fur lined hooded parka he was wearing attracted no more than a casual glance from Jack. His friend couldn't see the thick, square, large-framed glasses, the £1,000 cash or the long-peak golf cap that were in the inside pockets. Benny had collected them from the unit earlier that morning.

As he sat on the subway train heading for Buchanan Street, he was lost in his thoughts for a few minutes. His mind drifted to the earlier business with Fiona Semple. The child with no shoes. He thought about the impulsive gesture he had had, when he blew her a kiss before she left in the Stack's car. He knew it had come from the earliest recollections of his own daughter. The paternal instincts that came naturally for any child in distress, your own or otherwise, when they are at such a young and delicate age, mentally vulnerable and physically incapable given their size. To see her – to see all of them – snatched from their beds and subjected to what they had been, he could feel an anger rising within. It came from the pit of his stomach. He knew the feeling well. It was familiar. He had experienced it many times before, in the aftermath of the death of his wife Emma, and he knew he would need to rein it in or run the risk of it consuming him.

Bringing his thoughts back into the present, Benny was now aware of a teenage boy sitting opposite him, watching with a degree of curiosity, as this middle-aged man sitting on his own stared off into space. The boy was with a teenage girl who Benny assumed was his girlfriend. She was absorbed in her phone although he wasn't sure what she could be doing on it. He was certain there would be no signal down here, in the bowels of the earth. As Benny turned his head and looked directly at him, the boy quickly averted his gaze to the advertising posters above the seats, looking at nothing in particular, in a way that almost suggested guilt for having been caught looking at something he shouldn't have. Such was life on public transport.

For now, Benny Fox had no knowledge of the existence of DS Jenny Mullen or DC Audrey Hannah, nor did they know of him. Benny glanced up at thc contemplative pose of the green-bronze Donald Dewar statue, as he walked up the hill to the Buchanan Galleries shopping centre donning his best 'easily forgettable casual' look, whilst the detectives were less than half a mile to the east, in the Freeman Building, in the Merchant City.

"As far as I'm aware, there isn't a caretaker as such. If we have a problem, we contact the landlord, and they sort things or send someone over. It's usually a man called Arthur. He's a bit of a handyman. A nice guy." The detectives had gone into a solicitor's office in the building and were speaking with one of the few members of staff who were still there. As it was mid-afternoon on a Friday, most had already left for the day.

"Do you have details of the landlord?"

"I have." The young man searched around his desk then handed over a business card with details of the letting company. "Here you go."

DS Mullen had opted for the solicitor's partly at random but partly by applying a little rationale. They were closest to where she had parked the car and they were the closest company to where the passageway cuts through the building. She thanked him then stepped outside and called the number on the card. It rang four of five times. Just as she thought the letting company people would also be finished for the day, a very efficient sounding lady answered.

"Roberts Commercial, good afternoon. Lorraine speaking. How may I help you?"

DS Mullen explained who she was and why she was calling. Without going into any specific detail, she said an investigation was underway and it involved the forcible abduction of minors. She then said it centred around the Freeman Building. She was looking for the fullest information possible on the building and its occupants / tenants, as well as details of the building owners. "I can of course obtain a warrant, but any help you can provide could give me a good head-start in our enquiries."

Lorraine said she understood and that she would send someone over immediately. She took an email address from DS Mullen and said she would forward the other information there. As a mother of two, the very mention of the abduction of minors meant there would be no question of her not doing everything within her power, to help.

The detectives started to look around but didn't have long to wait. From the street at the front of the building, they had recognised the passageway from the CCTV footage. They both went through and stepped out into the service area at the back. It was a lot colder there. There wasn't a lot of heat in the late afternoon autumnal sunshine in general, but in this area, which would be locked in perpetual shadow until the following spring, the temperature never got the chance to come up at all.

A quick look around didn't tell them anything. It was a deserted service area. No people, no vehicles, no signs of life other than a series of commercial bins.

It had been less than fifteen minutes after ending the call, when a silver Renault Kangoo van with no markings hurriedly drove in through the opening and came to a halt in front of the detectives. A man in blue overalls stepped out and introduced himself as Arthur.

DC Mullen explained to Arthur that she was looking to get a handle on the place. Who worked in the building; The types of businesses; Maybe one or two spaces would be vacant, awaiting new tenants? She didn't elaborate but she was thinking of somewhere four children could have been held for a few days without anyone noticing. She was recollecting the conversation with Donald Stack and trying to establish a timeline back to when the first abduction would have taken place. She had considered speaking with the families of the children first, then coming here. She then reconsidered the order in which she would do things, and decided coming here first, then visiting the families second, would be best as firstly, a lot of the businesses would be closed up for the weekend if she left it too late and, she thought any recollections or descriptions from the children would be more helpful if she had already been here and could visualise it first-hand.

Arthur said, "There are no vacant offices but there is a section of the building that is currently under redevelopment. Well, I say that. The redevelopment work has ground to a halt and the place is lying empty."

Donald Stack's driveway hadn't seen as much traffic in as long as he could remember. There were the family cars; His own, his wife and his father's; There was Marion's friend's car; Two vehicles from the Police Crime Scene Examiner's and a van from the security company. Thankfully he had a big place and there was room for everyone.

Marion's friend Anna had arranged to come and take her and the kids out for the afternoon / evening, while Donald and Freddy dealt with the other stuff. It was partly to give them some space but mostly to take Marion's and the children's minds off things for a while. She had offered for them all to stay at her home overnight, but Marion thought it best if they didn't. The security company people were here to try and get to the bottom of why the system had not worked even though it had been set the night before. Regardless, Donald had instructed them to replace the entire system to the best that they had available. He was spending a considerable amount of money with them and as a result, they didn't mind waiting in the van until the police had finished their work.

From the first vehicle, there were scene examiners who were gathering everything they could from Kyle's bedroom, the stairs and hallway.

The officer from the second vehicle was dealing with fingerprints from the door, the area around the hall table and the alarm system. Not that he could contribute anything, Donald felt the need to remain in and around this area in case any of the officers needed anything from him. He was getting a proper education in all things 'Fingerprints', as the officer made polite conversation with him. He now knew all about Ridges, Substrate, Matrix, Development Medium, and Distortion. By the time they were finished Donald was confident he could have gotten himself a job at the Scottish Crime Campus at Gartcosh in Lanarkshire.

When the police were finished, they loaded their equipment into the two vehicles and left at the same time. Before they did so, Freddy had signed for a copy of some paperwork for Donald.

When they moved out, the security company team moved the van into one of their spaces.

First to get to work was a tech using a laptop with diagnostic software in it. It quickly confirmed that there was no fault with the system, but it had in fact been switched off using the alarm code that is selected by and known only to the customer. Donald explained in no uncertain terms that he set the alarm and did not unset it at any point afterwards.

"The way that system is right now, is exactly as it was left when I went to bed. I set it as always and have never touched it again since."

"Well, according to the diagnostics, it's been switched off."

Donald was getting angry. The resultant tightening of his vocal cord and muscles gave his voice a higher pitch.

"I just told you, no one here switched it off."

"Is there a possibility you or another family member might have written the number down or maybe gave it to someone else, and you've forgotten?"

The dialogue was on the verge of becoming accusatory when the older man from the three-man team, hurriedly came down the stairs and interjected. He had been checking all the points and the PIR's upstairs when he heard how the conversation was going. Clearly, more experienced than his younger colleague, he felt it prudent to take over and try to diffuse things before they went from bad to worse.

"Mr Stack, please, if you can come with me for a moment, there's something I want to show you." The man had introduced himself as Charlie on the way in.

Donald followed Charlie to the van. Charlie reached in and lifted out a piece of kit, showing it to him.

"Firstly, let me apologise for young Christopher, he didn't mean any harm. He's good at his job technically but he's young and I understand he needs to learn that there's a way to speak with people. You have an expensive system with our company, and you need to know that it will do its job when it's supposed to. It didn't and I know that's not good enough."

Turning to the piece of kit in his hand, he continued, "This thing here is what we use to over-ride a customer's code where there is a problem. I couldn't say for sure at this point, but there is a possibility that someone has used something similar in your house to turn your alarm off. When that laptop gets plugged into the main system back at our office, we will know if the alarm was manually unset or if something like this disarmed it. From what you said, I have no doubt it is the latter of the two."

By the time Charlie was finished, Donald was less annoyed with Christopher, but he was now considerably more anxious about the fact that someone could simply switch the thing off and come in. Again, Charlie took his time and walked through what could be done to lessen the likelihood of the same thing ever happening again. He told Donald there was an irony in all of it. It came down to high-tech versus low-tech and in the end, low tech would have won. There was no forced entry. The front door had simply been opened with a key or similar. Had there been an £8 surface bolt or a properly placed chain on the inside, the only way in, would have been to smash a hole through the front door glass or wood and manually unlock them. Either that, or kick the door in. In either case, the PIR motion sensor would have done its thing and the intruders wouldn't have had the chance to over-ride the alarm code. It would have triggered by then.

By the time they were finished, a new system had been installed at Donald's insistence, even though there was nothing wrong with the original one. He got no arguments from any of the team. Charlie explained that although there were no systems that were linked directly to the police in the UK, any activation on this system would automatically be received by specially trained security controllers in the Alarm Receiving Centre, which operated 24/7. A second detector would be triggered, and this would be the confirmation for the Alarm Receiving Centre to contact the police.

Motion sensors were installed around the outside of the building, and these were connected to newly fitted security lights. By 05.00 pm, the security installation team were finished. Christopher and the third man sat in the van while Charlie undertook the orientation tour of the newly installed system with Donald Stack. As Charlie was leaving, he said, "What you have here Mr Stack is right at the top end of home security. It doesn't get any better. I'm sure my bosses wouldn't be happy with what I'm about to tell you, but if it was my house, I'd still get a couple of old-fashioned bolts for my front and back doors." He took a few steps away then without the slightest hint of irony, turned and called back, "Either that or get a dog… better still, get two. One with a loud bark and the other with big teeth."

As the security system installation team van was heading for the citybound M74, two cars were leaving the Russians warehouse yard on South Street, Glasgow. A metallic red Ford Kuga was carrying Fedir and Pavlo, heading for the Clyde Tunnel making their way back to Govanhill. At the same time, a black V-Class Mercedes carrying Olek and three dead Russians, was heading in the opposite direction.

The 'child snatchers' - cum - 'watcher murderers', had carried out their instructions from Yegor via Artem.

The two men and one woman had been tasked with one job only, and they failed. For this, the price was two bullets in the head from a HK VP9 9mm handgun. The direct thread mounted suppressor ensured there was no sound. There had been no instruction on who was to carry out the killings, as long as it was done.

Pavlo was more than happy to oblige. He didn't need to be asked.

There are, give or take, 300 crematoria in the UK. Approximately one third of these are privately owned. One such crematorium located on the outskirts of Glasgow is owned by a company that is registered offshore. Join enough dots and you would not be surprised to learn that company is owned by a Russian called Yegor Omelchenko.

By 06.30 pm, with the help of another 'inner circle' operative, there would be no hint of the three watcher's bodies ever having been there. Every detail, right down to trace metal from fillings; from the woman's wedding ring; from the six 9mm bullets, was collected and properly disposed of.

Arthur the Handyman showed the detectives to the empty section of the Freeman Building. He produced a set of keys that looked surprisingly small in view of the fact he had told them he had the keys for every door in the building.

The first time he produced them was to open the heavy metal plated door that led into the fire escape stairs from the service area. It was nothing more than coincidence that it had been the same stairs used by the Russians.

The stairway gave access on to each floor and the offices of the tenants located there. The detectives were only interested in the empty space at this point.

Neither Arthur nor the detectives could have known, but the watchers had been meticulous in clearing out behind them. There was no trace of them, or the children having ever been there.

Except there was.

Two things, actually.

Slowly sliding his fingers over the doorframe of one of the new rooms, near the lock, Arthur said something wasn't right. He was mindful not to get skelfs from the tiny splinters and slivers of wood.

"This door has been damaged, but it looks like someone has tried to hide the fact. It should be a smooth finish, but it's not. The door frames come ready made from the timber suppliers. They are cut to size in the factory, and they come out pre-sanded."

As DC Hannah moved in for closer inspection, she asked, "Are you saying it looks like someone has forced their way in here?"

"No. That's the strange thing. It looks like the damage has been done from the inside. Like someone inside was trying to get out."

Both detective's immediate thoughts were that it had been the children trying to get out of this room. They could never have known that Benny Fox had already got them out of the room next door, and away over the rooftops.

The damage here had been the watchers trying to get out after he had tied the door shut with a length of his climbing rope, and locked them in.

The second thing was the keys, or the lack of them in this case.

"Both of these rooms normally have a key in their lock. I know that for certain, I've seen them lots of times. Their gone and the only person who would do that would be me, and I haven't touched them."

DS Mullen had seen enough to know a visit from the scene examiners would be required and it would not wait until Monday.

"Arthur, as of now, this area is out of bounds to everyone unless you have my say so. I'm going to need you to keep yourself available with your keys if that's ok."

He replied by way of a nod, and they took a note of his mobile number.

To her colleague she said, "Audrey, if you had any plans in place, it might be an idea to change them. It's going to be a long weekend for you and I."

10

After his shopping trip, Benny went home. He had his Skype with his daughter and two grandsons in Surrey. As always, it was good to speak with them. Living so far apart was difficult for him at times but ordinarily, it isn't something he dwelled on.

Having been so close with the children earlier in the morning however, had brought on a sense of melancholy and he knew that speaking with his own family would help him shake it off. It did the trick. He felt better by the time he was finished.

He had laid his shopping bags on the sofa when he came in and went straight to his tablet and logged on. Now he was finished, he went back to his purchases. Among the various items he had bought were two burner phones. He had purposely chosen old style, cheap, pre-paid mobiles and he had deliberately used a corner shop that was set a few streets back from the main thoroughfare. It was the type of shop that stocked everything you could imagine, and his purchase was not out of the ordinary. Using cash and keeping his head down and away from the security camera, he would be anonymous if anyone ever felt compelled to check the footage. Ever vigilant, he kept the phones in the packaging so as not to get fingerprints on them. They would stay there until he was ready to use them, should he ever need to. He was thinking ahead and covering his bases.

The plan was to keep his routine as normal as possible for the foreseeable future. The only difference tonight was that he would not go for his usual run. He would sort some dinner, have an early night to get caught up on his sleep and tomorrow afternoon he would be at the pub with his friends like any other Saturday.

As a 19-year-old, Martin Connor was typical of hundreds, if not thousands of young men his age across the country. He had a job, was in a steady relationship and he had lots of mates. He was also the product of a broken home. After years of fighting and arguing, his parents Jim and Irene, had divorced when he was ten. He had lived with his mum and saw his dad at the court-appointed times. Sad as the situation had been, it didn't do him any harm. Some of his closest friends had been in exactly the same position.

He had moved into a rented flat with his girlfriend, Laura about six months earlier. Since they had moved in together, they had been in the habit of going to his mum's house most Friday nights, for their dinner. It was a regular thing and they all looked forward to it.

This Friday was different. He couldn't get his mum on the phone. It was going straight to voicemail. He tried calling the house but there was no answer there either.

As the afternoon became evening and he still couldn't get in touch with his mum, his concern had moved up a gear and he was starting to worry. At her insistence, he still had a key to her house.

He went there and let himself in but there was no sign of her. He toyed with the idea of calling the police but thought she would be annoyed if she was out shopping or visiting friends then came home later to find he had made a big fuss over nothing.

He wondered if she had been called in to work. He knew she worked in the care sector and would sometimes do back-to-back shifts that could keep her away for a day and a half or two days at a time.

He decided to leave it for now and just keep trying her mobile, off and on.

Although Martin Connor knew his mother had lived her whole life in Kaluga, Russia before coming to Scotland where she met and married his father, there was much that he didn't know. He'd seen photos of where she grew up near the Oka river.

For one thing, her name wasn't Irene. It was Iryna. She had been born Iryna Kushnir. She didn't work in the care sector. She worked for a Russian thug called Yegor Omelchenko. As part of the inner circle, her job of late had been a caretaker of kidnapped children. She wasn't shopping or visiting friends or pulling another back-to-back shift.

She was dead and her recently cremated ashes were literally in the wind.

Saturday morning was busy for DS Mullen and DC Hannah, and it didn't look like it would slow up any time soon. Between interviewing the families of the other children, reviewing the reports from the Scene Examiners from the previous day, visiting the Freeman Building with the Examiners today and reviewing the reports from the tech's who had gone over the widened search area from the CCTV footage, they had their work cut out.

DS Mullen was walking through what they knew so far, with her younger colleague.

"What we have here are two lines of enquiry. We have our mystery man, Mr John Johnstone, who by all accounts liberated these children from their captors, before any ransoms were paid. Then we have the kidnappers. As things stand, we know absolutely nothing about them. Would you agree?"

Again, Audrey Hannah felt like she was being tested.

"Yes, I would. To a point. We do know that they, whoever they are, are highly organised. The way they got in and out of the four homes tells us this. We know there is a connection between the four children and that is most likely to be the school."

She paused for thought then continued.

"Although the school is a connection, it would be wrong to assume it is the only connection. We need to explore the idea of there being anything else that they have in common. Anything in common, apart from them all being incredibly wealthy, that is. We know the children were held in the Freeman Building, so again, it's logical that there is a connection between the kidnappers and the building. Perhaps the Scene Examiners will shed some light on that. Then there's the ransom notes. That has an old-school feel to it, in my opinion."

"How so?" asked DS Mullen.

"I don't know exactly, it's just a feeling. Modern day situations like this one tend to involve modern technology.

Parents receiving anonymous instruction by phone or untraceable email. This feels like it's from another time. Maybe the Document and Handwriting people at the crime lab in Gartcosh will come up with something."

"I hope so. We could certainly do with something to go on. Although this John Johnstone character is not our primary focus, it would be good if we could speak with him. I'm sure he could fill in a few blanks for us."

"I agree with that. We have to assume though, that his reason for being there in the first place was not anything legal and as such, I can't see him volunteering to come and speak with us.

"Me neither, but we live in hope."

As Benny Fox was making his way to meet up with his friends, Martin Connor decided he had waited long enough, and he went to the nearest police station. After explaining his concerns and the fact that the last time he had any contact with his mother was Thursday, he was taken to a room to make a statement. When he was providing the details they required, he realised that he did not know where his mother actually worked. He had always known she was a nurse and was certain it was in a care home. He had never had any need to ask and it didn't come up in conversation. She never talked about her work. He thought his father might know, so he passed his contact details on too.

When the meeting was finished, the officer explained what would happen next and said someone would be in touch as soon as they learned anything. Likewise, Martin said he would let them know if he heard anything or his mother got in touch with him.

Like all of his colleagues, the young officer had received the memo from DCS Cook in Specialist Crime only yesterday, laying out in no uncertain terms that unsatisfactory communication would not be tolerated, regardless of what department it related to. He said it affected the Force's effectiveness, as a whole.

As soon as he completed his report, he made sure the information was placed on the system and was relayed to the relevant people. Despite his efficiency, not everyone took DCS Cook's instruction with the same level of enthusiasm. A similar conversation to the one he just had with Martin Connor had taken place at another police station on the other side of the river, only an hour earlier. A lady had reported that her husband went to work on Friday morning and never came back. She has not been able to contact him since, and this was completely out of character for him, she said.

That report was not completed nor was the information placed in front of anyone. The officer concerned there, was more interested in finishing his shift and placed the paperwork in his 'to do' tray with a view to giving him something to do when he came in on Sunday. Among the information that the lady had provided was her husband's occupation. He was a nurse in a care home. She knew it was called 'something' House and was in Glasgow, but for some reason, she couldn't immediately recall exactly where it was.

Over the course of Saturday, the detectives garnered everything they could from their various reports, meetings and conversations with colleagues. In summary, it didn't move them much further forward than where they were when DC Hannah laid out their position, as she saw it.

They did have a few things confirmed by the Scene Examiners at the Freeman Building, but these raised more questions than they answered. They were able to confirm that the two partially completed rooms in the area that was under redevelopment, had been thoroughly cleaned. The lead examiner said they were completely free of dust and debris compared to the rest of the area which, by comparison, hadn't been cleaned in over a year, maybe two. Another observation she had made was the window.

"All of the windows in this area were locked except for one. There are fresh footprints in the dust inside, on the windowsill and on the floor. The shoe size is a nine which places it right in the middle of 'average' for UK males, assuming it was a male. What is not average, is the tread – or lack of tread – to be exact. The sole is completely smooth. This type of footwear is typically used by certain athletes, climbers or on rare occasions, very specific Special Forces people."

Beyond this, the examiner would not speculate, saying she preferred to deal in facts. What she did say was, "I can tell you there were no fingerprints."

DS Mullen replied, "Nothing unusual about that Christine. Criminals wear gloves all the time."

"I don't mean there are no 'usable' prints. I mean there are no prints.... full stop."

Based on the information I have, you have four children, your unknown man who got them out, at least two kidnappers according to the children and the handyman who confirmed he was in and out of here over the last month. There is not one single fingerprint in this entire area. The place has been seriously wiped clean from top to bottom. Doors, walls, handles, rails. Every surface is spotless."

The detectives said nothing.

Having taken care of the watchers, Artem moved his attention to finding the man who had freed the children. Having reviewed all of the CCTV that his contact had provided, his train of thought was not entirely dissimilar to the detectives. He had watched Benny arrive, move through the city streets with the children, open the shop as easily as a man who has a front door key, pass them over to the man called Donald Stack and disappear back into the darkness.

He paused the footage on the clearest image he had of Benny Fox, which wasn't much, and once again spoke to his laptop.

"Who are you and what brought you here?"

Artem was certain this had not been a rescue mission. This man had not come here with the intention of freeing the abductees.

"You were here for another reason my friend. Finding the children was an accident for you. Lucky for them. Not so lucky for you. I look at you and I see a thief. Not only a thief, but an accomplished thief. This is not your first time. You have done this before, maybe many times before. That is where I will start. The clock is ticking for you, Mr Man in Black."

Artem got to work pulling in information from all across Yegor's extensive network of contacts. As the thief was not in prison, it was a fair assumption that he had not been caught for many years, maybe he had never been caught. Also, this was predominantly a commercial district. The thief was not a common housebreaker nor was he an opportunist. From this, he knew the thief was organised. Artem tasked everyone to start looking for burglaries that had taken place over the last two to three years; which yielded a good payday; which may or may not have been reported to the police and most importantly, for which the case was still open as no one had been caught.

It didn't take too long for information to start coming in.

There had been a jeweller who put diamonds in the safe at night and was last out of the shop. He was first in next morning, but the diamonds were gone. No sign of anyone having been in the shop; no sign of the safe having been opened; no sign of the alarm having been tampered with; and yet, the diamonds were gone.

There had been the Spanish drug dealer, Juan Pedrosa, who chose to keep a six-figure sum of cash in his Clydeside penthouse apartment because he was nine floors up, the money was in a safe, and it was safer than the bank, according to him. Despite the safe being locked and him being the only person who knew the combination, and the fact that there had been five other people sleeping in his apartment, he opened it in the morning only to find the money was gone. After much finger-pointing, shouting and cursing – which was entirely in Spanish – the only word his girlfriend understood was 'fantasma'. According to Juan Pedrosa, whoever took his money must have been a ghost.

Benny's afternoon with his friends was a welcome distraction. They had their usual table reserved and the day, as always, was filled with laughter. Every weekend saw more outrageous stories told about at least one member of their group. These were always exaggerated, invariably funny and unfortunately at someone's expense. For all that though, there was never any malice, and whoever was the butt of the comedy took it in the spirit it was intended.

As the afternoon yielded to the evening, the alcohol was taking its effect. The crowd started to split off in different directions. A couple stayed put in the Chip and a few stayed out but decided to visit other bars in Ashton Lane. Another couple decided to go for a curry. Benny, the only one who did not drink, was heading home. He said his goodbyes and was back in the flat within thirty minutes.

At around 09.30 pm, his mobile rang. It was his friend Jack. For Jack to call at night was unusual enough. The fact he had been with him for most of the day up until a couple of hours earlier, made Benny sit up. He muted the tv.

"Hi Jack, how's things? Is everything okay?"

"I'm not sure Benny." Jack was mindful to guard his words on phone conversations with his friend. It wasn't code, but he knew Benny would understand. For years the plan was the same. Although very unlikely, if they were ever put on the spot about conversations they had, it was just a retired crime reporter regaling his friend with stories. It wasn't exactly cast iron, but it would be hard for someone to disprove.

"Remember we were saying that this isn't Los Angeles or New York?"

Benny knew he was referencing the guys with the machine guns.

"Yeah."

"I just learned from a reliable source that today, someone has been looking into unsolved burglaries in and around

Glasgow, and I think it might be the same people. I know they don't know who they are looking for, if you catch my drift, but the fact is, they are looking. Apparently, they are pulling in information from all across the city."

Benny moved into character. "That sounds like another good story Jack. I'm looking forward to hearing the rest of it sometime."

Jack understood. They made some unrelated light chit-chat then ended the call.

Benny thought about the two burner phones he had bought. It looked like he was going to need them after all.

11

Benny had a restless night's sleep and was wide awake almost an hour before the first signs of daylight would start to appear.

After pulling on his running gear, he locked his flat and quietly left the building, being careful not to wake any of his neighbours.

It was dry and not too cold. A good morning for getting some fresh air and clearing his head. I say, 'fresh air'. It's as fresh as you'll get in any urban centre the size of Glasgow.

He crossed the road, went through the park gate and cut down through the trees on to the Kelvin Walkway. Turning right, he made his way north, following the river towards Maryhill Locks. He veered left for Dawsholm Park, turned left at Bearsden Road, followed that then turned left again at Anniesland library. He made a good pace along the A82 Great Western Road, back to the Botanic Gardens, from where he made his way back to the flat.

After adding a few small detours to his main route, he had totalled just over 6 miles and covered that in 40 minutes. It wasn't as long as he would usually run but it served its purpose. He had got his heart rate up, got a good sweat on and had cleared his mind. A bit.

Jack's phone call, the night before, had started what could only be described as a chain reaction of scenarios running through his head. He would think of one thing, which gradually changed into another, then another. Before he knew it, he was picturing the worst. The negativity was out of character for him, and he didn't like it. He wouldn't get those thoughts out of his head until he was able to separate facts from fantasy and to that end, he would need to know what Jack Buchanan knew. At the end of that call, they had agreed to meet up this morning. Not in their usual place, but this time in a café near Kelvinbridge.

Benny got there first, just before 10.00 am. He ordered a coffee and took a seat outside in the lovely autumn sunshine. The lady who owned the place brought out his latte, made some polite conversation then left him alone to read the newspaper, that he had picked up on the way. As always, he had dressed for the weather. Coat, hat, scarf and gloves.

There was no one else around to see the smile that formed as a random thought popped into his head from nowhere.

Looking around him, and thinking about the weather, he heard his wife Emma saying, "You'll need to get properly wrapped up Benny. It's cold. Not cold, cold, but cold." She had a way with words. He missed her. He missed her every day.

He had barely gotten the paper opened when he heard the voice from behind him, "Why are you sitting out here? It's Baltic. Have you eaten yet? I'm starving."

Benny laughed and replied without turning round. "Two questions and two statements all in the one sentence, without coming up for air. Good morning, Mr B. How are you?"

"I'm fine thanks, but I'm not sitting out here. I need my home comforts Benny boy. Let's get inside for a heat."

Moving inside, it wasn't busy, and like outside, they would have the place mostly to themselves. Another hour and a half, and you would be lucky to get a seat here, inside or out. After ordering coffee and bacon rolls, they made some small talk, mostly about Jack and the rest of the gang's antics from the night before, after Benny had left. Despite it being funny for the most part, it reminded Benny that making the decision all those years ago, not to drink alcohol, had been a wise move.

After the breakfast came, they got down to business.

"As you are aware, I still keep in touch with a few people here and there from my days at the paper. It comes in handy, especially when I'm sourcing information for you. I know we spoke about this, and you said not to go looking into anything. I didn't. However, last night, big John and I ended up in Michael Ross's place at Charing Cross and I met a good friend from those days. He still does freelance work for the Associated Press. One thing led to another, and he told me, someone high up in one of the city's organised crime gangs has put feelers out for information. They are looking for someone who has carried out big score burglaries – one's like the ones you would do – but has never been caught. Like you."

"Does your friend know who these people are?"

"No, not yet, but here's the thing. This only started yesterday. Just over 24-hours after your surreal version of the Pied Piper of Hamelin, cutting through the city streets with the children in tow. It doesn't take a lot for me to make the leap, from you - an anonymous burglar, crashing the machine-gun men's party and ruining their payday – to some heavyweight gangsters looking for an 'anonymous burglar', the very next day. Of course, it could be unrelated. It could be nothing but coincidence. It could be my imagination, just adding two and two to make five. At the end of the day though, I don't think it's any of that. My instincts are telling me loud and clear, that these two things are one and the same.

"Me too. I wish it wasn't, but I'm with you on this. I've no doubt it's me they're looking for."

Benny was deep in thought as Jack ordered more coffee.

"Okay. On the plus side, I'm careful. I'm always careful. For the same reasons that the police couldn't find me, I can't see how these people could find me either. Having said that, if the police ever did find me, the worst that would happen is, I would go to jail for a long time. These people? Whoever they are, if they catch up with me, jail would be the least of my worries."

"So, what do we do then?"

"Well firstly, there's no 'we' here, Jack. Not in this. I know you've always had my back and I love you for it. We're like brothers, and I know you'd always be there for me. This is different though. If it is the same people, and logic tells me it is, I'm not prepared to put you in harm's way. Kidnapping children and walking around with machine guns? I think these people would kill you – and me – without a moment's hesitation. What I'm going to do is stop them before they get anywhere near me."

"And how do you propose to do that?

"I don't know yet. I'm going to have to give this a lot of thought, but I have an idea where to start."

The genuine sincerity in his friend's voice was clear to hear. "Whatever you decide to do Benny, just be careful. I wouldn't want anything to happen to you."

"I know that Jack."

Jack thought this would be a good time to lift the mood a little. "It's not just that. I'd miss you of course, but more importantly, who'd keep me topped up with Chateauneuf de pap down the pub, every other day."

When they finished and went their separate ways, Benny went by his place, picked up the two burner phones and a few other things he had bought, then made his way to his unit.

He changed out of his normal clothes and put on his leathers. Having replaced the bike's ringer plates for the proper ones, he lifted the bike seat, plugged in the two new phones to the two USB ports located there, and started to charge them up. He put the ringer plates from the Freeman Building job, a pair of heavy-duty pliers and his unassembled flip phone, along with the battery and SIM card, into one of the panniers. He rolled the bike out, locked up and set off.

He hadn't had a specific destination in mind as he rode out. He thought he'd just go with the flow in whatever direction took his fancy and see where he ended up. He did know however, wherever he went, at some point, it would need to include somewhere fairly remote and somewhere that would be by the woods or overgrown.

He ended up out for almost three hours and took a route that headed southwest, away from the city towards Prestwick and the coast. Before he got there, for no particular reason, he decided to veer left and ended up riding through the East Ayrshire countryside. After passing a farm called Corrie Mains and a picturesque village called Sorn, he found a remote spot, pulled in and took his things from the pannier. First, he took the pliers and snapped the number plates into a dozen small pieces that would mean nothing on their own. These would be discarded one piece at a time over many miles, into hedgerows, trees and undergrowth. Not very environmentally friendly, but for now, that wasn't high on his agenda.

Bringing out the burner phones from under the seat, he could see these were fully charged. Selecting one, Benny inserted the SIM card and when it was ready, dialled 101.

"Hello, my name is John Johnstone. I need to speak with the detective in charge of the investigation into a kidnapping incident that took place in and around the Freeman Building in Glasgow two days ago." He gave the operator the number of the new phone and ended the call without waiting to hear the reply or waiting to be connected, if that was indeed something that would have happened. He didn't think he would have been connected to the lead investigator straight away, but that was okay. It was the call back that he wanted.

He decided to sit parked up where he was for a bit and see what happened. He didn't have to wait long. In less than ten minutes, his new phone rang. His first thought was he would need to change the ringtone to something less annoying and reduce the ringing volume. The small display window simply said 'call'. There was no number. That was okay. He let it ring. It rang for what seemed like a long time. He was starting to wonder if there had been something that he should have done beforehand, to engage the voicemail. The ringing ended.

A few seconds later, the display showed there was a new message. He opened it. The message confirmed that he had a new voicemail.

He followed the instructions and set up his first-time password for retrieving voicemail. When he was done, he pressed and held the number 1 on his phone and the system told him he had one new voicemail. As instructed, he pressed three to listen to it.

"Hello, this is Detective Sergeant Jenny Mullen. It's a message for Mr John Johnstone. Mr Johnstone, can you call me as soon as you can please? It's very important. My number is 07..."

Benny wrote the name and number on a piece of paper then deleted everything. The call out; the call back; the message saying there was voicemail, and the voice message itself.

When he was done, he disassembled that phone and assembled his own flip phone. A few minutes later he was calling Jack. It went to his voicemail. Benny read off the name and number and left a message asking Jack if it was possible for him to find a home address for this woman. He ended by saying, "If you fancy another bacon roll and a coffee, tomorrow around 10.00 am, would be good." More code. More arrangements being made, that would make no sense to anyone but Benny and Jack.

He was done for the day. It was a good Sunday out on his bike. It was productive, and it had gone to plan. He took his own phone apart, put everything away in the pannier, got his helmet back on, fired up the big black Kawasaki and set off through the countryside, heading in the direction of the motorway. Being as much old school as he was paranoid about security, there was no Sat Nav. Despite this, he knew from instinct and experience, he would be back at the unit in less than forty-five minutes.

Just like the day previous, Benny arrived before Jack. Human nature being what it is, he automatically went inside and got comfortable in exactly the same seat he had sat in the day before. The same lady stepped forward, said good morning, and asked if he was having a latte again. Human nature.

There is a notion that is impossible to be defined as anything other than mythology, but for millennia, academics, scholars and theologians alike, from many cultures, have debated their beliefs in their own version of the same thing.

The Japanese tell of the legend of the red string. An invisible string, tied to the pinkie fingers of two strangers who are destined to meet and be soulmates for evermore; The Moirai of the Greeks - the three weaving goddesses, apparently hold a thread of gold for each person on earth, which is suddenly cut when the death of that person is imminent; There is reference to a red string in the Kabbalah that talks of tying believers to the Holy Land, of Jerusalem.

Whether we are believers in such things, or not, there is no doubt that some things, whilst seeming unconnected and unrelated, absolutely are.

Jack was only five minutes behind Benny when he reached the cafe. At the very same time they were placing their breakfast orders, there were situations and conversations and actions taking place all over the city, that were inextricably linked.

Magical, invisible threads? Almost certainly not. Connected? Without a doubt - Yes.

Artem and his network of informants; DC Mullen and her boss, DCS Cook; DC Hannah and the CCTV techs; Information about two missing persons that were not connected on Saturday afternoon, but now may be, on Monday morning; A freelance journalist mid-call with a source about his latest story, intending on making another call to an old friend as soon as he is finished; All linked, all taking place simultaneously, and all centred around one man.

Benny Fox.

Artem had brought his boss up to speed with his enquiries. "We are receiving information on a continuous basis Yegor. There is no doubt this thief was there for reasons of his own. I will find him and when I do, you decide his fate."

DS Mullen apprising her boss, DCS Cook of the progress of the enquiry so far. By far the biggest step forward had been the man who calls himself John Johnstone, calling 101 and looking for her, the previous afternoon. "He reached out when he didn't need to sir. I have no doubt he will call again. It is my belief he holds the key to this whole case. He was there and saw whatever there was to see, first-hand, before the kidnappers had the chance to clean up."

DC Hannah had been called downstairs by one of the tech's reviewing the wider CCTV after their main person of interest had disappeared. "It may be something, maybe not, but I found this and think it's worth looking into. Just after our jogger disappears around 6.00 am, in the streets behind Ingram Street and Virginia Place, I monitored all traffic emerging from that area. I discarded taxis, buses and work vehicles. Across eight cameras, I noted every vehicle that left within 15 minutes. I cross referenced this with all traffic coming into the same area within 15 minutes before we first saw him. I got one hit. A black Kawasaki motorbike."

A missing person report had been made in person by a son in relation to his mother and was logged on the system on Saturday. Another missing person report made in person by a lady in relation to her husband, also on Saturday, had not been logged onto the system until late on Sunday afternoon. It was apparent that there were similarities which could mean a possible connection between the two, and questions were now being asked as to why the latter report was not logged until almost 24-hours after the statement had been taken.

Jack Buchanan was halfway through his second bacon roll when his phone rang.

"Excuse me," he said to Benny. "Hello, Jack speaking."

It was his friend from Saturday night. The journalist.

"Hi Jack, it's Peter Mann here. I have that address for you. It'll cost you two bottles of malt. One for me and one for the guy that got me it. The good stuff mind, none of your rubbish. And remember, if you get anything I can use in my piece, you let me know. Agreed?"

"Agreed. What's the address?" He wrote it down. "Thanks Peter, that's appreciated. I'll get a couple of bottles of 15-year-old and drop them off to you. I'll chat with you soon."

He turned to Benny, "The address you were looking for? This is it. I hope you know what you're doing."

He passed Benny an address for a street in East Kilbride.

"It was my friend Peter. He's the guy I was telling you about. He used to work on the crime desk with me many years ago. He's probably more connected today than I ever was."

"I find that hard to believe."

"Believe it amigo, it's true. He is putting together a 'spotlight' piece on Glasgow's organised crime gangs. I said I might be able to feed him some information going forward. Obviously, he only gets to know what you want him to know, if anything. By the way, you probably heard, the address will cost two bottles of 15-year-old."

"That's no bother at all Jack. I'll sort that out. If what I'm thinking is right, it will be a small price to pay.

12

Benny was focussed on only one thing for the rest of Monday, and that would employ all of his attention. Detective Sergeant Mullen.

He formulated this section of his plan as he walked home from the café, after leaving his friend. Taking a slight detour, he made his way to the Hillhead Library on Byres Road. As someone who used the library a lot, he was very familiar with the layout. He went straight to the Reference Section and quickly found what he was looking for. Maps.

With the recall ability that his memory was capable of, he took in the information he needed and left the library less than fifteen minutes after going in.

Back in his living room, he got comfortable on the sofa, closed his eyes and did his 'cerebral walkthrough' of possible scenarios, mentally closing doors as he went along.

His paranoia radar was running on full power and given the circumstances, that wasn't necessarily a bad thing.

Since the time he encountered the men with semi-automatic weapons, who chose to make a living out of snatching 8-year-old children from their beds, wrist-tying them and putting blackout hoods over their heads, he found it easier to simply refer to them as 'Thugs', when thinking of them.

He began. "The Thugs are trying to find me. They don't know who I am, which is good. Why are they looking for me? Because I took the children before they got their money. Donald Stack had confirmed they hadn't been paid. Assuming this is the case, what is their game-plans for after they have found me? There's no money in it for them. Logic dictates therefore, its good old-fashioned revenge. Taking that to its logical conclusion, the plan is to kill me. So, what's the best way to ensure that doesn't happen? I could run. Run where? I couldn't take all this baggage to Surrey and run the risk of involving my family. That's never going to be a serious option. Where else would I go? No-where was coming to mind, so running wasn't a realistic consideration. I could do nothing and just hope they don't find me. Maybe, but what if they do – it brings me full circle right back to where I am now. Again, not a realistic consideration either. If I'm not running and I'm not hiding, the only thing left as far as I can see, is to fight. Not fight, literally, but put wheels in motion to find them before they find me. Using the resources of the police to do that would heighten the chances of a good outcome, considerably. Jack said the Thugs were 'pulling in information across the city'. What if some of these favours come from within the police? It's not inconceivable. Law of averages tells me that of all the people who could be on the payroll of the Thugs, it's unlikely to be the lead investigator. Not impossible, but unlikely. So, when it's all broken down, my earlier instinct to buy two pre-paid burners was correct. Engage in dialogue with this DS Mullen lady on a one-to-one basis. Help her to apprehend them, and that can only be good for me." Satisfied he had a plan of sorts, he got to his feet and set about putting it in place.

Unaware that the police now had a black Kawasaki Z1000 on their radar, Benny was oblivious that he was taking a slight risk as he drove along the quiet residential streets in St Leonards, East Kilbride. The risk being that the lead detective on the case lived there.

Having perused a map of the area earlier in the day, he knew exactly where he was going as he rode along St Leonards Road past the Catholic Church and took a left into Calderglen Road. The street he was heading for was one of the cul-de-sac's that branched off it.

It was a nice enough area. It wasn't his cup of tea though. It had a 1970's feel to it and as a result, most of the house designs differed from each other. Detached, semi-detached, bungalows, split levels, two-stories. "A world apart from the new estates that were being thrown up these days with their regimented lines of identical houses, street after street," he thought.

Arriving at the street he was looking for, he went to the end, turned without stopping and drove out again. The drive-by was enough to tell him what he needed to know. The house he came to see, backed on to the woods, had good, mature gardens and was two-storey. That suited him a lot better than a bungalow. There were no cars in the driveway, but it was the afternoon of a workday. It didn't tell him anything, but it wasn't a problem either. Given the size of the house, it was a reasonable assumption that it was a family home. A husband or a partner? Children? Maybe, maybe not. He noted there was an alarm. He would have been surprised if there wasn't. He put the property in the £250,000-£275,000 bracket. Assuming there were two incomes, it looked reasonable for a detective on her salary. Nothing to suggest she was living beyond her means. Not on the Thugs payroll, was what he was driving at.

He knew it was supposition for the most part, but instinctively, it made sense.

When he was finished, he rode back to his own home in Glasgow, parking on the other side of the river as he always did on the rare occasions that he took his bike there. It would be dark soon and he would be heading back out to his unit around 09.00 pm.

He got there at 09.10 pm. In much the same way as he had when he readied himself for the visit to the Freeman Building at the end of the previous week, he went through the same process organising clothing, equipment and changing the number plates on the bike.

Turning the lights out at 11.15 pm, he'd get a few hours of sleep on his three-seater sofa.

The alarm went off at 02.30 am. He had calculated his movements step-by-step, and knew he would be dressed, bike out, unit locked up and journey covered to his destination, in fifty minutes. He allowed another ten minutes to change clothes at that end, and a further fifteen minutes to jog from where his bike would be parked, to the cover of the woods behind, and to the side of the house of Detective Sergeant Jenny Mullen.

His timing was perfect. He arrived as planned at 03.20 am, parked up in the secluded place he had picked out earlier that day and changed clothes. As he jogged from the bike to where he planned on entering the woods, he never saw a soul on foot. A few vehicles had passed him but as far as he could see, no one took any notice.

Under cover of the darkness and the shrubbery, Benny got himself to the treeline on the edge of DS Mullen's garden and stopped. He regulated his breathing, waited five or six minutes and listened. Completely still, completely, silent he was listening for the tiniest sounds of life. Doors or windows opening or closing; voices; footsteps; a car engine coming at speed.

There was nothing.

Satisfied he was alone and not at risk, he quickly removed the jogging gear. From Benny the Runner to Benny the Thief in sixty seconds. With the assortment of items that he had brought in his backpack, he went from Benny the Thief to Benny the Professional in another sixty seconds.

His lock-pick gun. A small alarm disabling device, not dissimilar to the one the Russians had used. A Yukon Advanced headset with fixed night vision goggles.

For all of Benny's expensive, professional equipment, the next three minutes would be 'make or break' time. In much the same way Charlie the security technician had explained to Donald Stack about high-tech versus low-tech, Benny knew this to be absolutely true.

Dogs.

Motion sensors lights were problematic but could be overcome. Get close enough to the cabling and it could be cut, rendering the lights ineffective. That, and the fact that they were so commonplace these days, people did not automatically react if they came on. Animals, birds, the wind.

There were a dozen things that could bring them on, none of them a concern.

Dogs however were completely different. No matter how deep a sleep you might be in, if you suddenly hear your dog barking, growling, becoming alarmed, you react. It only takes seconds for that trippy state of sleep to dissipate and full consciousness to resume.

Stealthily, Benny moved around the darkest edges of the garden. No lights came on. So far, so good. Dressed completely in black, he would be invisible to the world. From his perspective looking out, it was the opposite. Through his goggles, the world he saw in its infinite shades of green was more than adequately lit for what he needed. Careful not to trip over anything or bump into anything, he made his way to the back of the house itself.

No lights. Good. No dogs so far. Better.

His earlier question of whether the detective had a family or not was answered with the oversized trampoline and the kids sized football goalposts that were there.

The back of the house had a set of bi-fold doors that led out on to an expanse of decking. The rattan furniture was still there but the cushions and back rests were gone, presumably stored away when the summer had ended. It would have been simple to unlock these doors and enter, but there was the alarm to consider. He knew it was on as he looked in through the glass and could see the blinking light from the PIR sensor, high up in a corner.

There wasn't much about home security systems that Benny didn't know. However, from the whole myriad that was available, there are essentially only two components that make up over 90% of home security systems. There is the PIR sensor – Passive Infrared. The little unit that is fixed high in a corner, standing sentinel over its protective grid monitoring heat changes or detecting movement.

Then there is Contact Motion which triggers the alarm if protected doors or windows are opened while the system is armed.

He went to the front of the house. It was only minutes after 04.00 am and the little residential cul-de-sac was fast asleep. He stepped to the front door. Doing its job, the motor of the lock-pick whirred but would be silent to anyone standing more than a couple of feet away. Benny felt the clicks more than he heard them. When finished, he was moving in slow motion as he gently pressed the door handle down and applied the slightest of forward pressure. He didn't want to open it. Not yet. He just needed to check it was unlocked. It was. Next, he had to check if there was a secondary set of security. There was a descending order running through his mind. No secondary lock would be the first prize. A chain would be an inconvenience, but fixable. A bolt would be a problem. A bolt would be almost as bad as a dog.

He let the door move forward in the frame but no more than two inches. No bolt. Good news.

Slowly, he let it move further another inch. Slowly for two reasons. One was, there might be a chain engaged and if there was, he didn't want it making any sound. The other reason was as important, if not more so. He was mindful of any motion sensors. If the moving door triggered the alarm, it would commence the countdown of the time he would have available to disarm the system. Just like any homeowner, coming in from work for example, unlock and open the door and you have, typically thirty to sixty seconds to unset the system.

When a crack appeared between the door and the frame, he saw it and stopped. There was a security chain engaged.

Back in his unit, he had an array of cutters, each purchased with different purposes in mind. They were all of the highest grade and were chosen based on the quality of the Jaw and the Steel. Another two considerations were the cutting force and the length of the handles.

He had brought one pair, with the job at hand in mind, but they would be used as a last resort. He had also brought a tool that he had fashioned with his own hands. At first glance it appeared both crude and rudimentary. It was neither. Benny was well practiced with it and could literally use it with his eyes closed. Working with only touch and feeling to guide him, he was both adept and accomplished.

The tool had started its life as nothing more than a cheap wire coat-hanger. After bending and twisting it into the exact shape and length he wanted, he covered every inch in black PVC electrical tape by winding the tape round and round, smoothing it on tight with his thumb and fingers, The tape gave it added rigidity, but more importantly helped suppress any noise when he was using it.

After bending the wire tool into an inverted 'L' shape, he slipped it through the crack and moved it into position. The small hook that had been shaped on the end, soon found the correct point of the chain. He twisted it slightly, one way then the other, and teased the end the of the chain out of the housing that held it in the locked position. Using the tool to lower the chain until it was hanging fully extended down the inside of the door, he turned it to the correct angle and quietly brought it back through the door crack. He placed the tool into the backpack and brought out the alarm device.

In one fluid movement he opened the door, stepped inside, located the alarm control panel, which was situated on the wall behind the door, plugged in the device and pressed the button. It had taken eleven seconds.

He closed the door over behind him but left it fractionally ajar. It would save a few valuable seconds if he had to get out in a hurry. Benny knew a few seconds head start could make all the difference. From the street, it would look closed, with nothing out of place.

He waited a full three minutes before moving. Certain that no one had stirred, he took a few tentative steps in through the door on his immediate left. It was the living room. Like outside, the room was awash in the green light world he saw through his night vision goggles. He looked around and found what he was looking for. Against one wall, there was a floor to ceiling glass unit with a selection of photos and ornaments set out on it. He unzipped one of the compartments on his backpack and removed two items that were the whole purpose of his being here. These were placed, one on top of the other, on one of the highest shelves beside and slightly to the back of a framed photograph that showed two primary school aged children smiling as they posed in their school uniforms. Almost certainly, a brother and sister.

Retracing his steps, he came out of the living room and closed the door. Using his device, he reset the alarm. Stepping outside, he went through the process of re-attaching the chain.

It was considerably more difficult to replace it than it had been to remove it. After a couple of minutes, it was done. He relocked the front door. The whole exercise had been partly an attempt to leave the house as he had found it, hoping no one would have known he had been there. His bigger concern was to make sure the place was secure again, for the benefit of Detective Sergeant Mullen and her family.

The process of the next fifteen minutes was virtually the same as it had been when he arrived, but in reverse.

Benny was back in his unit in Kinning Park before 05.30 am. He undertook the usual routine of cleaning, wiping and sorting the equipment and the bike. By 06.15 am, he was settled on the sofa with a cup of tea, thinking about the next stage of his plan.

He waited until 07.15 am, got his new burner phone, walked through the estate to his blind spot and sent a text to DS Mullen on the number she had called him from two days earlier in Ayrshire. Photographic memory. Nothing written. Nothing stored.

The message simply read, "DS Mullen, I have left two items beside the children's school photo in your living room. One of the items is a pre-paid phone. There is one number stored in it. It is mine. Can you call me please? John Johnstone."

Within minutes the burner rang. He thought it might and he hadn't moved from the concrete bollard he was sitting on. The display told him the incoming call was not from the pre-paid he had left in East Kilbride. It was from DS Mullen's own phone.

"How fucking dare, you. You break into my home and think that's acceptable? I will find you and arrest you. We'll see how acceptable that is."

Before she got the chance to reload and continue, Benny cut across her.

"Hang up and call me on the phone I left you. I won't answer a call from this one again."

He ended the call without waiting for a reply.

His phone rang again less than a minute later. It was from the pre-paid he had left her.

He answered and launched straight into what he had to say, before she got the chance to speak. He had given this a lot of thought in the unit, in the last hour.

"Firstly, I apologise for coming into your home. As for finding me and arresting me, trust me when I tell you, that would be a lot more difficult than you think. I made a judgement call and I believe it was the only decision I could take, given the circumstances. I think one or more of your colleagues is corrupt and in the employ of the people who kidnapped those children. In the fullness of time, I will explain why I think this to be the case. For now, however, you are the only person that I will deal with. I know from experience that phones, like every other electronic device can be hacked. They can be cloned. They can be tracked. You have called me twice from your personal phone DS Mullen. The number is in the public domain. It's the reason I found out where you lived. Absolutely no one, except you and I, are aware of the two pre-paid phones we are speaking on now. I would like to keep it that way please. The other item I left, the box of colouring crayons in the plastic food-bag, could have the fingerprints of one, possibly two of the abductors. The only other person to have handled the pack was Clark Munro, one of the children. I will call you again in a few hours with a description of two different abductors and of the vehicle they were driving. When I give you the vehicle details and an exact time, I'm sure you will have no difficulty in tracing it from CCTV. I understand you will have many questions and I will do my utmost to answer them when we speak later."

Benny ended the call, removed the battery and SIM card and went back to his unit.

13

As a thief, Benny would only steal from institutions. 'Insured money' was how he made his peace with it on a moralistic level. This, however, was not always the case. It was only ten years earlier that he had made this decision. The twenty years or so, prior to that, were different.

For Benny, it had always worked on an ethical level. He was a principled man. Always had been. He would steal from people whom he considered less than 'wholesome'. Stealing from criminals sat easy with him. Corrupt jewellers, drug dealers, loan sharks, anyone who accumulated their wealth from the exploitation of others. He was more than happy taking it from them.

To try and typify him as some Robin Hood figure would be a gross overstatement. He wasn't. Most of what he stole, he kept. Having said that, he wasn't averse to incredible acts of kindness and generosity, and over the years has given tens of thousands of pounds to worthy causes and people in need. Always anonymously.

There were two main reasons that brought about the change. One was, stealing from dangerous people wasn't an ideal pastime and he knew the longer he did it, the more he was riding his luck, regardless of how meticulous his planning was. Basic law of probability. The other reason was, when he took anything that wasn't cash, it had to be moved on. Fenced. It meant the involvement of a third party.

With hindsight, he couldn't understand why it had taken him so long to arrive at this conclusion. Nonetheless, he had come through it unscathed. Now, after ten years, the chances of anything coming back to bite him from those days, were almost zero.

Almost.

There was a particular job from eleven years earlier that was more standout for him, than the others. In fact, there is a possibility that job was the one that made the decision for him.

Benny had learned of a particularly nasty piece of work who was living on one of the leafier fringes of Glasgow and was in the process of reinventing himself. The story the crook had to tell, had been heard a thousand times over. He had walked the same path as so many before him. Local hardman to petty criminal to serious criminal to number one in a small criminal gang to number one in a bigger, more organised criminal gang, to carving out his own little empire, operating on every level of crime that he was capable of. He had a viciousness to him and everyone in his world knew it. He was not averse to getting his hands dirty, dirty being a metaphor for bloody.

Then came the inevitable day when the crook realised, he had more money than he had ever dreamt of, and suddenly he wanted respectability. He didn't just want it. He craved it. Rubbing shoulders with the affluent, respected wealthy at every opportunity, he wanted to be part of that life. In his quest for acceptance, he thought he could buy it.

The biggest, the shiniest, the newest, the loudest, the most expensive, he had to have it all. On this journey, he had discovered that buying art was a marvellous sign of respectability.

He bought art legitimately. He bought it, and Benny Fox stole it from him. Could there be anything more ironic?

Although there was an eleven-year gulf between then and now, the parallels and synergies between that crook's story and the Yegor Omelchenko story were remarkable.

Started with nothing; preying on society for your own gain; growing a criminal organisation and increasing personal wealth exponentially; Seek social acceptance; End up a victim at the hands of a mysterious thief; Pump every resource you have at your disposal into finding him.

A week before one particular Christmas, he had attended the opening display of Leonardo's Madonna of the Yarnwinder at the National Gallery of Scotland. After a few introductions from a good friend, he found himself at a private viewing in an Edinburgh gallery less than a week later.

As a complete novice to this world, naivety would always bring the risk of being exploited by the unscrupulous. However, in his particular case, that would never be a concern. He knew - that they knew - who he was. His reputation preceded him and that was enough to guarantee the paintings would be the real deal.

He made two purchases at a combined cost of £420,000. They were given pride of place in his home and were prominently displayed on the morning of Christmas Day. Perfect timing.

He could never have imagined he would wake up three days later to find them gone.

The paintings, as well as £100,000 worth of jewellery, and a substantial sum of money, were taken. The police were called but scene examiners were having great difficulty. There was no trace of anyone having come into the property, other than the family. No prints, nothing out of place, no disturbances or breakages outside or in. The items in question were there one day and were gone the next. Like they had simply vanished.

Every snitch was leaned on, every tree was shaken, bribes were offered, threats were made. It all amounted to nothing.

Benny had moved the paintings and the jewellery on at 20 pence in the pound. It was less than the normal rate, but anonymity was more important than money here. How did it end? Benny ended up netting over £100,000 for the paintings and jewellery, plus the cash. The criminal-cum-art lover ended up with nothing and the paintings ended up in a private collection in the South of France.

Now, eleven years on, Artem's search for burglary cases that had never been closed, returned a fairly extensive list. Among that list was the theft of two paintings plus cash and jewellery.

There was nothing exceptional about the items stolen, but the fact the thief had gotten in and out without leaving a single trace, caught his eye. He looked deeper and explored the items that had been stolen.

Like many paintings, the two had been given names by the artist. A quick Google search told Artem they had resurfaced, having been sold by a private collector three years earlier.

There was no name but with his contacts, it took less than an hour to get one. Via the agent that handled the sale, Artem now had the name 'Mr John Miller-Mackie' with an address in Kensington, London. The information made no reference to Mr Miller-Mackie's country house outside Cap Benat, an hour's drive to the South-West of St Tropez in the South of France.

It didn't take much for Artem to trace the steps. From Mr Miller-Mackie, back to who he acquired them from, all the way back to the person who first sold them. The thief. It was an easy process in Artem's mind. Mr Miller-Mackie would provide the name of the agent who handled the original sale when he bought the paintings. The agent would provide the name of the fence who supplied them. The fence would provide the name of the thief who stole them.

He considered getting a phone number and calling this man in London, but decided against this, thinking it would achieve a better outcome if the conversation was face-to-face. That is usually how it worked for him.

He filled Yegor in on what he had found and said he would go to London to speak with this Mr Miller-Mackie. He said he would take Pavlo Volkova with him. "Whatever he knows, I will find out and we will be closer to finding this thief before the day is out."

After having someone in the organisation make the necessary arrangements for them both, they flew BA and arrived in London Heathrow's Terminal 5 before 01.00 pm. Picking up their Mercedes hire car, they took the M4/A4 city-bound and using the built-in sat nav, were driving into The Royal Borough of Kensington and Chelsea at 01.40 pm. It was the name given on the on-screen map, courtesy of the integral

COMAND info-system. Artem missed the tiniest upturning at the corner of Pavlo's lip that placed him part-way between displaying disdain and sneering. Clearly, Pavlo was not a fan of 'Royal' anything.

Finding their destination without any trouble, they slowly drove along Thurloe Square in London's SW7 with the park on the right and the properties on the left. No ascending odd or even numbers here. The houses were simply numbered 41, 42, 43 etc. Glancing into Thurloe Street as he passed, he saw what he was looking for. As a one-way street with no entry from his end, Artem drove past it, stopped at number 43, and reversed back around the corner. There was an empty parking bay there. It was stencilled in white paint as a City Car Club bay. It meant nothing to Artem. It could have read 'Disabled Parking Only'. It would have made no difference. He parked in it and they both got out.

They made their way to the house they wanted and Artem pressed the buzzer. A lady answered. She sounded well to do.

"Hello, can I help you?"

Artem put on his most charming, clipped English voice, "Good afternoon, madam, I need to speak with Mr Miller-Mackie. I apologise for not having an appointment, but it is rather important."

"I'm sorry, that won't be possible. May I ask what it is in connection with?"

Artem saw Pavlo's face and could read his mind. He knew each thought would include violence in one form or another.

He carried on and lied, "It's in connection with two paintings that he sold three years ago. It appears there is something of a problem with the validity of the sale."

"What problem?"

"It is rather sensitive madam and in the interest of privacy, yours as well as mine, it would be preferable if we could continue this conversation inside."

Silence. He waited but there was nothing. As he was getting ready to speak again, the door buzzed and clicked open from the electro-magnets as it was momentarily unlocked from within.

Benny Fox could have told the Russian Thugs and Mrs Miller-Mackie that there were only two types of these doors. Fail Secure and Fail Safe. This door was almost certainly Fail Safe.

As Artem and Pavlo stepped inside, closing the door behind them, they heard the lady's voice.

"Up here." The Miller-Mackie's lived on the first floor, and she had stepped out on to the landing. The property had originally been one house but like many others in the area, had been split into two.

After entering the house at her invitation, they followed her to the main reception room. Artem noticed it was bright and airy. There were meticulously preserved high ceilings and ornate cornicing. Clearly original. A big white marble fireplace dominated the room and the general décor suggested family wealth, generational wealth. It exuded a certain timeless charm without having to try too hard. As one house with seven or eight bedrooms, it would easily have sold in the region of twelve million pounds. Now, split as it was, it would still be worth at least half of that amount.

Pavlo noticed there were no other people present apart from the three of them. There was more open plan to the place than he would have expected, and he concentrated his hearing on the rooms that were out of sight, for any sounds. So far, he heard none.

Without formal introductions the lady, who Artem assumed was Mrs Miller-Mackie, spoke first.

"So, what is this problem you are referring to?"

"It's to do with the validity of ownership of the paintings I'm afraid. Mr Miller-Mackie may have sold something that doesn't belong to him. It's imperative that I speak with him."

She looked at him smiled and said, "I do apologise. Where are my manners? My name is Lydia Miller-Mackie." She extended her hand.

Artem took it, shook hands, smiled and lied again, "My name is Arthur Brookes."

Pavlo stood to the side and said nothing.

"Well Mr Brookes, unless you have brought a Ouija board with you, I'm afraid you've had a wasted journey, and this is as close as you will get to speaking with my husband."

She extended her left arm, motioning towards the marble fireplace behind Artem. He turned and saw the Murano Blue ceramic pot sitting atop, front and centre.

It took a few seconds for his otherwise excellent command of English to grasp the Ouija board comment, when he realised it wasn't an ornament. It was an urn, and it held the ashes of the late Mr John Miller-Mackie.

A dead end for the Thugs and a bullet dodged for Benny. Literally.

14

It had just gone 10.00 am when DS Mullen heard the phone ring in her bag. It wasn't the ringtone of her own phone and for a split-second, she thought it was someone else's. Then she realised it was the pre-paid. In the seconds it took her to retrieve it from her bag and answer it, a troubled sensation coursed through her at the thought of the man who she knew was calling, having been right inside her home, when he left it for her. The two words that summed up how she felt about that were Anger and Violated. Not in equal measure. It was more the latter than the former.

She was at her desk in the Clyde Gateway building in French Street. She got the phone, accepted the call and spoke without looking at the display. She knew exactly who it would be.

"Wait one minute."

She lifted her notepad and pen and was moving towards one of the interview rooms that would be empty and would give her some privacy.

From her own desk, DC Hannah, saw what was happening but didn't say a word.

As she entered the room, the newly fitted energy saving lights came on automatically without needing to find the switch. She laid her things on the desk and looked at the small phone. It was cheap but one of the features it had was a speaker. She engaged this and sat the phone down in front of her.

There were no formalities.

"So, you told me you would have descriptions for me." Violated had gone and emotionally, she was back at Anger.

Benny heard it but made no reference. It was perfectly understandable.

"I did. I also told you I think one or more of your colleagues is corrupt and working for the people who kidnapped the children. I told you I would explain why I think that. Let's begin there."

Benny had taken the usual precautions at his end, to ensure any trace placed on the call would not harm him. If she'd had a trace put on it, they would find the location quickly and a patrol unit would be dispatched. It wouldn't be futile, but it would be pointless. He specifically chose a spot where he would see them coming but they would not see him. There were no cameras, no people and no traffic. No witnesses. He would destroy the burner and disappear.

He gave the detective enough credit for having thought this through too.

She had. Arriving at a very similar conclusion, she thought it would be useless where he thought it would be pointless. She knew the dialogue would stop and that would not help her or the case. There was no tracing in place.

She also knew she was not in control here and that did not sit easy with her. For the time being, however, there was nothing she could do.

"So, tell me."

Benny gave her a condensed version of the information that he had, including what he'd received from Jack, via his friend, Peter Mann. "Within hours of me leaving that building with the children, the criminals had started pulling in information from contacts all over the city. They were looking for me. That is without question. There was no contact with me at any time, at that building, yet they knew of my existence. This tells me there is only one possible way they could have known."

She said it before him, "The CCTV."

"Exactly, and you know, as I know, where operational control sat that early in the proceedings. Your people took the reins and everyone else was shut out."

She knew it was right. It made sense.

Benny continued, "Detective Sergeant, I am genuinely sorry for coming into your home. It was a necessity for me. I came in the front door, I took no more than a dozen steps, I placed the phone and crayons, and I left again. I know it doesn't make it right, but the least I could do was make sure you were 100% safe before I left. If my instincts are correct, no one is aware that we have these two phones yet, apart from us. I couldn't risk leaving it for you somewhere other than your home and someone else coming across it. If you can accept that as a fact and we can move on, I genuinely want to help here, and I believe I can. The 'two phones' thing is because I trust you only. Pure and simple. You can call me paranoid, and it would be justified, but it has served me well for a long time, and I won't change now. Especially now."

There was a pause then DS Mullen spoke, "Okay, John, if that is your name, I will go along with it for now, but you should know this. You are a fundamental person of interest in this investigation, and we are committed to finding you. There is a lot of resource committed to that and it won't stop."

"That's okay. It's probably better that way. It would raise suspicions if the search for me stopped suddenly for no good reason."

If her statement had been designed to elicit concern from him, it hadn't worked.

"So, these descriptions?"

Benny took the next five minutes to lay out what he knew. She took copious notes. Some of what he told her was already filling in gaps. The rest, she would get to work on, as soon as they were done here.

When the call ended, DS Mullen walked back to her desk. She now had something of a dilemma on her hands. Could she bring DC Hannah and DCS Cook into her confidence with regards to the conversation she just had with Benny? She would need to do something. They were both part of the investigation and he was in the middle of it.

She trusted her boss implicitly. As for DC Hannah, she had no proper working relationship with her before this case and as such, couldn't form an opinion one way or the other. She didn't really know her. Her guess was that she would not be a threat, but this was not about guessing. It was about facts.

Even if the other detectives were straight down the line, the issue would still be, something being said or information being passed on, inadvertently. Carelessness.

She knew she would need to include them to some degree, and she decided how she would move forward.

She would confirm that John Johnstone had been in touch. There would be no reference to the two burner phones. The assumption, therefore, would be that it was to her own phone. In the event that anyone was rogue, and her phone was cloned, it would yield nothing.

As for the burner, Benny had put in place a protocol for them both to follow, when they had spoken a few minutes earlier. He said it was for their own safety. He asked DS Mullen to remove the SIM and battery immediately after the call was terminated, saying he would do the same. Going forward, they should both assemble their phones respectively and leave them on for five minutes before disassembling them again. He said this should be done four times every twenty-four hours. 02.00 pm; 06.00 pm; 10.00 pm and 10.00 am. That gave them both four windows to contact the other, if necessary, after which the devices were invisible.

"If we miss one, we simply wait until the next one," he said.

"Christ," she thought, "No wonder no one can find you."

Later that day, there was something of a confluence and three things that were not obviously linked came together that would propel the case forward, considerably. A box of colouring crayons, gobbledygook and missing persons.

The first thing DS Mullen had done when she came into work that morning, was pass the crayons on for fingerprint analysis. Like a lot of what happens internally in police forces the world over, she has a friend who works in that very department and asked her if she could put it to the front of the queue and rush it through as a personal favour. Her friend did and the results were back within a few hours.

From an investigation point of view, it was fantastic news. The little box of crayons returned four usable prints. Three full and one partial.

Of the four, one was clearly a child. Of course, there would be nothing in the system, but it was assumed this would belong to Clark Munro and was ignored. The other three were in the system. The two full prints were from the same person, a woman, and the partial which provided an 82% match, was from a man.

A quick search of the police database flagged up two different missing persons reports that had been filed the previous Saturday and Sunday respectively. These were their fingerprints. Both were Russian.

DS Mullen looked back at her notes from the earlier conversation with Benny. She had written down the 'gobbledygook' as he called it. Many sketch no set him.

She did a quick Google search. No results. She added 'Russian' to the search. Again, no results. She was about to put this line of enquiry to the one side then she had another thought.

She sat looking at the screen for a moment. Many sketch no set him. Maybe it wasn't English. Maybe it was something Russian that sounded like that.

After four or five minutes of trial and error using Google Translate, she got a result.

Mne skuchno s etim. It was Russian for 'I'm bored with this'. That's what he heard and assumed they were talking English.

Crayons. Missing persons. Gobbledygook. Confluence.

DC Hannah had been following up an enquiry of her own. A black Kawasaki Z1000. The tech working the CCTV search told her there was good news and bad news. She was tempted to say that she wasn't in the mood for games and maybe it would be easier if he just came to the point. She didn't.

"So, give me the bad news."

"The bad news is that the system isn't dynamic enough to run the CCTV search ad infinitum. It means we can't tell where the bike came from or where it went to, outside a few miles in any direction. There are too many variables. We'd need every camera, for every street, for every frame. Without an exact time and place, it's impossible."

"Okay, what's the good news?"

"The good news is we got the number plates. The bike is currently registered as being for sale by one of the dealers here in the city."

The details were taken from the tech. DC Hannah went to her desk and phoned them.

She placed a call to the dealer and was passed initially from reception to the main office, then she was put through to the Sales Manager. It took less than four minutes for her good news to change to bad news.

It was quickly established that the details she had were indeed correct. "That's right Detective, it's a Diablo Black Kawasaki Z1000SX. That is the number plate. I can tell you though, that your other information is incorrect. This bike has been in the middle of the showroom for the last two weeks. I'm looking at it right now. It hasn't turned a wheel."

"Is there a possibility it was taken out, used and brought back without your knowledge?"

"It's a possibility, yes, but it's very unlikely. It will be easy for me to confirm that one way or the other though, just to be sure. Every bike's milage reading is taken when they come in here. Also, we have 24-hour surveillance cameras on a continuous feed, and these have a digital seven-day backup. I'll check both and phone you back."

DC Hannah thanked him for his help and ended the call. She wasn't holding out any hope of getting anything positive from him. Then another thought occurred to her. There was one positive. What it told her was, if that bike hasn't moved, it means the rider of the other bike in the CCTV footage has deliberately replaced its proper number plates with copies of those from the one in the showroom. If someone has gone to that trouble, she knew with 99% certainty, the man in the camera was their mysterious man in black. At least one of his chosen modes of transport was a motorbike. She had already run a search and there were no bikes of this description reported stolen in at least the last six months. Therefore, there is a high probability this guy has bought the machine which means he must keep it somewhere. Ideally at his house, which could provide an address.

Benny Fox's earlier assertion that the police had a mole reporting to the kidnappers, was right on the money.

Another package had been couriered to the top floor offices in Bath Street. It was a sealed Manila Envelope and contained a series of photographs of the black motorbike and its rider, and with these was a handwritten note. The photographs had been lifted directly from the CCTV footage and were the clearest that were available. Each one was time and date stamped. They corresponded exactly with the incident at the Freeman Building. The envelope, marked private and addressed for the attention of Artem was sitting on his desk, awaiting his return from his fruitless trip to London.

The photos would not move him much further forward than the CCTV images had moved DC Hannah, but next to the Manila Envelope was a second, smaller envelope. It was also marked private and addressed for the attention of Artem.

This one contained a name. Peter Mann.

15

Just after 01.00 pm, DS Mullen had her meeting with her boss, DCS Cook. This was now a regular thing and as per his request, she kept him abreast of ongoing developments. She was mindful that she would need to be back downstairs before 01.59 pm as she had questions, she wanted to ask John Johnstone and needed to fit in with his 'five-minute window of paranoia'. On some base level, it annoyed her having to comply with something as banal as this, but on a higher level she accepted it actually wasn't banal at all, and he was probably right.

They finished up at 01.40 pm. She hadn't mentioned the two burner phones nor the pre-arranged, five-minute slots, four times a day.

On her way to her own desk, DC Hannah stopped her and filled her in on the situation with the black motorbike. The Sales Manager from the city dealership had already called back and confirmed their bike had never moved. The milage and security footage confirmed it, but he did something else. Belt-and-braces, he had called it. He had counted how many bikes would need to be moved in the showroom to get that one to the entry/exit doors. Seven. Someone would need to have moved seven other bikes, got this one out, rode it about town then undertook the whole process again, in reverse, to put it back. And clean it back up to showroom condition. None of those things happened, he assured her.

DS Mullen acknowledged that it was significant, regardless of whether they got an address yet or not. DC Hannah said she was already working on tracking down all UK sales of that particular make and model, for the last 12-months.

"That's good work Audrey. I'll let you get on with that. I have a call I need to make."

She said it was a personal call. This would explain why she didn't simply call from her desk.

It was 01.58 pm. She discretely removed the pre-paid burner from her bag and took this with her notepad and pen into the interview room she had used earlier. The indicator was switched from 'vacant' to 'in use', to ensure privacy.

02.00 pm. She had the SIM card and battery in place and was already dialling.

It was answered on the second ring.

Since their earlier conversation, she had thought a lot about how much she was prepared to share with him. She didn't want to tell him anything. This man was a thief, and she was a serving police officer. Her professionalism told her it was wrong to tell him anything about an ongoing case, and it went against every instinct she had. However, her experience told her it was necessary, and she knew a two-way flow of information would result in her getting much more from him, than it would if it was simply a case of take, take, take.

With this in mind, she was first to speak, when he answered.

She couldn't bring herself to call him John. Mr Johnstone was difficult enough.

"Mr Johnstone, I got the results back from Fingerprint Analysis and we got a positive result. Two results, actually. We got two full prints for a female and one partial for a male. That was good foresight you had in lifting the crayon pack and putting it in the bag."

"It just made sense at the time Detective. The children had confirmed the crayons and colouring books had been provided by a lady and they said a man had been present. He was the one who brought them food and drinks. Are you able to tell me anything about either of them? I'm guessing positive returns means they are both in your system."

There were no names or addresses. No reference to the Missing Persons reports that had been filed.

"I can tell you they were both Russian."

There was a brief pause. Benny was thinking about the conversation he had with Jack, about how his friend Peter Mann had first mentioned there were criminals pulling in information. He also said Peter Mann was working on a 'spotlight' piece for the newspaper and it was organised criminals here in Glasgow. Could it be Russians he was talking about?

"Hello, are you still there?"

"Sorry Detective, I was distracted for a moment. Yes, I'm still here. Russians? Does that fit in with anything else you have in relation to this?

"No, not yet."

"I see. Well, I remembered something. After I gave you the description of the Black Mercedes earlier, I remembered part of the number plate. One number and three letters, in sequence."

The search for the car was underway with the CCTV technicians, after DS Mullen had passed on the information Benny had given her. There were no results back yet.

"That's good. That should help narrow things down a little. Earlier, when you said someone had spoken, what you called 'gobbledygook', do you know if that was a man or a woman?"

"Yes, it was definitely a man."

She didn't elaborate on why she was asking but she was now certain it was the same Russian man she had a partial fingerprint for.

"I wanted to ask you something else. It's partly personal but mostly connected with the case."

"Sure, fire away."

"When you gained entry to my house the other night, am I correct in saying the alarm was set but you were able to unset it, then reset it again?"

"Yes, that's right."

"So, did you have our passcode?"

"No. I have a piece of equipment that alarm company engineers use on site to unset an alarm without the passcode."

"And does this piece of equipment work on all alarms? Is it universal?"

"No, not exactly. If you're familiar with modern day car mechanics in a garage workshop, think of it like the diagnostic machine or laptop they plug into your car's ECU –

The Engine Control Unit. If it was a Ford garage for example, their machines would work across the whole Ford range. They wouldn't be expected to work across the Porsche range, however, or BMW. I already knew what alarm system you had as the logo is emblazoned on the Bell Box cover on your outside wall. I knew, to bring the Ford kit and not the BMW kit. Like the car diagnostic equipment, there are generics which do a little of everything but don't do all of anything, if that makes sense. Those would be too much of a hit or a miss thing. It would be like a professional tradesman using DIY tools."

DS Mullen didn't reply. He could hear her thinking at the other end of the phone.

"If I may Detective, I think I know where you are going with this. Is it the homes of the kidnapped children you're thinking about?"

"Yes."

"You're wondering if the system could be determined from the outside covers of those properties."

"I am, yes."

"That's an excellent question and well worth pursuing if you don't mind me saying so. These are wealthy people. I would hazard a guess at their systems being right at the top end, and if so, it's very unlikely those systems could be properly determined from a drive-by. I would go so far as to say, your kidnappers had details of the systems, beforehand. Assuming, all four families had the same Alarm Company, the information could have come from someone who worked there and had access to that information. That's a real stretch though. The odds of that would be astronomical and it's my guess, the details of the systems could only have come from someone who had actually been in all four homes."

When Artem came into his office, he was relieved to see Yegor was not in. The trip to London had been a dead end. He knew his boss was very black and white about these things. There was no grey for him, no middle ground. This would be received as bad news. Artem had always found it easier to deliver bad news if it could be followed up with good news. He hoped one, or both, of the envelopes on his desk would contain the good news he sought.

Opening the big one first, there were photographs and a handwritten note from the Russian's inside man, in the police. He spread the photos out across his desk. Each was of the same man riding a motorbike, the only difference being they had been taken seconds apart from different CCTV frames.

As he read the note, it explained that the man in the photographs was the man Artem was looking for. The note further explained that the number plates had been ran through the system but yielded nothing as they were ringer plates from another bike that was the same make and model. He was very familiar with this process. They did the same thing with cars and vans on a regular basis.

The note also said a search was underway for a black V-Class Mercedes.

He hissed through his teeth. This was more bad news. It was not what he was hoping for.

Turning to the smaller envelope, the note inside had been typed and was from one of the organisation's many contacts. It explained that an investigative journalist was writing an article on organised crime in the West of Scotland but focused mainly on Glasgow. It said the Russians and their relationship with the Asians on the city's southside, was a significant portion of the article. The name of the person writing the piece was given as Peter Mann. It confirmed his movements that were routine for most days of the week. He was a creature of habit. The name of the pub owned by Michael Ross featured, more than once.

Artem made a mental note to see that both sources were paid for their information. Without lifting the phone on his desk, he pressed the speaker button which served to secure an outside line, whilst putting the phone onto handsfree. The number he punched in was recalled from memory. Like most of the people who worked for him, he memorised numbers rather than writing them down or storing them in his own phone. It was another small level of detachment.

The phone was answered by Pavlo. Artem spoke to him in Russian as he often did when it was only the two of them. Artem told him he had two things he needed sorted. He wanted Pavlo to get Fedir and Olek, and for all three of them to come to his office right away. He also told him to put the black V-Class out of sight and not to drive it again.

The three of them arrived in less than twenty minutes. Pavlo and Fedir took the stairs up to his office while Olek found a parking space for the red Ford Kuga he was driving, explaining he would only be minutes behind them.

When everyone was gathered, Artem gave his instructions. Firstly, The V-Class was now obsolete. He had considered having it run through a 'chop-shop' where some value could be gotten from it, whether stripping for spares or cobbling it together with a different V-Class, rebuilding it, painting it and selling it on. It wasn't lost on him that even second hand, the car would still command a price of around £30,000.

With the advances of modern forensics as they were, however, he was thinking of how it had ferried the children from their homes to the Freeman Building, and how there would almost certainly be trace DNA, regardless of how well it was cleaned. He decided against these options and told them he wanted it completely destroyed, immediately.

Another tentacle of Yegor's network was a scrap metal business that he owned. It was thirteen miles to the east of the city, in North Lanarkshire. The car would be driven there first thing in the morning when the roads were quiet. By the time most people were hurrying through their breakfast cereal or morning toast, before getting on with the rest of their day, it will have gone through the Baling Press Compactor, resulting in a non-descript 3,000 kg metal cube that would disappear into the recycling process along with hundreds of tonnes of other scrap ferrous metal.

He moved on to the journalist, Peter Mann.

Olek was instructed to secure a van that could not be traced back to them. This would work in exactly the same way as Benny's bike. The van would be stolen. The plates would be changed to those of an identical vehicle, and unless serial numbers and VIN numbers were cross-checked, it wouldn't attract more than a second glance from the police or anyone else.

The information Artem had received from his source had been photocopied and a copy was passed to each of his foot soldiers. Starting with the Charing Cross pub owned by the man called Michael Ross, the journalist should be visually identified. From there, a plan would be put in place and when it was safe to do so without attracting attention, he should be lifted from the street, hooded and using the stolen van, brought to the warehouse at South Street.

It was another dry, cold morning and the first signs of daybreak were coinciding with the automated switching off of the streetlights.

Other than the occasional car or the man walking his dog, the streets were empty as the black V-Class made the last few hundred yards of its life's journey. Approaching the entrance to the scrap yard, Olek slowed the car and indicated. As he did, the big gates started to open. There were only two people here as the car swung in through the opening, which was immediately closed behind him. There was himself and the only scrap yard worker who knew the whole set-up was not entirely what it seemed. He too, was Russian. The other workers, who would not start their shift for another hour, were either Scots or Polish, and they didn't actually know who their employer was, other than JCG Metals, which was nothing more than a front. As long as their money was in the bank at the end of each month, they didn't really care.

The plan was easy. After the car was destroyed, the second man would lock the place up and drive Olek back to Glasgow. There was no one to see what was going on.

Except, there was.

Danny Manuel was on the last break of his shift having started at 02.00 am and would be finishing at 10.00 am. It was nothing more than coincidence that saw him sitting in the half light, half dark inside the cab of his Scania S650 V8, with the engine and lights switched off. As a matter of course over an

8-hour shift, he would take two short breaks and one longer break. If it had been his first short break, the engine would be running, and the interior lights of the cab would be switched on as he would pour himself a coffee from his flask and be on the move again in 15 or 20 minutes. Similarly, if it was the longer break – his 'lunch' break – although it would only be 05.45 am, the cab lights would be on, but the engine would be switched off unless it was particularly cold, in which case he'd leave it running for the heater. This being his last break, he didn't want anything else to drink or eat. He would usually use this time to have a 'power nap' as he called it. He had read that term a few years previous but couldn't remember where. He always set the alarm in his phone for 20 minutes in the unlikely off chance that he drifted off into a deeper sleep.

His truck was parked up in the same place each night in an industrial estate, the farthest edge of which was separated from the scrap yard by a chain link fence. From his position, he had an interrupted view of more than half of the yard. Ordinarily, there was never any sign of life from the place as he would stop, park up, have his power nap and be on the move again, over an hour before the first scrap yard worker arrived.

Not today though.

He had only been stopped with the engine powered down for two minutes, three at the most, when the yard's big sodium lights burst into life and illuminated everything, including his cab. Although it was getting light, there was still enough darkness to allow the motion sensor technology to auto activate when a car had driven in through the gates and stopped. The driver got out, left the engine running, walked back and closed the gates behind him. Danny looked on for no reason other than curiosity. It was different from every other morning he had been here over the last two years.

He watched the man get back in his car, drive round to the office building and park in the bay nearest the front door. Rather than going into the office itself, the man walked firstly to the crushing machine and powered it up, then moved to a crane and powered that up.

Danny's interest was now piqued, and he followed the movements of the man.

After a few minutes, the man walked back to the gates and opened them again. As he did, a black Mercedes entered, and the gates were closed behind it. Danny was thinking how smart the car looked and assumed it belonged a manager or maybe the owner. It pulled up outside the office but didn't take one of the parking bays. The gate opener came to the driver's window and there was some conversation.

Of all the things he could ever have imagined happening next, this would not have been one of them.

The Mercedes moved forward and stopped. As the driver got out and took a few steps back, the gate opener climbed into the crane, swung it round and positioned the big grabber claws immediately above the car.

"What? Surely not." He was talking to himself, and at the same time he was reaching for his mobile phone.

In the single fluid movement of someone who has done this many times before, he was able to open the camera app, shift to video, zoom in and start recording, with nothing more than a glance at the handset. As the digital seconds were counting up on-screen, confirming he was recording, he watched the scene in front of him unfold, through the phone screen.

The crane claws closed in on the car roof, grinding metal and showering shattered glass all over the ground as the windows imploded and exploded simultaneously. It picked the car up as easily as you or I would pick an apple or an orange out of a fruit bowl. The gate opener was clearly experienced in operating this machinery. In one movement he lifted the car, swung it round until it hovered over the crusher and dropped it in. He switched off the crane, climbed out, walked over to the other machine, and pressed a few buttons on the panel attached to the side of it. With the same ease and lack of effort that was evident with the crane, the crusher did its thing and within a few minutes all that was left of the black Mercedes was a giant metallic Oxo cube.

The crusher was shut off, the two men got into the car that was in the bay, left the yard and within seconds the sodium lights switched themselves off. By comparison to the previous few minutes, the yard was eerily silent. It was as empty as it was every other morning.

The surreal scene he had just witnessed was running through his mind when he realised the phone in his hand was still recording.

16

Eighteen hours before Danny Manuel recorded the incident at the scrap yard, which was just after the meeting with Artem, Olek drove Pavlo and Fedir back to their flat in Govanhill and dropped them off. From there, he went on to the warehouse and made the necessary arrangements for the stolen van and the V-Class Mercedes, for the next morning. He had drawn the short straw. The other two would get to go socialising for a few hours. They changed clothes into something smart but casual and had someone pick them up and drive them to Charing Cross. There was a pecking order within the organisation, and although they were not quite at the top, they were a long way from the bottom. When they called for a driver, someone would stop whatever they were doing and come for them.

They were heading for Michael Ross's pub.

The place was surprisingly busy for a mid-week afternoon. No one gave them a second glance as they entered the bar. Finding an empty table, they sat down, ordered a couple of beers and picked up two lunchtime menus. The food was typical bar fayre, but it must have been decent. Most of the patrons were, or had been, eating. The choice was always the same in most bars like this one. Steak Pie, Fish and Chips, Macaroni, Chicken. It never varied much from place to place. They had been in Scotland for many years now, but they still missed the food of the motherland. Kamchatka crab, Pelmeni, Kvass, Borscht.

They placed their order and engaged in mundane chit-chat about nothing in particular. It allowed them to blend in. It didn't take too long to find their man. Within earshot, there were four men grouped at the bar, one on a stool and three standing. It seemed like they had been in the place since opening time, and it didn't look like any of them had eaten. To say they were drunk wouldn't be accurate, but the way they were going at it, they would get there soon enough. The drinks were flowing. As is always the case in most places, the more they drank, the louder they became.

From the conversation they were having, the Russians learned there was a Joe, an Arthur and a Peter. When they heard the name Peter, Pavlo and Fedir discretely tuned in a little more intently. The crunch came almost an hour later when Peter was suddenly referred to as "Mr Mann" by the one called Arthur. Peter Mann. The correct name in the correct pub. This was their man.

The two Russians ordered beers but drank them slowly. After another two hours, Peter started his 'goodbye' routine as he was getting ready to leave. In true drunk man fashion, it took almost 10 minutes to do that, and he said to his friends he would see them tomorrow, same time, same place. Pavlo and Fedir looked at each other. Without speaking they both understood. They now knew who they were looking for and where he would be in 24 hours' time. They stood up and stepped out the door before Peter Mann.

Crossing the road, they found the best vantage point and a few minutes later their man emerged. Following him from Sauchiehall Street into Elmbank Street, they watched him move on to another pub. They didn't need to follow him any further. They had what they needed. Cutting straight through Elmbank Street, at right angles, is Sauchiehall Lane. In 24-hours' time, this is where they would park the van and take him as he passed.

After his shift, Danny Manuel went home and as he did every other day, went straight to his bed. He would fall asleep quickly and not wake until 06.00 pm. He'd get up, get dressed and join in with everyone else who was just coming home from work. The routine suited him, and it gave him a sense of normality. Other people slept then worked. He worked then slept.

As he was sinking deeper into a dreamless sleep, the Russians were in the South Street warehouse, running through last minute rehearsals for today's plan.

The Mercedes had already been destroyed in the early hours. Olek had prepared a stolen Peugeot Boxer Hi-Top van. It was non-descript white and the plates had been changed to those of an identical make and model which was registered to a company in Stirling. The only obvious thing that would separate the two vans was on the inside. The stolen van had been fitted with black tarpaulin and a metal bracket had been secured to the floor.

It would blend in completely with the hundreds of other white vans that criss-crossed the city every day, going about their business.

Forty minutes before the time they expected Peter Mann to be walking along Elmbank Street, the van rolled out of the warehouse yard gates on to South Street. Turning right for the city centre, they made their way to the A814 Clydeside Expressway and joined the flow.

In a few minutes, they had reached the on-ramp for the M8 motorway. They took this and exited at the next junction. A few lefts and rights brought them to their destination. Each of them knew their part in what was to come. Fedir got out of the van, and it drove away. He wore a heavy coat and a hat, making sure to keep his head down the whole time. Just like Benny Fox, he too was very aware of the plethora of CCTV cameras in the city.

He positioned himself adjacent the pub on the assumption that Peter Mann was inside, and he waited. He wouldn't go in, as that might draw attention. Without losing his line of sight with the pub door, he stepped into a coffee shop and bought a latte, to go. With no urgency at all, he slowly walked up and down the street, always observing with peripheral vision or occasionally looking in shop windows and using the reflection as a mirror to keep watch.

Olek and Pavlo had driven the van around a few streets in the immediate vicinity. When they were ten minutes from when they expected their target to appear, Olek brought the van on to Sauchiehall Street and turned right into Elmbank Street. Fedir saw the van but made no eye contact.

The day previous, their target had walked along the left-hand side of the street. Olek turned the van into the lane on that side, stopped tight against the building on his right and put the hazard lights on. It left more space on the left side of the van. Pavlo got out and opened the side sliding panel door, then got back in. Fortune was with them today on two counts. Peter Mann had decided to leave his friends a few minutes earlier than the day previous and stepped out of the warm pub into the cold afternoon air, buttoning up his coat as he did so.

The first piece of good fortune was that they were in place and hadn't missed him. The second was that Elmbank Street was relatively quiet compared to most other days.

Fedir already had a text message composed and ready to go. It simply read, 'He is on his way'. As he saw the man emerge from the pub, he sent it to Pavlo. Pavlo's own phone pinged as the message arrived almost instantly. He got out of the van again and walked to the back which was level with the street. He saw their target approaching with Fedir walking closely behind him. Like Fedir, Pavlo was also wearing a heavy coat and a hat. It would have been virtually impossible for either of the Russians to be identified from any subsequent CCTV footage review that might follow.

Less than ten strides away, Peter Mann was approaching the lane oblivious to what was coming. One last look, up and down the street told Pavlo there were no other pedestrians in close proximity. Five strides, then four, then three. Pavlo turned towards the target, looked at him and said "Peter." As he did so, he took a few steps back into the lane. As Peter Mann stopped to see the man who had just called out his name, he felt the push from behind as Fedir closed in on him and bundled him into the lane. It happened in an instant. Fedir pushed from the back, Pavlo pulled from the front and in less than five seconds he was forcibly thrown into the van. Pavlo climbed in after him. Fedir slid the side door closed and got in the front beside Olek. The hazard lights were turned off and the van moved forward. Olek had already gauged the width of the lane in front of him and knew he would get through, despite the line of cars that were parked nose to tail down one side. It was tight but his judgement was perfect. He managed to squeeze through without scraping any of the parked cars on the right or the wall to his left.

At the end of this section of the lane, they emerged onto Holland Street at the Renfield Centre – the old St Stephen's Parish Church. As a one-way street, they turned left, moved forward to the T-junction and turned right, once more joining the flow of traffic on Sauchiehall Street.

In the back of the van, Peter Mann was understandably terrified. He had no idea what was happening to him. Surrounded in draped black tarpaulin, he was hooded, and wrist tied. Tethered to the newly fitted bracket on the floor, he was protesting that there had been a mistake. They, whoever they were, had the wrong man. In return, Pavlo clenched his right fist and smashed it hard into Peter Mann's face. The hood stopped the blood from spattering. Later inspection would confirm that his nose was broken.

Pavlo told him he would kill him if he spoke one more time. Of course, he wouldn't have. Artem may well have killed him, if he did. Peter Mann didn't know this though. With the pain from the punch surging through his body, he didn't speak again for the rest of the journey.

With this part of the plan complete, the van and its occupants made its way back to the warehouse.

Two nights every week, Danny Manuel met up with friends and played five-a-side football at the local floodlit pitches. As autumn rolled on into winter, the weather would get worse and the pitches would close for the season, until the following spring. For now, the weather was fine, and they took the fullest advantage. Tonight, was one of the two that he played football.

It was after the game, in the changing rooms, he confided in two of his closest friends.

"Wait until you see this on my phone. It was this morning when I was on my break. Watch it and tell me there isn't something shady going on. It's unbelievable."

One friend worked in a bank. The other was a uniformed police officer with Police Scotland.

DS Mullen and DC Hannah were going over everything they had in relation to the case at hand. They both needed to be on the same page and this meeting took place every morning, before the day got underway. Most days they partnered each other but it was inevitable that there would be times they would have to work independently of each other. The meeting ensured they both had the most up to date information and were not working at cross purposes.

After Benny had given the detective the partial number plate, the vehicle was quickly traced back to the owners. It was registered to an offshore company which turned out to be a dead end. Nonetheless, instruction was passed throughout the force for all units to be on the lookout for the V-Class, with a full description being provided.

It was part of a normal, routine day when the young police officer who played five-a-sides two nights a week, was going about his business. He saw the communication that referenced the black Mercedes and immediately recalled the footage in friend's mobile phone. The instruction had a contact name attached to it. Detective Sergeant Mullen who could be contacted at the Clyde Gateway building in Glasgow. He called her, explained what had happened and arrangements were made for the detectives to contact the truck driver, Danny Manuel.

They went to his home and caught up with him just before he was going to bed for the day.

Danny gave DS Mullen his phone and she watched the video clip. She couldn't make out the registration number nor identify the two men from the footage but there was no doubt in her mind this was the car they were looking for.

Satisfied they had as much information as they could get from Danny, they thanked him for his help and left. Before they did, the clip was forwarded from his phone to DS Mullen's. In the car, they discussed what they had seen, and both put forward suggestions as to how this fitted in with the investigation. They theorised, they speculated, and they postulated. For now, that was all it would be until they had more facts.

There was one fact however that DS Mullen did not discuss with DC Hannah.

If this was the same vehicle, and she would bet everything she had, that it was, they destroyed the car. This told her, they knew the police were looking for it. There was more than that though. There was an underlying niggle she couldn't put her finger on. She knew it would come to her eventually. In situations like this, it always did. She just hoped it would come to her sooner rather than later.

This time it came sooner. It took no more than 15 minutes. They were still in the car, heading back into the city, when the thought popped into her head. She knew what was troubling her. It was the timing.

She had gotten the partial registration number from John Johnstone. It was passed into IT support to run a trace on the owner and tie it back to the CCTV footage of when the car had arrived back at the Freeman Building. The fact that the investigation into the vehicle owners turned out to be a dead end, came to light AFTER the car had been destroyed.

Why would they destroy it? The only logical reason was that they knew the police had identified it and were looking into ownership. The fact that they knew this before the dead end came to light brought her back to the conversation she had had with John Johnstone. There was a leak. Someone on the inside was feeding the information back to the kidnappers.

This was a problem that would need to get sorted fast, before the whole investigation was compromised.

DC Hannah interrupted her thoughts and brought her head back into the car.

"Of the two people in the footage at the scrap yard, it's clear that one of them knows their way around the machines and has keys. I wouldn't imagine there are too many people who work there. It should be easy to narrow it down and to trace ownership of the business. I think that's a good place to start."

"Yes, I agree. You can get onto that when we get back. I have to have my daily meeting with DCS Cook."

The meeting with DCS Cook didn't take long. She brought him up to speed and explained the rationale behind her concerns about there being a leak. He said he had no doubt her thinking was correct. He suggested she carry on with the investigation as normal and he would discretely look into things from his end.

When she got back to her desk, DC Hannah had already established ownership of the scrap yard belonged to a company called JCG Metals. She spoke with the manager who told her the company had originally been owned by a man called John Graham, but he sold the business two years earlier to a bigger company and retired. The manager was very accommodating and provided all the details he had for the bigger company. He said he didn't have a lot of dealings with them directly. He explained that they were fairly autonomous at JCG, on a day-to-day basis. Any correspondence was sent to, or received from, the company's Chartered Accountants in Glasgow which was also the company's registered office address. At DC Hannah's request, he said he would email her a list of all employees.

The list came through in a matter of minutes and she printed it off. There were 12 names on it and of all of the information it gave, there was one standout for DS Mullen. The majority of the names on the list looked Scottish. Jim Smith; Neil Gribben; Iain Stewart. The first nine names read in the same vein. There were two that she guessed might be Polish, but she would need to confirm this. There was a Lewandowski and a Jaruselski.

The standout was Anatoly Lysenko. She hadn't come across this name or anything similar before, but every instinct she had was telling her with absolute conviction, Anatoly Lysenko was a Russian.

17

"What's happened Jack? When I heard your voice on the phone, I knew something wasn't right. Now seeing you here, I know there's definitely something wrong."

Jack had called Benny and asked if he could meet up with him as soon as possible. That was less than thirty minutes ago, and now they were back in the café at Kelvinbridge.

"I was speaking with a friend this morning. You don't know him, Benny. His name is Jim Ferrin and he's a taxi driver. He was telling me the city is buzzing with news of three murders. Have you seen or heard the any of it yet?"

Benny said he hadn't.

"Have you ever heard of a Russian called Yegor Omelchenko?"

"No, who is he?" Benny's mind was instantly drawn to the fact that DS Mullen had told him the fingerprints lifted from the crayon pack belonged to a Russian man and woman."

"According to Jim, this Yegor guy runs a real heavyweight organised crime outfit here in Glasgow. They're into everything and he is a particularly nasty piece of work by all accounts."

"Okay. I'm missing the connection though. What is it about this that's got you rattled?"

Jack looked around him to reconfirm that no one could overhear him, which of course, they couldn't as he continued to speak in hushed tones.

"These are the same people that Peter Mann is doing his article on. That means they are the same people that are trying to track you down. Remember, he told us they were pulling in information from their contacts? Now, three people who work for him have been found in a southside house with their throats slit." He paused then said, "It wasn't you, was it?"

"What? Of course, it wasn't me. Don't be daft."

"I know it wasn't you. I'm winding you up. I've been trying to get hold of Peter all morning, but his phone is switched off. And before you ask, I'm careful. I'm using the old burner phone that you gave me, so nothing can be traced back to me."

"Good. Where is that phone now?"

"It's in my pocket, in bits, like you said to do. It's kept like that all the time when I'm not using it."

Benny nodded and said nothing. He was thinking. Trying to join the dots, but he couldn't. It was too fragmented. He would need to speak with DS Mullen. That would be another two and a half hours before the next agreed window.

Benny went home and put the tv on. It was muted and on the channel that the Scottish lunchtime news would be on shortly. He had reasoned that if it was as Jack said it was, three murders in one house, it wouldn't matter what channel he was on. This would be headline news everywhere.

His assumption was correct. The national news was broadcast at 01.30 pm with the Scottish news coming on at 01.55 pm. When the national news came on, it was the first article at the top of the programme. The newsreader gave an overview then they cut to a reporter who was on site. The on-screen scene was typical of its kind. Police personnel and vehicles everywhere; The street taped off; The white tent with white suited Forensic Services people coming and going.

He watched until the next article came on. Something about time and money over-runs for a government contract. He turned the tv off. The gist of the report was that three men – two in their thirties and one in his forties - were found dead in a house they shared in the Govanhill area. Early indications were that they were of Russian origin and unconfirmed reports said all three men had died from fatal knife wounds. A Police Scotland investigation was underway, and the reporter said they would bring more details as and when these were made available.

01.36 pm. Just over twenty minutes before his 02.00 pm window. He noted down a few things on a scribble pad that he wanted to talk to DS Mullen about then grabbed his Parka and left the house.

With his hood up, he made his way along the Kelvin Walkway until he found a spot that was remote enough for his liking and was far enough away from his home that he was satisfied. On the stroke of 02.00 pm his phone was assembled, and he dialled the only number in it. It was six or seven seconds before it was answered. DS Mullen seemed slightly out of breath. She said she had needed to find somewhere with a bit of privacy.

Benny said he had seen the murder case on the news.

"The news report said the victims were Russian. Are you able to tell me if there is a link between them and the kidnapping case?"

"I'm not at liberty to discuss it with you." Abrupt and to the point. Benny hadn't expected anything different.

DS Mullen knew it was all connected. There was the lorry driver's video footage from his phone. One of the two people at the scrap yard – Anatoly Lysenko – was Russian. The missing persons reports from the weekend. The fingerprints from the crayon box. All Russian. It all connects. Now all she needed was hard proof.

He looked at the scribble pad page he had brought with him from the flat.

"Maybe I can help then. Does the name Yegor Omelchenko mean anything to you?"

There was a pause. Not a yes or a no. This told him that it did.

"Why do you ask?"

"I'm asking because his name came up in conversation a few hours ago and I have it on good authority your three dead Russians worked for him. There is also a strong possibility that they are the people who kidnapped the children."

"Where did you get this information from?"

Now it was Benny's turn not to answer. He moved the conversation on. "I understand you can't discuss things, that's fair enough. Let me ask you this. Assuming it is connected to the kidnapping, what would you need specifically, to take things forward?"

She wondered if mind-reading was another of his talents.

"Proof," she answered.

"And as a detective, where is the logical place to start looking for that proof? Do you start at the bottom, do you start at the top or do you just go through without structure and see what turns up?"

"Right at the top. I'd start there and make my way down the food chain, until I had enough that tied it all together."

The stolen van with the ringer plates was driven to the warehouse at South Street, where Peter Mann was unceremoniously dumped out of the back onto the ground. Still hooded, he was taken to a small windowless room and locked in. To all intents and purposes, it was a makeshift cell. He waited a few minutes, unsure if he was alone, before he moved to take the hood off. Fortunately, his hands were tied at the front and not behind him. Slowly and tentatively, he was half expecting another punch to the face like the one he had received earlier, but as it turned out, he was alone. There was a table and two chairs. Unlike some cells, these were not bolted to the floor. He sat in one of the chairs and reached to his face. It was tender and still stinging. The blood was already clotting and any breathing through his nose brought an uncomfortable wheezing sound. It was definitely broken. If he had been part-way drunk before, he was as sober as a judge now. He still clung to the thought that this was case of mistaken identity.

It took a minute before he realised his mobile phone was gone. One of the abductors must have taken it from his pocket when he was bundled into the van or when he had been punched in the face. It had been in the outside pocket of his coat and within easy reach.

As it was, it was Pavlo who had lifted it. It had been passed to Fedir just before the sliding van door was closed. As Olek had started to drive, Fedir had dismantled it and threw it out the window. Peter Mann's phone was in bits, scattered up Sauchiehall Lane.

The plan had been for Artem to talk to him because he wanted to find out what he knew about the organisation and the people associated with it. Who had he been talking to? Artem wasn't entirely sure at this point whether this journalist would die or whether he would be 'persuaded' to drop the whole thing and let go.

He was in the process of wrapping things up at his Bath Street office before leaving for South Street, when his mobile rang. Before he had the chance to answer it, line 1 on the office phone display lit up, then line 2. It was nothing more than instinct, but he knew these calls were linked and something was wrong. Something was very wrong.

He answered his mobile as his secretary dealt with the landline calls. It was Pavlo calling to inform his boss about the situation in Govanhill. It was normal practice for the Russians to work in three-man teams. This would normally be a driver and two others who did most of the 'heavy lifting'. The murders had been another of the three-man teams. Pavlo explained that someone in the building had heard the commotion and called the police. Things had escalated rapidly from there. He said Olek and Fedir had gone to find out what they could, and they would report back directly to Artem.

"Early indications are that this was not random or trouble that got out of hand boss. It appears to be targeted and professional."

"Is there anything to suggest it is linked to the kidnappings or the thief?"

"I can't be sure, but I don't think so. I think this is something else."

"Okay Pavlo. Stay with it and keep me updated."

As with any organisation there was a pecking order. Someone informed Pavlo, he informed Artem and now Artem would need to inform Yegor. The last thing he wanted was for Yegor to learn about it from the news on tv or from someone else.

They didn't know yet, but they would before the day was out. It was nothing to do with the kidnappings or Benny Fox. It was the Asians who were seriously pissed at Yegor having pulled the plug on their people trafficking enterprise. Unlike him, their operation wasn't as varied or diverse and they did not have anywhere near as many legal businesses, or other illegal businesses to fall back on. This had put a serious dent in their cashflow. There would be no need to dig deep to determine who had done this. The Asians were about to make it crystal clear that it was them.

It was stupidity on so many levels. The Asians whose weapon of choice in this case was a Damascus Knife, had just kicked off a turf war with Russians who not only outnumbered them as a criminal enterprise, but had a favoured weapon of their own.

The Heckler & Koch SP5K semiautomatic.

Start at the top. That was the detective's advice. Benny got in touch with Jack and asked if he could discretely find an address for Yegor Omelchenko. With such an unusual name for someone living in Scotland, Jack said it shouldn't be too difficult and that he would be in touch as soon as he had it.

He wasn't joking when he said it shouldn't be too difficult. He called Benny in less than 15 minutes with an address.

In less than an hour, Benny was through the Clyde Tunnel on his Kawasaki and passing through, Anniesland, Bearsden and Milngavie, leaving the city on the A81. He was heading for the eastern edge of the Kilpatrick Hills and the village of Strathblane.

It wasn't a huge place, and he was confident he would find his destination easily enough. When he reached the village, he was to take a left, then left again onto the Old Mugdock Road, so he was coming back on himself. Jack had told him if got lost, he should stop a local, preferably someone slightly older, and ask for directions to the big houses that sat between the Punchbowl Dam and the Deil's Craig Dam. It meant nothing to Benny, but it would mean something to anyone who was born and raised in the village.

He found the road he was looking for without needing to ask for directions. The first thing he noticed was that every house he passed seemed to be bigger than the one before it.

"How the other half live," he thought to himself as he slowly rode by.

Autumn had firmly taken hold and the myriad of stunning colours it had brought with it, was something to behold. The most beautiful hues of yellow, gold and brown, interspersed with red, purple and orange, lined the road he was on as well as the two or three roads that ran off it. Most had names on the gates, the gateposts or on the stand-alone house signs that were positioned outside the property access on the manicured grass verges.

He soon found the place he was looking for. On his first pass he noted the electric gates, the high box hedge that still had enough foliage to screen most of the house, and through the gates he saw a Range Rover Autobiography sitting on the drive. He was more interested in what lay behind and to the sides of the house. Benny was planning on paying Mr Omelchenko a night-time visit, not that he or his family would know anything about it, and this meant finding the best point of access.

After he had what he needed, he made his way back out to the main road. Picturing the geography in his mind's eye, he turned right and headed down the Old Mugdock Road in the opposite direction from the village until he was level with the area where he knew the back of Omelchenko's house would be. He found a spot that would serve his needs and made a mental note of where it was, as the next time he would be here it would be in complete darkness. Somewhere between 03.00 am and 04.00 am.

18

It was 02.55 am as Benny pulled the bike in off the road, dismounted and pulled it up on to the centrestand. He was in tight against the metal gate that gave access to a farmer's field. It would be very easy to miss as it was covered on both sides and above, with trees and undergrowth. This was the spot he had picked out 10 hours earlier. It was as good as he would get on this stretch of road as the ground itself was hard-packed earth after a long hot summer, a dry autumn and a two-and-a-half-ton tractor having driven over it repeatedly. He had noticed that the galvanised heavy metal field gate was closed with the slide in place but there was no chain or padlock. He had considered opening the gate and rolling the bike through it, so it was out of sight from the road. Given the hour and the remoteness, he decided against that and packed his cammo cover with his other things when he left the unit in Glasgow, instead. The cover was similar to many others that completely envelope a motorbike to protect it against the elements when it is being left outside for a prolonged period, especially over the winter. The only difference was, this one had a camouflage design.

He readied himself, got his fully stocked backpack, covered the bike and crossed the road into the field on the other side. In the ten minutes or so he had been here, there hadn't been another vehicle in either direction. Thinking about it, he could count on one hand the number of vehicles he had seen since he left the A81 and took the road out past Mugdock Country Park.

He found an opening in the fence at the road edge, cut through it and started to cross the field towards the houses. He couldn't see them from here, but he knew exactly where they were. He engaged his night-vision goggles and took a minute for his eyesight to adapt to the surreal world of green. There were other sets he could have purchased that were considerably cheaper than this one, but Benny was definitely from the school of 'you get what you pay for'. He had paid a lot for these and never regretted it for a second. The quality was first-rate.

It didn't take long for him to reach the back of the Omelchenko property boundary. It's how he saw this. At DS Mullen's place, it was the 'edge of the garden'. Here, it fell far short of being an estate, but it was considerably more than a garden. The word boundary seemed appropriate.

The goggles went in the pack and his mask, and an array of tools came out. These were clipped onto his belt or placed in the small fabric pouch that was strapped diagonally across his torso with a strap running from his right shoulder down under his left arm. Everything was secure, nothing was loose and none of it restricted his movement in any way nor would it make any noise.

He went through the same procedure as he always did. Sensory Acclimation, and thinking about motion sensors, dogs, alarm system, door and window lock mechanisms, and other exits from the place, in case he had to get out quick.

He never got close enough earlier in the day, to determine the type of alarm or the locks.

There was good news and there was bad news.

The good news was there were no dogs to worry about and although there was an alarm system, it was switched off. The bad news was the reason why he knew it was switched off. Yegor Omelchenko had decided to engage a bit of muscle in and around his home. Benny couldn't have known but two days earlier, there would have been no one here, apart from the family.

Since the murders in Govanhill, he had decided to beef up his personal security.

A lot of the gardens here had mature trees. Benny picked out a Sycamore that easily stood at 60 ft tall, maybe more. With ease, he quickly and quietly climbed this until he had an uninterrupted view of most of the gardens and the back of the house. Dressed in black from head to toe, high in the darkness of the tree he was invisible, despite the fact it was almost devoid of leaves due to the time of year.

Benny counted two men in the grounds and through the floor to ceiling windows he could see another two moving around inside, which told him the alarm was off. There could be more, and he would have to tread carefully. Very carefully. From his vantage point high in the branches, he used a small but powerful monocular and zoomed in on the guards outside then right into the house itself. On closer inspection, the bad news just got worse. All four were wearing shoulder holsters and already, he saw a handgun in three of them. The fourth man had disappeared somewhere inside the house. It was a reasonable assumption that his holster would not be empty.

The lighting was subdued, both inside and outside. It was more than adequate but there were no bright lights. There was no sound either, as the guards patrolled without speaking. The family would be fast asleep, and the guards would be mindful not to wake them.

Benny was weighing up his options. He knew he didn't have to gain access to the house. It wasn't imperative and he could take it or leave it. These armed guards had added a whole new dimension to the situation, and he was leaning more towards leaving than staying. That was until something else caught his eye.

To the right of the house, near the front, there was a three-car garage that backed right up to the neighbouring property. He could see the roof of the garage was in touching distance with an extension that wrapped itself around that side of the house. It was substantial. Benny wasn't sure if it was a conservatory with a solid pitched and tiled roof, or if it was an orangery. Either way, he could easily take himself up through the neighbour's garden, get onto the garage roof and step on to the conservatory roof. From there, there was a reachable balcony from one of the upstairs bedrooms. Above that there were fixed external vertical timbers attached to the walls that ran up into the eaves. Aesthetically, they enhanced the look of the building but from a security perspective, they were like a climbing frame. For someone of his agility, it would be a simple manoeuvre from there to roll up and onto the roof itself. The only reason he was considering this was because he saw at least four separate skylights in the roof and any of them would be more than sufficient in size for him to slip inside.

Now that he had some direction and a possible way into the house, the deciding factor was the guards themselves. He would hazard a guess at everyone having retired to their beds by midnight, possibly earlier. There was no possibility of any of these men having taken a quick nap. With their employer being who he was, they wouldn't dare. Benny knew they would have been patrolling for at least four or five hours. That's four or five hours of mundane nothingness. The boredom would be all consuming by now. Psychologically, it would feel like they had been patrolling for eight or ten hours straight. Now, at just after 04.00 am, their alertness levels would be between low and almost non-existent.

It was decided. He got himself out of the tree and found a way into the neighbour's garden.

It worked exactly as he had visualised it. In approximately four minutes he had gone from the tree to the garage roof, to the conservatory roof, to the balcony, to the timbers, and onto the house roof itself. All without the slightest sound. The guards on patrol were oblivious. In the dead still of the night, Benny really did move like a cat.

Once on the roof, he made his way up and over the apex stopping at the first skylight. He was as careful about not loosening anything underfoot that could fall off and down to the ground, as he was about not making any noise.

He looked inside through the glass. It was nothing but darkness with the odd tiny green or red electric light here and there. He was certain these were from a PC or something similar. Benny powered up his night vision goggles, brought them down over his eyes and looked in again. This time he could see everything. It was a study and his earlier guess about the PC was correct. It was a big room. He couldn't see all the way to the four inside walls but from what he could see, he was sure at least one other skylight would be above this room. Among other things, he had brought a length of his climbing rope, although he was limited as to what he could have secured it to on the roof. The house was very modern and there were no chimney stacks or anything similar. He wasn't convinced the skylight frame was robust enough. That wouldn't matter here though. The big desk was immediately beneath the skylight and Benny knew if he held on to the window frame with both hands and was at full stretch, his feet would reach it. Having brought a few small tools, he had the roof window open in a matter of minutes.

The first thing he did was lean his upper body in and check out the whole study. It confirmed it was empty. He eased himself in and reached the desk comfortably. He brought the skylight window down to give the appearance of it being closed from the outside, but it wasn't secured. One push would open it without any problems.

Stepping down from the desk onto the floor, he was thankful for the deep pile of the expensive carpet. It helped muffle any footsteps and reduced the risk of any squeaks from the flooring itself. The first thing he did was move to the door. Despite the size of the room, there was only one door. He lifted one of the chairs that was nearby and wedged it under the door handle, ensuring it was solid and secure. It wouldn't take a lot for someone sufficiently motivated to kick it in, but it would buy him a few seconds and that was all he would need.

The second thing he did was lift another chair on to the desk and position it under the window in the roof, he had just come through. Neither this one nor the one under the door handle had wheels which meant they would be secure enough. Thirdly, he got back up onto the desk and reached up and removed the bulb from the ceiling light. Again, anyone coming in would automatically reach for the light-switch. In the inevitable confusion that would follow when it didn't work, it would buy him another valuable few seconds.

He started searching the study. He did not know what he was looking for, but he would know it if and when he found it. With plenty of experience, he knew where to start looking. It didn't take long before he found a safe inside a sliding door in one of the built-in units. He was familiar with makes and models like Chubbsafes, Securikey Euro, Phoenix, Burton Eurovault, which were in this size range. He didn't recognise this particular safe but figured he should be able to access it relatively quickly, if the kit he brought in his backpack worked.

It did.

Opening it, he lifted the contents out for a better look and placed them on the desk. There were ledgers, files, folders and dossiers that included photographs.

And money. There was a lot of money.

Having handled big sums many times, Benny looked at the denominations, the thickness of each banded bundle and the currency – Sterling and Euros – and put the amount at approximately £300,000 to £400,000.

He looked at the ledgers first. Still wearing the night vision goggles, he opened one and could make out most of the text, but not all of it. It didn't mean much to him but there were names, dates and amounts of money listed beside each entry. His first thought was that these were a record of transactions. The dates in the top book were current. Turning the pages, he saw they were laid out chronologically. There were three similar ledgers. Opening the bottom one of the three, he saw the dates went back five or six years.

This was the proof DS Mullen had been speaking of. He was certain of it and decided in that moment he was taking everything with him, including the money. After all, what self-respecting burglar wouldn't take the money. He metaphorically kicked himself for not having had the foresight to bring a bag with him, and there was no room in his backpack. He looked around and found something that would do. In one of the corners of the room, lined along the wall, were the spoils of a rich man's shopping trip. There was an array of rope-handled, laminated paper bags neatly lined up, mostly with the contents still in them. They were emblazoned with the names of various top-end luxury boutiques. Benny took the four largest, removing the contents, twice putting one bag inside the second, giving him two that were doubled up for extra strength. He placed in the money and documents. It was a good fit. They were both full but not overflowing or in danger of splitting. The doubling of the rope handles would also make them easier to carry. He placed the bags on the desk beside the chair and was getting ready to climb up and make his exit when he heard movement outside the door. It stopped him in his tracks.

He stepped nearer the door to hear better. He saw the slightest of movement on the door handle as someone tried to open it. The wedged chair was stopping the handle from opening fully. He couldn't have known but it was one of the inside guards who had been periodically checking all the rooms in the house, except the family bedrooms, as part of his patrol.

What happened next took only seconds but resulted in mayhem.

Benny had seen a pen holder on top of the desk and in addition to an assortment of pens and a letter opener, it held a big pair of scissors.

After another unsuccessful attempt at opening the door, the person on the other side had now put his shoulder against and tried to push. The wedged chair was holding. For now.

Benny pulled off one of his rubber soled, treadless climbing shoes, grabbed the scissors and moved to a plug socket on the wall. He partially opened the scissors to the correct width, wrapped the rubber shoe completely around the handle, lined up the two blades with the top socket hole, and the bottom-left socket-hole, turned his face away and pushed as hard as he could. The shoe was 100% rubber without any holes or tears, and it served as a perfect insulator.

The result was a flash and a simultaneous bang. The effect, as Benny expected, was that it fused the entire house. There were shouts from the other side of the door as the guards from outside ran into the house, the family woke abruptly and there was a lot of confusion.

It took between a minute and a minute and a half for the first guard to make the connection with the locked door and returning his attention to it, he didn't mess around. He lifted his boot and smashed it in. He had his gun out of the shoulder holster. As with the rest of the house, the room was in complete darkness. It could have been floodlit like a football stadium and it would have made no difference.

Benny was gone.

By the time Yegor had pulled his trousers and a top on, Benny was down from the roof and over the back of the three-car garage, into the neighbour's garden.

By the time someone had brought him a torch and he realised his safe had been opened and everything in it was gone, Benny was over the field and back at his bike.

By the time Yegor reached Artem on his mobile phone, Benny Fox was back in his leathers, and gunning the big Kawasaki down the Old Mugdock Road, heading for Glasgow.

19

The built-in alarm in DS Mullen's phone went off at 06.30 am as it always did. She reached from her bed to the bedside table and snoozed it.

Her husband Steve, would get up first as he had to be ready, and on his way to work by 07.30 am. After he left, her routine never varied much. She would get the kids up, organise some cereal or toast for breakfast, sort them for school and sort herself for work. Like clockwork, they would all leave the house at 08.20 am, she'd drop the kids at school and would be in the office for just after 09.00 am. Every weekday was the same.

Except today.

Today she was in the kitchen at the stage between getting the kids up and organising the breakfast. Her mobile phone vibrated confirming she had an incoming call. The display read 'caller unknown'. She couldn't be certain and didn't know why, but she thought she knew who it was. She answered and simply said, "Hello."

"Detective Sergeant, apologies for not sticking to our agreed time slots, and for calling you on your personal phone, but this could not wait until 10.00 am. I have left a package for you in the garden, under the children's trampoline."

Without asking him to elaborate, she opened the bi-fold doors and stepped out onto the decking. She had the phone in her hand as she moved towards the trampoline, knelt down on one knee and looked under, doing so as if this was all perfectly normal.

"There's nothing here," she said.

"There is, you're kneeling at the wrong side. It's at the other end beside the yellow Mitre football."

She stood suddenly, looking in every direction. Her voice increased a few octaves, as the anger started to flare up.

"Are you here? Here at my house, again. Where the fuck are you?"

Benny remained calm. "I didn't come into your house again. Be thankful for that Detective. When you see what is in the package, you will understand that I could not afford to leave it without ensuring that you physically had it in your hands. The contents came directly from Yegor Omelchenko's home. I broke in and took them from inside his safe. I believe this is the hard evidence you need. This is the proof from the man right at the top."

Standing in the garden, unaware her mouth was open, she was speechless. She wasn't entirely sure what to make of what he had just told her. She is a Detective Sergeant in the CID, and this man on the phone just told her he has left her the contents of something he stole from someone's safe. The fact that person was a criminal himself was irrelevant.

Regaining her composure, she walked around the trampoline and stopped by her son's football. Kneeling down again, she looked under and this time she found it. It was one of the original two boutique bags.

There was no need for the second bag as Benny had the money. The bag in DS Mullen's right hand contained everything else.

With the phone in her left hand, she was talking to him for at least fifteen seconds before she realised there was no one there. The call had been terminated and Benny was gone.

The detective took the bag into her house, placed it on the table, sat on a chair and looked at it without opening it. She was very experienced and was more than capable when it came to doing her job. This was different though, and she was slightly at a loss on how best to proceed. Should she have forensics people look at it before touching it again? Should she get her gloves on and take out the contents to see what was actually here? Should she take the package exactly as she found it, straight in to work? Should she leave the decision to her boss?

Four choices. She opted for the last one.

DCS Cook's mobile number was listed in her phone. She called him and got connected quicker than expected.

"Detective Sergeant, I'm in the car on hands-free on my way into the office. What can I do for you?"

There was no reason for him to tell her he was using hands-free, where he was or where he was going, but he did. It was nothing more than habit. She told him what happened in the last ten minutes or so, said she was considering bringing the package in unopened, and said she would appreciate his advice on whether that was the correct thing to do, or not.

"I don't think sending forensics out to your place would achieve anything. Bring the package in and we will go through it together. I'll see you when you get in."

She told the kids to sort themselves while she took the bag to her room and got ready. Taking it to her room was only to ensure that they didn't touch it.

By 09.35 she was sitting in DCS Cook's office. She had kept him apprised of the investigation at every stage leaving nothing out except the burner phones and the four time slots. She hadn't had the chance to speak with him about the conversation with Benny from the previous day. That would have been covered at her normal meeting with him this morning.

The bag was sitting on the desk still unopened as she brought her boss up to speed.

"John Johnstone called me yesterday sir and asked if the murders in Govanhill were connected to the Russians. I told him I could not comment. He then asked me if the name Yegor Omelchenko meant anything to us. I didn't answer him. I asked him where he got that name from, but he avoided the question. He then asked me where the best place would be to find evidence. I thought he was asking from a procedural perspective. I simply said I'd start at the top and make my way down from there. I didn't think for one second he would go and break into someone's house."

"Not just someone's house DS Mullen, but Yegor Omelchenko's house, no less. And he definitely said to you he broke into Mr Omelchenko's house, opened a safe, removed the contents and left them in your garden?"

"Yes sir, that's exactly what he said."

"Well, let's see what Mr Johnstone's criminal efforts have produced."

With both detectives wearing standard issue gloves, DCS Cook carefully lifted the contents out of the bag and laid them on his desk side by side.

There were three ledgers and four different coloured foolscap cardboard document wallets, each with its own label and containing a series of beige square cut folders which were filled with all manner of paperwork, some with photographs attached.

The first thing DS Mullen noticed was that there was handwriting on some of the documentation, partly in English and partly in a language she did not understand. She recognised it as Cyrillic and was in no doubt it would turn out to be Russian.

The document wallets were labelled as follows - People; Property Deals; Finance; Miscellaneous.

After twenty minutes of poring over what they had, they arrived at a conclusion that was not easily discernible when they had started. Their initial thoughts were that it was simply record keeping as you would have with any business or set of businesses. The more they read, the more apparent it became that everything they had here, could be used for leverage in one way or another. In fact, it was the very opposite of what would be routine record keeping for a business. It's why all of this was kept in a personal safe at home and not in an office filing cabinet or on a company computer.

The information held in the ledgers fell into two distinct categories. One part held names, dates, times and monetary amounts for 'off the books' transactions. The other part held similar levels of detail on people who had been paid money for a plethora of different reasons. Everything from pay-offs for information, to bribes.

When they finished, DCS Cook sat back in his seat, raised his eyebrows and let out a barely audible whistle.

"Talk about painting a target on your own back. If this really has come from Yegor Omelchenko, and from what I have just read I am 99.9% certain it has, he will hunt this John Johnstone guy to the ends of the earth, there's nothing surer. There might be a small window for us – and for Mr Johnstone – if Mr Omelchenko thinks what was stolen is still out there and there's a chance the Russian can get it back. I can't see him thinking the first thing the thief would do is pass it all on to us. I mean, why would he? And of course, that begs the question. Why would he?"

He was looking at DS Mullen and she realised it wasn't rhetorical. Her boss was asking her why Benny would go to the trouble of breaking in at considerable risk to himself, just to steal everything and pass it on to the police.

"My first thought sir is that it is because John Johnstone is aware the Russians know he wrecked their kidnapping plans, he knows they are looking for him, or at least trying to identify him, and he wants to see them locked up before they find him. That seems logical to me."

DCS Cook was nodding in agreement. "It seems logical to me too. That being the case, we need to act on this straight away."

"I agree sir. Where do you want me to start?"

"Firstly, I need you to complete a report laying out how this documentation came into your possession in the first place, so we can get that into the system. As you know, we can't get warrants based on this information alone as it came from an anonymous source. I know we have a name for him, but until that is confirmed, technically he is anonymous. What we can do, is this. We can follow up on the information in terms of research. From whatever that gives us, we take what can be validated, corroborated and is determined accurate, and that can be used to secure the necessary warrants. I will assign more people to you starting this morning. We know the kidnappings are linked, and the murders are linked, but for now, they become secondary from your point of view. Dealing with this information is time-critical and must take precedence."

Satisfied that DS Mullen had the package from under the trampoline, Benny terminated the call, pulled the battery and SIM card, got back to his bike and headed to the unit. When he got there, it took less than an hour to go through his process of removing all trace and potential evidence from himself, his clothing and his equipment, including the bike. When he was finished, all that was left was the money he had stolen from Yegor's safe. It sat on the desk, stacked up in neat piles. He was a bit off the mark when he'd estimated the amount to be between £300,000 and £400,000. It was the Euros that had thrown him. Allowing for the current exchange rate, the amount in front of him totalled £540,000. It was just short of that figure and Benny had rounded it up.

His immediate thought was that he was going to need to get himself more space at the safety deposit box company, and he was going to need to have a sit-down with his 'money man'.

There were two standout things about Benny Fox that no one knew. For obvious reasons his family didn't know. Less obvious was that his best friend, Jack Buchanan, the man who he would trust with his life, did not know. Firstly, Benny had flawless documentation that provided him with another identity. An identity that would stand up to all but the most rigorous of investigations. It's little wonder the documentation was flawless. and it would pass most forms of scrutiny. It cost him £75,000 a year to ensure it did. He had been introduced to a man who lived in the north of England by another man who lived in London.

The second thing was that Benny had a net worth in excess of £18 million, if he encashed every single thing he had.

It started around fifteen years earlier, when he was routinely using the services of a fence to move all manner of valuables that he had stolen. Understandably, there had to be a considerable element of trust between both parties in order for the relationship to be a success. Purely by chance, he came across a man called Manus Quinn who originally came from Belfast but had lived in Glasgow for most of his adult life. Manus fenced the valuables Benny stole and that relationship had gone from strength to strength. Even today, Benny and Manus are good friends. By the time Benny had made the decision to start dealing only in cash jobs, Manus had expanded into other areas and the loss of fencing for Benny was less of an issue for him than it might otherwise have been. Mere coincidence, but the timing was fortuitous.

In the circles Manus Quinn moved in, everyone knew a man – or knew a man, who knew a man.

As Benny's accumulated wealth was growing at a considerable pace, he was running out of places to hide it. He spoke with Manus about his 'problem' and of course, Manus knew a man. They both took a trip to London where they met Colin Campbell. Colin was primarily involved in Financial Services but being based in the City, he had his fingers in many pies. Benny took to the man easily enough but as was his nature, he was on his guard. He was prepared to give Colin Campbell the benefit of the doubt, but it would be in small transactions and over a period of time. Fast forward seven years, and the relationship between both men was on a solid footing.

One of the earliest things Colin put in place was the concept of using diamonds as a means of holding wealth. He was connected to a few of the savviest people who operated out of the diamond world's most famous address, 100 Hatton Garden.

Hatton Garden is famed worldwide for everything connected to jewellery and the diamond trade. Number 100 was the home of The London Diamond Bourse and Club. The most influential and people in the know, were members.

Benny took Colin's advice and invested some of his money in diamonds.

He read up on everything he could lay his hands on, about the subject. He quickly learned that at the beating heart of the diamond world were the 'C's. When he started reading there were four. Carat; Cut; Colour; Clarity; As time moved forward, his proficiency in the subject saw him progress from novice to intermediate and now he was close to expert. In the same timeframe, the 'C's kept coming. Certification came along. Conflict diamonds introduced Conscience. Under it all lay the other 'C' no one spoke of. The vulgar one. Cost. In the diamond world the famous quote attributed to J.P. Morgan ran true. "If you have to ask the price, you can't afford it'.

At his first foray into that world, Benny exchanged tens of thousands of pounds for diamonds. In less than a year, that became hundreds of thousands, and within three years, Benny was making purchases in the millions between diamonds and other precious stones.

Although it was not the primary driver for starting down this road, from an investment perspective, it was very lucrative. Their year-on-year increase in value was anywhere between 10% and 15%. Compared to the bulk of money, they took up no space at all. Add to this the portability, the ease with which they could be transported, and in most cases how the stones could be rendered untraceable, it was perfect.

Today, Benny probably held around 80% of his net worth in precious stones and these were located in half a dozen places up and down the country. In order to maintain an element of detachment between himself and the safety deposit boxes that held the stones plus the cash, it was apparent very early on that he would need another identity.

Everyone knows a man, who knows a man.

Colin Campbell, the man from London, knew a man in Leyland Lancashire, who specialised in that very thing. Hugh Kane. Hugh made it clear the first time he met Benny that 'you only get what you pay for in this world, son'. That sat well with Benny who had lived by the same sentiment his whole life. For a price, a substantial price, not only was an identity created but more importantly, it was continually used and added to until it became as real as the identities of everyone else.

This fictitious man had a job, a driver's licence, paid tax, rented property and rented safety deposit boxes. He had a mobile phone contract, had a Sky TV package and even paid the BBC for a TV licence.

From time to time, he bought and sold diamonds. His name was Ian Walker.

That's what £75,000 a year bought you. A living, breathing, ever evolving identity.

These days, Benny was more than comfortable operating in the diamond and precious stones world without the need to involve anyone else. He had his own network of buyers and sellers well established.

What he needed from Colin Campbell now, were investments and accounts set up overseas which he could securely access from anywhere in the world. Colin had suggested they do this very thing many times, over many years, but Benny never had any real intention of moving out of Glasgow, let alone Scotland.

That was before he had gone to check out the viability of burgling the Head Office of a payday lender in the Freeman Building in Glasgow's Merchant City.

Before he met four 8-year-old children who would change his life forever.

Before he crossed paths with a gang of Russian thugs, whose lives he would most definitely change forever.

20

Since the meeting DCS Cook had with DS Mullen in the morning, things were moving at a considerable pace. There was an energy around the Gateway Building that seemed almost frenetic at times. What started out with two detectives looking into a foiled kidnap attempt, was quickly growing into a task force that would pull together many different facets of what were initially believed to be unrelated cases but were now very much intertwined. An area on the second floor was commandeered with the number of available computers and telephones continually being added to, to accommodate the increased number of personnel. The people who were drafted in from other departments or investigations were assigned tasks, the first of which was to ensure every single page of the ledgers and every single sheet of paper or photograph from the folders was securely scanned onto the system, which would be held in one central place. The number of technical support people was expanded, and by early afternoon information was steadily coming in.

The fact there was a mole in their ranks who would now have access to all of this information, was not lost on DS Mullen. She was hoping they would get far enough ahead of the game, quickly enough. that it wouldn't matter if word got out or not.

To that end, DC Hannah had been tasked with gathering as much as she could from the ledgers for cross-referencing to see if anything tied back to what they already had. Her plan was to have a high overview, giving the ledgers a quick onceover to see if anything jumped off the page, then go back to the start and go through each entry in detail, line by line. The entries in the ledger were for payments that had been paid out by the Russians for information.

The high overview of the first ledger threw up two names that she recognised. One was from somewhere early in the investigation, but she couldn't immediately place exactly where or when.

The other name was instantly recognisable. It was a man who had received eleven payments in total, over the last three weeks. The most recent was dated two days ago.

His name was John Muir, he worked in a technical support role with Police Scotland, and he was sitting at a computer less than thirty feet behind Detective Constable Audrey Hannah.

Peter Mann's assessment of his situation had shifted more than once already and was now in the process of doing so again. He was still locked in the small room that he now saw as a cell. There were no windows, no clock and he didn't wear a watch. He normally used his phone if he needed to know the time, but of course, that was gone. He wasn't entirely sure if what started out as hours had now turned into days, but the disorientation it brought was beginning to overwhelm him.

At first his thoughts were dominated by the idea that his captors had the wrong person and unfortunately for him, they meant to do him harm. The broken nose was testimony to that.

Early on in his plight he needed to relieve himself, but he held off as long as he could. When he couldn't wait any longer, he put his hood back on and knocked on the door to catch someone's attention, in the hope they would let him use a toilet. He caught someone's attention sure enough, but they didn't show him to a toilet. What they did do was pass him an empty bucket and close and lock the door without speaking.

No one needed to speak. Although the scene unfolded like a surreal mime, the instruction was clear enough. If he needed to go, it would be there, in the cell, in the bucket.

As time passed without no point of reference, the disorientation got worse. At first, he hoped no one would come in as that may mean another beating. That was until hunger set in and then he found himself hoping someone would come soon with food. The hunger pangs suggested he had been there for at least eight or ten hours. As if on cue, he heard the lock turning and quickly pulled his hood back on. He heard footsteps coming in, something being placed on the table, the footsteps retreating back through the door and the door being locked again. Slowly he removed the hood and there on the table sat a tray with food and water. It wasn't cooked food. It was a selection of pre-packaged sandwiches, crisps, a cake and a 500ml bottle of water.

He had unconsciously accepted the broken nose and didn't think about it so much now. The food and water that was periodically brought in over the coming hours was more than adequate sustenance. Now his thoughts were entirely preoccupied with sleep, or the lack of it, to be precise. There was nothing he could use that would offer any relief and let him sleep. There was no bed, not even old paper or cardboard or tarpaulins. Nothing at all, that he could lay out on and sleep on for even a few hours, other than the bare floor.

It's been said many times that we see what we want to see. It's how the mind works. Peter Mann came to consider his immediate surroundings as a cell, but it wasn't a cell, it was a room. Nothing more. Had he had the foresight to investigate, he would have found that the back wall was nothing more than a timber stud partition lined with Gyproc Fireline plasterboard. Had he considered this he would have found that the plasterboard sheets would have given way with very little resistance.

Even if he had known his captors were Russian, he could never have known they were pre-occupied right now with three of their number having been murdered by their Asian former business partners, by the burglary on their boss's house and by the police net that was tightening around them. He could never have known that the very building he was being held in had only one living soul in it. Him. It was mere coincidence that there was someone there when he had knocked on the door to use the toilet. That person left and only returned on occasion to bring food and water. For the time being, the Russians had all but forgotten Peter Mann.

With no one to stop him, he could have kicked out the back wall, made his way out of the warehouse, cut across the yard, gone out through the gates and walked all the way home.

Since they had started working on the case together, a form of friendship had developed between both detectives. In public or in any professional context it would always be

Detective Sergeant or Detective Constable. When it was only the two of them however, it was Jenny and Audrey.

"Are you sure this is the same John Muir?"

"I'm absolutely certain Jenny. His bank account is listed in the ledger with the payment dates and amounts. I have checked our records with Human Resources and it's the same account his salary goes into. It's him, there's no doubt about it. I've cross-referenced the dates of the payments and four of them coincide with when he was working on the John Johnstone / Freeman Building CCTV footage. Another payment coincides with when I had requested a query run on the black motorbike footage. Again, it was him that was working the footage that day. There's no doubt in my mind he's been taking copies of our investigation material and passing it on for money."

"I'm still struggling to get my head round who would be stupid enough to have any money like this paid into their own personal bank account. The guy must be an idiot."

Audrey smiled and replied, "I know what you mean but to be fair, I guess he never thought in a million years his paymasters would write the details in a book only for that book to end up in the very police office he works out of."

"True. Okay, let's get this sorted before he gets wind of what's going on and does a disappearing act on us."

They stepped out of the side room they had used for privacy. Audrey went back to her desk, keeping Muir in her peripheral vision. He seemed oblivious and was working away on his computer. In less than a minute later, Jenny Mullen, flanked by two uniformed officers made her way directly to his desk. As Audrey got to her feet and moved to join them, it was becoming obvious to everyone else in the big room that something was happening. People stopped what they were doing and turned to watch. Ironically, the last person to see what was happening was John Muir who was busy bashing away at his keyboard. When he saw them, he stopped what he was doing and sat back in his seat in the way of someone resigned to their fate. Audrey would have bet money that he knew he was caught, and the game was up. His body language said as much.

"Mr Muir, I want you to stop what you're working on and come with me please."

Ordinarily, most people would have asked why. It's human nature. If you are innocent and a detective accompanied by two uniforms asks you to go with them, your immediate response is "Why?"

There was no protest. No asking why. Nothing. He simply stood up and went with them. As he was escorted out of the room to be taken to an area where he would be detained until he was questioned, DS Mullen addressed everyone who had been looking on. "Okay ladies and gentlemen, the show's over. Can we get back to what we were doing please? Thank you."

Audrey went to her own desk and went back to working on the ledgers. The other name she had recognised was Ben McAdam. She was going through her notes from day one of the investigation and visualising in her mind as the scenes played out in her head. She hadn't actually had cause to write the name down, but it didn't matter. When she recalled the Friday afternoon, they had first visited the Freeman Building, she remembered.

They had parked the car and the closest business that was open was a Solicitors. The young guy on reception had been looking around his desk for a business card with the details of the letting agent, Roberts Commercial.

Audrey had noticed a few personal items sitting between his PC and the desk phone. There was a mobile phone, a small keyring with two or three keys on it, and a credit card sized blue Scotrail Smartcard. She recalled the card clearly. His photo was on the bottom left with a name, a number and a date on the right. The name was Ben McAdam. Not Bernard, but Ben.

Ben McAdam was in the book with one entry against his name.

Audrey Hannah had never placed a bet in her entire life. Not even so much as buying a lottery ticket. Today she was placing imaginary bets with the frequency of a seasoned punter. She was willing to bet Ben McAdam knew more about the Freeman Building and the handyman Arthur, than he had let on. She was also willing to bet he had been paid for sourcing the building as a safe place for the Russians to hold four kidnapped children.

John Muir was taken to an interview room by the two uniformed officers while Jenny Mullen let her boss know about this latest development. He said he wanted to sit in when she questioned him.

As the detectives entered the room, the officer who had been standing just inside the door, left. Muir looked very apprehensive. In fact, it was more than apprehension. Jenny Mullen thought he looked scared. She wasn't sure if it was because he knew what was coming or if he was worried about possible repercussions from the Russians. Her gut told her it was the latter. In the end it didn't matter. Before the interview got fully up and running, she had laid out the gravity of the charges involved. Murder, kidnapping, bribes. Even housebreaking was thrown in for good measure. She told him she had physical evidence confirming he had received eleven payments in less than three weeks and that was sufficient for her to obtain a warrant which would allow her to do a deep dive into his banking history.

"There are eleven payments here, John. That places you right in the middle of this. You are an accessory all the way down the line. Are we likely to find more payments when we take your account apart?"

She knew from his reaction the answer was yes. To coin a phrase, he visibly folded like a deckchair.

He provided as much information that he was capable of. Both detectives knew from experience that he was holding nothing back, especially DCS Cook whose experience was considerably more than DS Mullen's. From everything Muir gave up, one thing stood out more than the rest. A single name with an address in Bath Street in the city centre. John Muir said he only knew the man as Artem. He was Russian and the address in Bath Street was his office.

"That's the only address I ever used. A courier service would be used and any envelope or package I sent would be marked for his personal attention."

This information alone was sufficient for warrants to be obtained. That process would be underway in less than fifteen minutes time.

When they were finished, John Muir was placed in custody, DCS Cook went back to his own office to sort the warrant request and Jenny Mullen pondered on what she had just learned.

In her mind she was having an imaginary conversation as she walked through this new information. "Artem. Another Russian. If he has his own office, then in all probability, he is somewhere near the top of the organisation with Omelchenko and I have you to thank for that Mr John Johnstone, or whoever you really are."

That thought brought her back to her four windows. She had missed the 10.00 am and the 02.00 pm, but under the circumstances that was okay. She would assemble her burner phone for the 06.00 pm slot and see if John Johnstone made contact.

21

In the early afternoon, somewhere between the new task force being assembled and John Muir giving up the Russians, Benny Fox had his backpack on and was hitting the road.

Not the backpack from the unit with his burgling equipment in it, but the one he kept in the hall cupboard in his home. That was the one that had his training gear, swimming trunks and a clean towel in it.

Having managed a few hours' sleep earlier, he left the flat and turning right, was making his way to the Glasgow Club in Maryhill. He was always impressed with the sandstone façade of the leisure centre with its attaching building, the former Burgh Halls. As he approached it, the frontage always made him think of a question that came up at one of the pub quiz nights he had attended with his friends from The Chip. It asked, 'What sculptor links The Kelpies at Falkirk, Arria at Cumbernauld, Rise at Glasgow Harbour, The Carmyle Heron at Cambuslang, and the former Maryhill Fire Station?'

The answer was of course, Andy Scott. At the former fire station specifically, he had created four sets of metal gates which filled each of the four sandstone archways that the fire engines once came through. Behind the gates and archways is the old courtyard that once housed the fire station itself but is now given over to the new leisure complex and the Burgh Halls. The metal gates depict firemen in period dress with equipment of its day.

He had measured and timed the route a few years earlier. It was a shade over a mile, door to door, and his average run time, allowing for easy traffic conditions, was eight minutes. His personal best was under seven, but he wasn't out to break any records today. He liked the 25m no-nonsense pool. It was a straightforward rectangle with a shallow end and a deep end. Perfect. He had the timings down to an art form and knew exactly when to come and when to avoid the place. The days, and more importantly, the times he chose to use the pool were the ones when he knew the day crowds were mostly gone, there were no school parties or classes scheduled and the 'after work' crowd wouldn't start arriving until 04.00 pm at the earliest. He would almost have the place to himself. His routine never varied. He spent the first thirty minutes in the gym weight training. He combined the resistance machines and the free weights. The machines took care of leg presses, squats, assisted chin-ups and lat' pull downs. The free weights were more concentrated, and he found they were better for curls and lunges.

From the gym, it was a quick change and into the pool. Again, his routine which never varied would see him in and out in a little over twenty minutes. That's how long it took him to swim a mile. Averaging just under twenty seconds a length, he knew it would take sixty-four lengths of a 25m pool to make a mile. The twenty minutes was simply multiplying the sixty-four by the time-per-length.

That's why Benny Fox was as fit as he was. One hour, give or take, and he had run two miles, swam one mile and put in thirty minutes of high intensity weight training. There were other people he had seen in the gym who spent almost half of that time organising their progress chart, getting wipe-down paper towels at the ready, filling the water bottle, arranging the correct playlist in their phone for their workout, then actually finding the first machine and sitting down to start.

When he got back to the flat, the sweat-soaked gear and wet towel went straight into the washing machine. He needed a shower and some clean, dry clothes. The facilities at Maryhill were perfectly fine and were more than adequate, it's just that he had a fairly hard mile run home and it would have been pointless showering there.

When he was finished and dressed, it was 05.40 pm. He wanted to see the TV News at 06.00 pm but he wanted to call the detective at the same time. He put his TV on to the correct channel then pressed the pause button on his control. Like all modern systems, it could be paused, rewound or forwarded to suit. That would let him leave the house to make his call without missing anything. His only real interest was any updates on the murders.

As before, he made his way up the walkway path to his favoured spot, assembled the phone and made his call. It was 06.00 pm exactly and was answered straight away. DS Mullen was sitting in her car in the Gateway Building car park with the engine switched off.

"Detective Sergeant, how are you?"

"I'm fine thank you. And you?"

Benny's first thought was that she sounded a lot less hostile than she had on previous calls. Mind you, two of those calls were after he had been at her home, one of those, actually being inside her home. The hostility had been understandable.

"I was wondering if the information I left you was helpful?"

"It was very helpful, thank you. As you know, I can't go into specifics, but I can say it led to us obtaining warrants and progressing the case considerably. Can I ask you something?"

"Of course."

"Why did you do it? Why did you break into that man's home, steal his documents and pass them to me?"

Benny thought for a few moments, searching for the right response.

"Self-preservation," he replied.

"Self-preservation, as in, we get them before they get you?"

"Yes." He paused then asked, "Will it work?"

"Will what work?"

"Will you get them before they get me?"

It was her turn to take a moment before she answered, "Honestly? I don't know. I won't lie and say you will be 100% safe. We will get this organisation here in Glasgow, I'm certain of that, but I don't know if it stops here or if there are others who will move in and carry on where they left off."

"I appreciate your candour Detective. Thank you."

Jenny Mullen was about to cross a line she would never have contemplated, not even 24- hours earlier. Aside from breaking into her house and the fact he was a thief she was very much aware this was the same man who had rescued four children from goodness knows what. She knew it was not unheard of for kidnappers to receive the ransom money and end up killing the hostages, regardless. Tying off loose ends, they called it. The very thought sent shivers down her spine. She was also aware that the investigation might still be in the dark without his help. Despite this, all he had to look forward to, was a lifetime of looking over his shoulder. It didn't sit right with her and on balance, she would share some information with him despite that putting her career at risk.

"I'm about to tell you something, two things actually, and I would ask that these remain between us."

"Of course."

"You were right when you said you thought we had a leak in our ranks. It was a technical support guy. He was working mostly on CCTV footage lately and was passing images and other information on to someone in the city centre, for money."

"Can you tell me the name or the address of who was receiving the information or have the police already closed that part of the investigation down?"

If she answered, she really was over the line and there was no going back. As she weighed it up in her mind, she knew it's only because he got to Omelchenko's house as quick as he did, that they had anything. If they had waited for warrants to be issued and the right personnel to be assembled before driving to Strathblane then executing their search, there's every possibility the safe would have been empty. The same thing might happen tomorrow. She knew there had been an issue with obtaining the search warrant before close of business today and the same issue was making it difficult to obtain an 'out-with office hours' warrant for tonight. The most likely outcome was that the search warrant would be granted for 09.00 am in the morning.

Metaphorically, she took the step forward and crossed the line.

"We are scheduled to execute a search warrant at 09.00 am tomorrow. If you had any reason to go there, you have until then."

He didn't reply. He didn't have to. She knew that he understood what she was saying. She gave him the address in Bath Street and said the name he was looking for. Artem.

At that, they ended the call, disassembled their respective phones and went back about their business.

As Benny walked back to the flat, his thoughts were on the Bath Street offices.

As Jenny Mullen started the car engine and got ready to drive off, her thoughts were on what she had just put in motion, and she desperately hoped it would not come back to haunt her.

Benny plated up some home-made soup with a crusty roll, put it on a tray and sat in front of the TV to watch the news. The continuing murder story dominated and was first up. The story confirmed the police had narrowed the enquiry into an Asian criminal organisation carrying out some retaliation against an Eastern European criminal organisation. It was as much as they had by way of facts and at best, was vague, leaving more questions than answers. Everything that came after, was nothing more than the usual sensational journalistic speculation. In typical fashion they produced witnesses who never actually witnessed anything, rolled out locals who didn't know anything and spoke with the odd 'specialist' who spoke at length without saying anything meaningful. He put the TV off.

He left it until after 07.00 pm to ensure the worst of the traffic would be away, then headed for the subway. After visiting his unit and changing into his leathers, he locked the place up and rolled the bike out of the storage unit yard into the quiet roads of the surrounding industrial area. The area was cold and dark, and with the majority of businesses being closed for the day, it had a soulless feel to it. Paisley Road West was a stark contrast by comparison. There were many businesses open, spilling their bright lights through the windows on to the street. Although the traffic was light compared to during the day, there were buses, taxis, cars, people coming and going, and it all created an energy that Benny was happy to merge with. He turned right, joining the city-centre bound traffic and disappeared into the flow.

He knew the area well and with the Bath Street address firmly in his mind, he could visualise where he was going. It didn't take him long to get there and as it turned out, he was only one junction away from the place he was looking for.

He moved the bike along to the address and pulled up to the kerb. At first, he thought he was at the wrong place. When the detective gave him the details, she said it was offices. He knew he had not misheard, and he had the correct address, but the building he was looking at was an upmarket hotel. It was only when he looked higher up, he realised the hotel took up part of the ground floor, the first floor and the second floor, but there was a third floor above that, that was in darkness.

He put the bike into gear and slowly set off. Following the one-way system, he took a right then turned right again, into Sauchiehall Lane. He had to keep his concentration levels dialled up to maximum as the place was like an obstacle course. The ground was a combination of old cobbles and patchy tarmac. Many of the cobbles were missing there were more than just a few potholes, some of them deeper than his bike could have coped with. There were buckled manhole covers, parked cars and industrial wheeled bins dotted along the lane, which brought their own hazard in the darkness.

Slowly weaving his way along the lane, he pulled up at the place he gauged to be the back of the hotel and offices, which lay on his right. His focus was on the top floor. Again, it was all in darkness. A few yards ahead on his left there was an area that was inset from the lane. Pulling forward to look, he saw there were a couple of cars parked and a look up at the windows confirmed this part of the block wasn't commercial. It was peoples' homes. He saw what he was looking for on the left-hand side of the area. He had seen enough for now, and he moved off to start the short journey back to his unit in Kinning Park.

As he readied himself for later that night, he was overcome with a real sense of déjà vu. Prior to the Freeman Building incident, he might have undertaken one or possibly two scores in a year. Compared to that, this was like a full-time job. Once again, he went through the same preparation process leaving nothing out, settled on the three-seat sofa and was switching the light off around 11.00 pm. His alarm went off at 02.45 am. An hour was more than enough and once again saw him rolling the bike to a slow, quiet halt just before the area that was inset from the lane, at 03.35 am. He had switched his lights off. On his earlier visit, he had seen part of this area, just to the left, where cars couldn't park as there were air-con units on the wall and residential plastic wheelie bins. No space to park a car but there was enough room to fit a motorbike without any trouble.

He switched the engine off and was able to silently push the bike the last few feet into the space. With all the weight training he did, he was a lot stronger than he looked. This made the task of manoeuvring the bike easy. He took off his helmet and waited without moving. If there was any movement or sound, he would know. He let a few minutes go by until he was satisfied the world around him was asleep. Quickly and quietly, he went from leathers straight to black spandex. He wouldn't need the jogger's clothing tonight.

After securing the bike, he got his backpack on and made his way along the few yards of the lane until he was behind the hotel and offices. Without any difficulty he got himself up and over the locked black gates that gave access to the back of the building. He moved into a shadowed recess that once again rendered him invisible and sat down to start his 'Sensory Acclimation' routine again. Slow breathing, taking in the smells, the sounds, acclimatising his vision to the darkness of his surroundings, all the while watching and hearing.

When he was ready, he moved for the building. There were two sets of metal fire escapes, one at each end, that went from the ground all the way to the top floor. He knew there would be no gates or locks or chains. It was a fire escape after all, and ease of use was the whole point. He went to the one on his right.

His first step onto the metal staircase was tentative. He needed to be certain it wouldn't make any squeaks, squeals, or metal to metal clunks or clanks. It didn't. Despite the age of the structure, it felt solid and robust. He slowly made his way up, one flight then a landing, another flight and another landing, and so it went on until he was at the landing just above the top of the hotel level and just below the offices level.

He was entirely focussed on the windows at this end and was paying no attention to the rest of the block that ran away to his right.

The windows on all levels of that side of the block were much older and may have been original. He hadn't looked to see who occupied the floors in that part of the block, when he was out on the front street earlier. Maybe residential, maybe commercial, or maybe a combination of both.

A lot of maybes. With hindsight, maybe Benny should have paid attention to who the next-door neighbours were because, right there, from one window along to his right on the second floor, he heard a man's voice. It was less than twenty feet away and when it spoke, Benny froze. He didn't move a muscle. He didn't turn quickly to look in the direction of the voice, but instead, slowly turned his head following the sound.

The man's voice simply asked, "What are you doing?"

22

The turning of his head in the direction of the voice was deliberately in slow-motion. No sudden movements. As the window came into his line of sight, a girl's voice replied, "I'm having a cigarette, if that's alright with you."

Relief washed over Benny. He thought the man had been talking to him. It was now clear, neither of them could see him despite the short distance.

"You know you're not allowed to smoke in here. If the landlord finds out, we'll get booted out."

"He won't find out. That's why I'm leaning out the window. Who are you anyway? The smoking Police?"

"Don't be an arse, Mandy. You know what I'm saying. Just hurry up and come in, and get the window closed."

As she lit the cigarette, the lighter illuminated the area immediately around her and Benny could partially see her face. He put her age at early twenties. Possibly students. That could explain them being up and about at this hour. That could be wrong of course, and they could be up for work in a place that had a really early start. He didn't think so though.

His gut told him they were night owls, and they hadn't gone to bed yet.

The smoke drifted his way and the stale, woody burning tobacco smell easily replaced the only other smell that had been there before. That was the dank, smell of moss and weeds, and the perpetual dampness that pervaded in an area that never saw much sunlight from one year to the next.

He continued to stand motionless, waiting for her to finish.

He didn't have to wait long. Mandy could only have smoked half of the cigarette before deciding to flick what was left into the night, without stubbing it out against the wall or the windowsill. His eyes followed the lit end as it fell away to the ground below. As he looked back to the window, she had moved her upper body back inside, closed the sash window and pulled the curtains closed.

He waited another two minutes, had a look around then carried on with his ascent towards the roof.

The roof was laid out in much the same way as the Freeman Building or a 1000 other roofs across the city. There were flat sections, pitched sections and structures. There were ventilation and air-con ducts, ariels and satellite dishes.

As always, he sat down and took a minute to orientate himself with the surroundings.

As a consummate professional, he knew getting out was every bit as important as getting in. Or, in this case, getting up and getting down. Benny looked for alternatives to the fire escape should he need to find another way off the roof in a hurry. Satisfied he had at least two alternatives, he carried on.

Locating the right office was going to be the problem here. The starting assumption was that not all the offices would be occupied by the Russians. They could be, which would make life much easier but better to start with worst case scenario. From there, things could only get better. A rough calculation on the length of the building frontage, doubled up to allow for the same at the back, he estimated eight offices, maybe more, maybe less. He knew eight wouldn't be far away based on his experience of having 'visited' offices like these, many times over the years.

He could get into one and move through the building an office at a time using his equipment, or he could rappel at the front and rear, looking in each window as he went. It's not like there would be a sign advertising what rooms the Russians used, so it would need to be a process of elimination. Eliminate the offices that looked like they were from a different type of business and concentrate on what was left.

Opting for the latter of his two choices, he used his climbing gear and the night goggles, and started at the front. He was above the glare from the sodium streetlights and was confident no one would see him. Moving to the first window, he took in the desktops first. Calendars, penholders, a cup, a diary. They all had logos he recognised. Schroders, Jupiter, Scottish Widows, Rathbones, Close Brothers. This was all aligned to Financial Services in one way or another. One down, who knows how many more to go.

He was able to tick off another four offices using the same logic. In one, there were certificates on walls referencing The Law Society. Solicitors was a reasonable assumption. In another, there was paraphernalia referencing 'the third sector'.

He'd never heard of it but there was also paperwork he could make out, that had information about charities, voluntary work and community organisations. Another one ticked off.

He had eliminated all of the front from his mental list and in the end, he was left with five rooms at the back. Interestingly, it looked like these were all connected with adjoining doors. Where to start also worked on a process of logic, as did most things in his life. He took in the furnishings of each room and decided to start at the most salubrious. He had made a mental note as he went, that there were no PIR sensors. He wondered if the doors were alarmed and there was no motion detection in place. If that was the case, it demonstrated either confidence, arrogance or stupidity, in his opinion. If it was the offices of the Russians, he reckoned it would be a combination of confidence and arrogance. Time would tell.

If the doors were alarmed, he could see the windows weren't. That's where he would start. They were modern UPVC units, the same as the hotel floors below. He could see the windows were internally beaded, securing the glass onto the frame on the inside, ensuring it couldn't be removed from the outside. Internal beading told him the corners, transoms and mullions would be fully welded. These were high security units and would not be easy to open from the outside.

Unless you were Benny Fox.

He had the first window open in under three minutes. Stepping in from the windowsill to the lush, deep carpet, he was reminded of his visit to the study of Yegor Omelchenko. In the air, there was the faintest lingering smell of a high-end cologne that had been present but more prominent in Yegor's study. Creed Aventus came to mind. He had no doubts. He was in the right place. As he looked around, he was taken by how neat and ordered everything was, then something caught his eye. It was a framed professionally finished family portrait photograph. It took pride of place on the desk and showed a confident man, a beautiful woman, and two handsome children.

For the first time, Benny knew he was looking at the face of Yegor Omelchenko, child-kidnapper and murderer.

The man's face was now imprinted on his mind as he moved on. Yegor wasn't the reason he was here. It was the other man. Artem. Benny figured if he was as high up the food-chain as he thought he was, his office would be the room next door.

Benny exited Yegor's window leaving no trace that he had been there, moved to the next window and let himself in.

There was nothing about this room that personalised it. It was all business. The big hardwood double pedestal desk had seven drawers in total. There was a central drawer which would be in line with the user's stomach. In each of the pedestals to the left and right, there were two small drawers at the top and middle, and a big drawer at the bottom. All seven were locked.

Two minutes later, they weren't.

Another déjà vu moment, just like the safe in Strathblane. Benny found files. Folders, envelopes and photographs. The only thing missing was money.

This time he was prepared. He had brought a canvass kit bag with him. Pulling it open, he quickly emptied the contents of the drawers into it and zipped it up. He locked the drawers, retreated out the way he had come in and re-locked the window, leaving no trace. He wasn't thinking about the Russian knowing whether he had been burgled or not.

As soon as he opened the first drawer, it would be obvious. He was thinking about DS Mullen telling him they would be there at 09.00 am. If they didn't know the place had been burgled, it should stop any spotlight pointing in her direction. No awkward questions about who knew what.

He got back up to the roof, unhooked his climbing gear from where he had secured it and quickly made his way down the fire escape. A minute later, he was over the gates and in the lane.

Another four minutes, and his leathers were on with everything securely stowed in the top box and panniers. Less concerned this time about the people in the flats, he started the bike, put it in gear and rolled out of Sauchiehall Lane for what he hoped would be the last time.

The first signs of early morning activity had already begun as he cruised past a newspaper delivery truck unloading at a small newsagent shop.

As he was taking the on-ramp to the westbound M8 motorway, starting his long, detoured road back to the unit, an earlier thought was running through his mind.

He wondered if the lax security had demonstrated confidence, arrogance or stupidity? He thought it had been confident arrogance.

He was now reconsidering that opinion.

"Your boss's house safe has just been emptied despite him being at home – with four armed personnel, the police net is tightening around you with every hour that passes, and you leave all of this paperwork in an office desk and go home for the night? That is way beyond stupidity," he thought to himself.

Benny smiled to himself as he had another thought, "Maybe I was giving these people more credit than they warranted."

With a quick twist of his right wrist, he opened the throttle and felt the big Kawasaki do its thing as he gunned along the almost empty M8 motorway towards Kingston Bridge, heading south of the river.

Benny sat on the three-seater sofa that sometimes doubled up as a bed and placed the canvass bag beside him. Wearing gloves, he removed the items that had come from Artem's desk drawers, one at a time, browsing through each as he did.

He hadn't gone through the items from Yegor's safe in any great detail and he couldn't have known what he had in his hands was basically the other half of a two-part criminal story. Between both sets of information, there was every chance the combined lot spelled the end of the Russians reign of crime in West Central Scotland. This would be passed on to the detective in much the same manner as the first package.

In what he had read so far, there were names and places, most of which meant nothing to him. He opened another beige-coloured square cut folder and what he saw stopped him dead in his tracks. What he saw was a photograph – of himself.

Benny's stomach lurched and for a few seconds he thought they knew who he was. They had him.

He took a minute, gathered his thoughts and started to read. It soon became apparent they didn't know who he was. They didn't have him. He breathed easier.

There were two separate sets of documentation in this folder. The first, the one with his photo, was stapled to the large manila envelope which it had arrived in. It was marked private and for the attention of Artem and included more photographs, all of Benny. He could see they had been lifted from CCTV footage and showed him riding his bike. There was also a handwritten note that basically told this Artem guy, the man in the black leathers on the motorbike, is the man he was looking for.

"The informant," he thought to himself.

Behind this paperwork was another set of stapled documentation. Again, there was an envelope, this one smaller than the first, with a note and one photograph. He didn't recognise the man in the photo, but he did recognise the name. Peter Mann.

He recalled Jack saying that he had been unable to contact Peter, and Benny felt an unsettling feeling run through him. There was another note attached. It too was handwritten, but it was different handwriting from the other notes or envelopes.

This note only had two words on it. South Street.

He knew South Street well enough and also knew it was long stretch of road. From memory it started around the Castlebank Street junction near Partick and ran parallel with the river all the way to Dumbarton Road on the way to Yoker. He knew it was almost entirely industrial and he couldn't quite get the connection with Peter Mann. It's unlikely the man lived there.

He was walking through various scenarios in his mind, the way he does. Lateral thinking.

He closed his eyes and thought to himself, "Firstly there are only two sets of paperwork in this folder. It's unlikely that's random. I don't think this Artem is a random kind of guy. Both envelopes had come from the same source, the handwriting tells me that. The source is the leak in the police. If the paperwork and photos are to help this guy find me, perhaps the paperwork for Peter Mann is the same. Perhaps they are looking for him too. They can't find me because they have no name and no photo that they can ID me from. For him, they have both. Now, according to Jack, he is unreachable? That seems too big a coincidence. So why South Street. It could be one of two things. Either he does live there which means they know where to find him, or they already have him, and South Street is where they have taken him. Of course, it could be none of these things and something different altogether."

He decided the first thing to be done was to contact Jack and see where Peter Mann lives. If it's not South Street, then Jack could use his contacts and maybe find out if anyone was aware of the Russians having business connections there.

He knew he should leave things to the police, and they would sort it. That would be the right thing to do, and the easiest. The only reason he was investing himself in it was because he knew what it felt like to be one man on your own with armed thugs and gangsters coming after you. If he could help Peter Mann, he would.

He wrapped things up at the unit and made his way out to join the rest of the world going about its business.

He got Jack without any trouble and told him what he needed. Jack said he still hadn't heard anything from Peter. He said Peter lived in the East End just off London Road. "It's near Celtic Park and the Chris Hoy Velodrome. Out that way."

Before the call ended, he said he would find out what he could about South Street and get back to him.

23

He went home, went to bed and fell into the deepest of sleeps, having set the alarm for 01.00 pm. He wanted to speak with DS Mullen at 02.00 pm, assuming she was able to make the window. He was sure she would have her hands full and wouldn't be surprised if she couldn't. He used his normal everyday phone as an alarm. Reaching to switch it off, he saw there was a text message from Jack.

It was short and to the point. "I'll be having a glass of wine or three today, if you fancy joining me."

Benny smiled at his friend's sense of humour, and he knew exactly where he'd be."

He got himself ready and took the burner phone with him as he made his way to the Chip. He'd timed it so he'd be where he wanted to be just before 02.00 pm. He cut into the Kelvin Walkway and followed the path that would cross the river and lead up the steps to the back of the Botanic Gardens. Stopping at a quiet spot he quickly assembled the phone. The call was answered sooner than he expected.

"Good afternoon, Detective Sergeant."

"Good afternoon, John."

"I know you explained you can't go into detail but if I may, was your morning visit to Bath Street productive?"

"As yet, that is still to be determined. Let's just say we now have plenty of paperwork and computer files to be sifted through, that may or may not help us in our investigation. I can tell you it all looks like routine office files and records for the most part. Talking of visits to Bath Street, I'm guessing you never got the chance to pay one of your own?"

"On the contrary, my night was very productive."

There was silence for a few moments, which felt longer than it actually was, then she spoke.

"I don't understand. There were office staff working away when we got there and there was no mention of any break-in or anything being missing."

"That's the whole point, when you do what I do. Was Artem or Yegor Omelchenko there?"

"No, neither of them, although the office staff were frantically placing calls while we were there. I'm sure those calls were to both of them, but as far as I could determine, there was no contact made."

"Well, I can tell you, there was nothing in Yegor's office but there was a lot of documentation in Artem's. I took it all and of course, you will have it before close of business today. There's something urgent I need to take care of right now, then I'll get it to you."

When the call ended, DS Mullen's mind was all over the place. She was consorting with a criminal and not only that, but she was also complicit in his actions. She was the lead detective in the current investigation into trying to find the man for goodness' sake. It wasn't lost on her that she had told him about Artem and Bath Street and suggested he might want to go there during the night before the police arrived in the morning. She had already rationalised this, and to some degree, justified it. Even still, hearing him say he was going to drop off the documentation he had stolen left her feeling she was getting herself further and further down the rabbit hole.

On one hand, the documentation he had given her from Yegor's house had catapulted the investigation forward considerably, and who was to say this new information he was about to provide wouldn't do the same. On the other hand, however, she was going to have to explain this to her boss, and that would need to be done in a way that didn't place any suspicion on her. Perhaps it was a calculated and thought-out decision, or perhaps she was just telling herself what she wanted to hear. Either way it wouldn't matter. She would take whatever John Johnstone had to offer and if it helped further the investigation into the Russians, she would continue passing him sensitive information and deal with the consequences if they came.

When Benny entered the Chip, he was just in time to hear Gavin the barman saying to Jack, "And that's from the man who buys his clothes from the Sunday Post. 'Stretch' this and 'easy fit' that."

Benny grinned as he approached the bar. "What did I miss?"

"It's your old mate there, trying to slag me off for what I'm wearing. He wouldn't know style if it hit him in the face."

Jack chipped in from where he was sitting, "Less of the 'old' or your clothes will be the least of your worries, son. You'll get hit in the face."

Gavin was already pouring a Chateauneuf de pap for Jack and asked Benny what he would like, still smiling at Jack's retort as he did so.

"A fresh orange and lemonade please Gavin, and for what it's worth, I think you look very dapper. Nothing at all wrong with what you're wearing."

"You hear that old fella? A compliment from a man with taste. A man who knows what he's talking about."

He turned back to Benny, "Thanks Benny. If you want to sit down, I'll bring these over."

As Benny moved to sit at the table with Jack, a couple came in and went to the other side of the open fire. Until then, Jack and Gavin had had the place to themselves. Despite the friendly banter, Benny knew Gavin was very professional at his job and that conversation would not have taken place had there been any other customers in.

After the drinks had been brought to the table, both men came to the matter at hand. There was no need for small talk.

"So, why were you asking about Peter?"

Benny explained about the folder he had found in the Russian's office and told him about the two stapled files in it. One centred on him and the other centred on Peter. He had no intention of referencing DS Mullen as the person who had given him the name and address, and he knew Jack wouldn't ask.

"I have a gut feeling that something is very wrong with your friend, and if I can do anything to help him, I will."

Jack nodded, as if to acknowledge that he knew Benny would help if he could. That was his nature. "Well, I can tell you, you were right about there being a connection between Russians and South Street. There is a big warehouse and yard on the river side, and my contact says he knows for a fact it's Russians who own it, or at least work in it. He works for the company immediately next to the warehouse and over the years, there have been many people and vehicles coming and going but he has no idea what it is they actually do as a company. He said it was during that hot spell we had last summer, that he and some of his mates were having a kick-about in the yard during their lunchbreak. He said he had seen a few of the guys who would come and go next door on a regular basis. He had heard them speaking one day and he made an assumption that he said nearly caused bother. Apparently, the assumption was that they were Ukrainian. The guy had seen the Ukrainian national team on tv over the years. During one of the kick-abouts he suggested they knock up two teams for a game of five-a-sides. 'Scotland v Ukraine,' he had said. According to him, the guy's face was like thunder, and he went off on one, making it abundantly clear they were not Ukrainian, they were Russian. Seemingly it wasn't so much what he said, but more about how he said it."

Jack gave Benny the address and told him the place his contact worked, for reference. They made conversation for another twenty minutes or so then Benny said he had to cut it short as there were a few things he had to take care of before the afternoon was over. As always, he paid the bill and left a decent tip for Gavin.

He walked out of the lane, turned right, then right again into the subway station. Forty-five minutes later he was riding the bike out of the yard at the unit. He'd emptied the top box and panniers and replaced the contents with three items. One of the three was the canvas bag containing the contents of Artem's desk drawers. He'd toyed with the idea of leaving out the folder with the two stapled files. He decided there was nothing to be gained as DS Mullen was well aware of his own situation and she would need to be brought up to speed on Peter Mann's, one way or the other.

He had a few stops to make and thought it would be safer to put a set of the false plates on the bike to ensure his anonymity should anyone be looking for him at a later stage.

His first stop was his safety deposit box company. He was going to need money for what he had in mind. The next stop was a printer's, off Eglinton Street in the south of the city. He arrived there just before 04.00 pm.

There were no customers in the shop and the only person in the place was the middle-aged man at the front desk. He gave Benny the impression he owned the business. It's very possible he did as it was a small independent firm and not part of any of the big chains.

Benny had replaced his helmet with his beanie hat that completely covered his hair and the top of his face. It didn't look out of place. He simply looked like he was well wrapped up against the cold.

"Good afternoon, sir, what can we do for you today?"

"Hi, I'm not sure if I'm looking for decals or stickers. I am in the process of setting up a motorcycle courier service and I'm looking to put the details on the top box and panniers of all the bikes. You know, the name and contact details, stuff like that."

"It's stickers you're looking for, I think. They are less permanent and can easily be removed if need be. Vinyl is best and we do them on-site. The adhesive is low tack making the sticker repositionable and they come with air escape channels as standard ensuring there are no bubbles, and you get a professional finish. They can be done on a clear or coloured background, whatever works best. Either you upload a logo and specify fonts etc, or I can provide that from our catalogue."

"That sounds perfect. The problem I have is time, and I'm hoping you can help me. What are your standard turnaround times?"

"72-hours is standard, but we have an 'Express' service which is a bit more expensive, and the order is ready in 48-hours. Then we have 'Express Extra' which is more expensive again, but it guarantees a 24-hour turnaround."

"The thing is, I'm competing with another company, a big company, for a fairly lucrative contract and if we got it, it would be a huge step in getting us up and running from a standing start. In order to be in with a shout though, we'd need to be ready for early tomorrow morning."

In the hope it would serve as an incentive, Benny produced a wad of money from his inside pocket.

"Is there any chance at all that you might have a 'Super Express Extra' service that could have the stickers ready before you close today?"

The man looked at the money, looked at Benny and asked how many stickers he would need and what details would need to go on them.

Keeping it as simple as he could, Benny provided a company name, a phone number and an email address, all made up on the spot. He said there was no logo as yet, but they could revisit that when he was properly established.

The man wrote it all down and took measurements of the size of stickers Benny would need. It was a reasonable sized order and not overly complicated. The reality was Benny only needed three stickers for his own bike and that was it. The rest was for effect.

"I know what it's like to be competing with bigger companies so I'll do what I can to help. Give me a minute."

The man popped his head into the back of the shop and Benny could hear him asking one of the operators if he would be able to do it. He laid out the requirements. The operator said he could have it ready in an hour.

"You're in luck mister. We can have this ready in an hour."

He went to work on a desktop calculator and said, "I'll run that through as 'Express Extra'. Including VAT, the total cost would be £248. How does that sound?"

"That sounds perfect. Let's make it an even £300. I really appreciate your help, and this will help me immensely."

"Benny paid the man and said he'd be back in an hour. Leaving the shop, he got on his bike and headed for his next two stops. A DIY shop and a Post Office.

The two places he had in mind were within a mile of the printers. At the DIY shop, it didn't matter what he bought. It was nothing more than a prop and the only proviso was it wouldn't be much bigger than the palm of his hand. One of the first sections inside the shop was plumbing. He picked something that wasn't too expensive as it would either be given away to a stranger in the next two hours or more likely, it would end up in the back of a cupboard at home never to be used. He saw something that was the right size and cost less than £10. He paid and left the shop with a 28mm Brass Compression Lockshield Gate Valve. He had no clue as to what it did, but it would serve a purpose. The next stop was the Post Office.

That was an easier shop. He picked up a self-seal bubble wrap lined envelope and a pen.

Outside, he wrote a made-up name on the envelope along with the address in South Street that Jack had given him. He took a guess at something that sounded Russian. He recalled the name Arshavin from Arsenal Football Club from years earlier and went with that. He picked a random first name. Viktor Arshavin.

Almost an hour to the minute later, he was back at the printers. The stickers were ready for him when he arrived. Taking them, he thanked the man and started for the door. He was momentarily confused when the man said, "Good luck", then he remembered the non-existent contract bid in the morning.

"Thanks very much," he said as he left.

Now he had to find a quiet spot, get the stickers on to his bike and get to South Street as quick as he could. It had just gone 05.00 pm and he hoped there would be someone in the Russian's warehouse until at least 06.00 pm. If they closed at 05.00 pm and he was too late, he'd need to come back in the morning. He knew he was taking a risk as they knew of the existence of a black motorbike but went on the assumption that it was highly unlikely, they would connect the bike in the photo with the courier at their warehouse.

Despite the rush-hour traffic, he made good time. He cut through Tradeston, joined the M8 motorway, took the tunnel and was exiting the Clydeside Expressway on the north side of the river in just over twenty minutes.

He found the place he was looking for without any trouble. The gates to the yard were open and he rode through them, pulling up at what looked like the main office. The big yard lights came on automatically as he rolled into the range of the sensors. The first thing he noticed struck him as odd. The gates were open, and the office lights were on, so the business wasn't closed for the day, but there wasn't a single vehicle in the car park. He understood of course that many people, people like himself, use public transport to get around so he wasn't overly concerned. It just struck him as odd in this setting.

He opened the top box and lifted out the envelope that was addressed to Viktor Arshavin and contained the brass valve fitment.

It only now dawned on him that a courier would have some means of getting a signature for the package, but it was too late to do anything about it. Having said that, he was sure there would be no Viktor Arshavin which meant he'd need to take the package away again, meaning no signature would be required. He walked to the office door with the confidence of a man who was just getting on with his job.

He tried the handle and it opened.

Stepping into what looked like a reception area, he called out for someone's attention.

"Hello. Is there anyone here? I have a package for Mr Arshavin. Hello."

Nothing. There was no reply. He tried another internal door which opened into huge empty space. If anyone questioned why he took it upon himself to walk around areas that were clearly out of bounds, his cover story would be that it was late in the day, and he really wanted to avoid a return journey the next morning. It sounded feasible.

Looking around him, Benny was struck by the emptiness. No stock, no machines, no vehicles. The words from Jack's contact came back to him. "He has no idea what they actually do as a company." Benny reckoned the answer was, "Nothing. They don't anything here, and this place is a front for something else."

He called out again and this time his voice took on an echo-like quality due to the acoustics of the cavernous space.

"Hello, is there anyone here?" Again, there was no reply.

At the other end of the warehouse against what he presumed was the back wall, he could see a series of doors. It looked like two toilets, a kitchen area and possibly storerooms. He was about to leave when he heard a sound from behind one of the storeroom doors. It was faint but he thought it was someone saying hello. He crossed the warehouse and stopped in front of the doors.

"Hello. Is there anyone there?"

One of the doors knocked from the inside and a voice came from behind it. It was louder this time. "Hello. Can you help me?"

Benny dropped the visor on his crash helmet. He couldn't say why, but he was certain the person behind the door was Peter Mann and he didn't want him to see his face. There was a key in the door. Unlocking it, he turned the handle. When he opened the door, he could immediately see it was Peter Mann, but he looked different from his photo. This man in front of Benny had an unshaven, gaunt, grey complexion and his sunken eyes gave the appearance of someone seriously sleep-deprived or that of a habitual drug user. He guessed it was the former. He also noticed the man had his wrists bound. The wrist-ties looked familiar to Benny. He had seen them before on the wrists of 8-year-old children.

"Come with me. Hurry."

He wasn't running but Benny was moving at a pace as he crossed the floor towards the door he had just come through. Peter was right at his back. At the first door, Benny slowly and quietly opened it to check no one had come into the reception area while he was in the warehouse. It was still empty. As he was about to move through to the main door, he saw something on a desk that he could use. He vaulted the counter with the agility of young deer. He lifted the scissors that were in the plastic penholder and vaulted back. He cut off the wrist-ties and they stepped forward toward the main door. As before, he slowly opened it and checked outside. Again, there was no sign of life other than his bike. Apart from that, the car park was empty. They both hurried out the front door and moved to the bike. Benny opened the top box and one of the panniers, bringing out the two other items he had brought. One was a second crash helmet; the other was a leather jacket. The helmet was two sizes too big and the jacket, three sizes. None of that mattered. Peter got them on and climbed on the bike behind Benny. He dropped it into gear and swung it around the yard, heading for the gates.

Some people say good fortune is with you, or it isn't. Today it was with Peter Mann in spades. As the Kawasaki was moving out through the gates onto South Street, a red Ford Kuga with four men inside, was indicating to drive in.

24

At work she was Detective Sergeant Mullen. Outside work she was just Jenny. Typical of a million other young mothers just like her, Jenny's day didn't stop when she left work. It merely took a different direction and she had to start all over again. There was a stop to be made at the supermarket on the way home, to pick up something for dinner and the kids packed lunches for tomorrow. When she got home, it would be the same ritual. Empty the dishwasher from the morning, put a washing on, get the dinner started, shout upstairs for the kids to come down and pick up their stuff that they'd dumped in the hall and lounge when they came in from school.

"I can't understand why we have to go through this rigmarole every night. It's like Groundhog Day. Just put the bloody stuff away when you come in. It couldn't be easier."

They'd stopped asking what Groundhog Day was, a long time ago.

When everything was as organised as it could be, Jenny put the kettle on for a coffee. What she really wanted was to pour a glass of chilled Chablis and kick back with her feet up but given her role in the current investigation, she knew that wasn't possible. There was no Monday to Friday, nine to five, routine in the middle of cases like this. She never knew when she might get a call to go back in to work if there had been a significant development. Day, night, weekend, you were always on call.

At the same time as she was pouring her coffee, Benny Fox was blasting the Kawasaki along South Street with Peter Mann clinging on to him for dear life. In a futile attempt to chase after the bike, Olek had spun the Ford Kuga around at the gate and made to follow, when Artem who was sitting in the passenger seat told him not to bother. The bike had already disappeared into the night, heading in the direction of the city centre. Pavlo and Fedir were in the back seat.

"He is gone. Take us back in to the yard," said Artem. Olek made a U-turn when he caught a break in the traffic. Fedir, who seemed the most rational of them all was thinking to himself how Artem had said, 'He has gone' and not 'They have gone'. He wondered if Artem's thoughts were on the journalist or on the man riding the bike. He knew it was the same man and the same bike from the CCTV footage. The one Artem had been looking for. He also knew the warehouse was empty except for the journalist. Without checking, he couldn't be sure the passenger on the bike was that man, but every fibre in his body told him it was.

When it was clear that they were not being pursued, Benny eased off the throttle and slowed to the same speed as the rest of the traffic. Peter felt it and automatically reduced his grip on Benny. Not entirely though. He was still holding on, just less tightly. Peter had no idea who this man could be, but the actions of the last ten minutes suggested he was one of the good guys and could be trusted. At least, that's what he hoped. He was also aware there was no practical means of communicating with him and for the time being at least, he could do nothing more than hold on and see where he was being taken.

It didn't take long. Fifteen minutes later Benny was rolling the bike over the lowered kerb on to the pavement and he stopped at the three flagpoles outside the Police Scotland Clyde Gateway building. He was still thinking about the Ford Kuga. A cold, foreboding feeling had coursed through him and he couldn't easily shake it off. As the arc of the Kawasaki's sweeping headlight had flashed across the car, the deep red colour momentarily made Benny think of blood. He had seen blood in its various hues throughout his life, from the arterial bright red, to the venous dark reddish-purple. The colour of this car sat somewhere in the middle.

Leaving the engine running, he motioned for Peter to dismount, got off after him and put the bike on its stand. Between the streetlights, the lights from the building and the car park lights, the area was as bright as a floodlit football pitch at a midweek night game. Allowing for that, Benny was confident that, if pushed, Peter would not be able to give a meaningful description, even with the visor up. The helmet obscured too much of the rest.

He raised the visor, extended his arm to shake hands, and spoke with Peter.

"Peter? Peter Mann? My name is John Johnstone. It's good to meet you considering the circumstances. Listen, I need you to go in there and report what has happened, but I can't come with you. Is that okay with you?"

Peter seemed slightly confused, trying to take everything in, but he nodded his head.

"Good. Just tell them exactly what happened to you. How you ended up in that building, how I let you out and how we ended up here. You'll be okay now. You're safe. Can you do me a huge favour please?"

"Of course, after what you've just done for me, anything at all. Just name it."

"I want you to find someone in there and give a holdall to her. Her name is Detective Sergeant Mullen. Will you remember that name?"

"Yes. Detective Sergeant Mullen. I'll do that no bother at all."

"Thanks Peter. If you can take off the helmet and jacket, I'll get the bag for you."

They swapped over what they had. The canvas bag containing the stuff from Artem's office came out of the pannier and the leather jacket went in. The helmet went into the top box.

Peter thanked Benny for his help, took the bag and walked towards the entrance. He had many questions but knew they would need to go unanswered, for now at least, as Benny had made it clear he wouldn't be able to stay around. He got on his bike but instead of riding off, he waited until Peter had gone inside then he manoeuvred the bike through two of the stainless-steel bollards nearest the barrier, that gave him access to the car park. He slowly rode around to the front entrance and stopped where he could see into the brightly lit reception area. Peter was speaking to what looked like one of two receptionists.

After a few minutes a man wearing a shirt and tie, with a lanyard around his neck, appeared from the side. He carried an air of confidence, and it was clear to Benny, he was an authority in this building. He spoke with Peter for a few minutes, took the bag from him then they both moved out of view, in the direction the man with the tie had come from. Benny had expected to see DS Mullen and seeing the other man, threw him slightly.

He put the bike in gear, slowly moved around the car park and went back out through the space between the bollards that he had come in. He crossed the pavement, rolled on to the road and turned left, taking the A728 over the Rutherglen Bridge. Following the road, he saw a big pub/restaurant on his right called the Jenny Burn. Making his way round to the car park, he found a quiet spot at the farthest corner and stopped. He readied his burner phone and messaged DS Mullen on her own phone. He knew she wouldn't assemble her own burner until 10.00 pm, but he needed to speak with her now if at all possible.

He sent a short text and hoped she would understand.

"Can you call me asap. JJ."

She did understand and within minutes his phone rang. She was using her burner.

"Detective Sergeant, apologies for breaking our arrangement, but I needed to speak with you before 10 o'clock. Are you at work right now? If you're not, I think you will get a phone call from them very soon, asking you to go back in."

"I'm not at work. Not yet at least, and they've already called. I'm getting ready to head back in as we speak. It was my boss, DCS Cook. He called to say we had a walk-in tonight who was carrying a bag filled with, what looks like incriminating documentation, provided courtesy of a Mr John Johnstone. He also said the man who brought the bag had a fascinating story about being bundled into a van in broad daylight, put in a hood and restraints, locked in a room, and left there for days until a man on a motorbike let him out. Apparently, the guy didn't know what day of the week it is. Not figuratively but literally. Would you care to shed some light on any of that?"

"I will, of course I will. I think it might be better if we spoke again tomorrow morning though, and I'll tell you what I know. That'll give you a chance to digest the contents of the bag and speak to Peter Mann beforehand. That's his name by the way, in case they hadn't told you yet. Peter Mann. The urgency in my needing to speak to you was the bag. I know I said before that I don't really trust the police but you're the exception to that. I trust you. I just wanted to ensure you knew someone else had it and you were okay with that."

"I am. It's my boss, and he is as straight as a die. 100%." She paused for a moment then added, "And thank you."

"For what?"

"For what you said about trusting me. I'll take that as a compliment."

"You're welcome and I'm only saying it because it's true. I'll let you get on Detective, and I'll speak with you again in the morning. 10.00 am sharp."

"I look forward to it. Goodnight, John."

The Ford Kuga stopped and parked outside the warehouse office in the same place that Benny had parked his bike. Artem instructed his men to check if the prisoner was still there. If he wasn't, they were to secure the place and lock it up. As they were getting out of the car, he was already calling Yegor from his mobile.

"Yegor, we have another problem. The bike man we are looking for has been to the warehouse. He was leaving just as we were arrived, and we missed him by seconds. We tried to give chase but, on his motorbike, he was too fast." He was always reluctant to give Yegor bad news, but with the way the day was going, more bad news couldn't really make things any worse.

"There's more. There was another person on the bike with him. It may have been the journalist. The men are checking the warehouse now."

He could see the inside lights were being switched off and at that, Pavlo stepped out of the door before anyone else. He looked towards Artem and simply shook his head. Artem understood. The journalist was gone.

"Pavlo has just confirmed, he is gone. What do you want me to do?"

"Come back here. There is no point in staying there if you don't know where he has gone. I will have someone watch his house in case he is stupid enough to go back there."

Yegor had said, 'Come back here'. 'Here', was another of his legitimate companies. It was a Haulage, Freight and Courier business on the Air Link Industrial Estate, by the airport and since the police visit to Bath Street, was temporarily the Russians new base of operations. At best, the premises could be described as functional. The two main reasons for choosing this place over any other were that it was under the radar and more importantly, it was a 24-hour, 7 days a week operation, which meant the place would never be empty. Yegor wouldn't have to worry about a thief getting in and out of this place unnoticed, assuming of course he ever learned of the place's existence in the first place. It was a constant hive of activity.

Apart from a select handful of men in the business, inner circle men, the workers were oblivious of the criminal connection. There was never anything to raise any suspicions and that was how Yegor wanted it. That was about to change however, for anyone who had an ounce of savvy about them. It was after 07.00 pm and for the most part, the place was quieter than other times of the day. Still busy, but just less so. It would get a lot busier later when the night shift people came on for the trucks that would start coming and going through the night.

The men on shift all knew one another. When Yegor had arrived, one of the inner circle guys circulated among the workforce that it was 'just someone from head office' saying he and a few others might be here for a week or two. It wasn't broadcast that he was in fact the owner.

After the initial curiosity, he was soon forgotten, and everyone went about their business as usual.

When the four men arrived in the red Ford, that was a different scenario altogether. Artem looked 'polished' in a similar way to the other guy upstairs. Head office men. Olek blended in. He looked ordinary and there was nothing that set him apart from anyone else. No one took much notice of him.

Then there was Pavlo and Fedir. People noticed them. Of course, the semi-automatic weapons were gone but their physical appearance caught people's attention. There were plenty of adjectives that sprang to mind, and they were all appropriate and accurate. Hard; Trained; Fit; Strong;

Focussed; All business; No nonsense; Tough. They were most definitely not head office men.

Benny left the Jenny Burn car park and took another circuitous route back to the unit. He undertook the usual wind-down measures, locked up and headed for the subway home.

As he stepped out of Hillhead station onto the bustling Byres Road three things came to mind in quick succession. After the relevant warmth of the train, he was struck with how cold it was and he adjusted the collar of his coat to try and compensate. Then there was the vibrancy to the place that he was very familiar with. There were all manner of businesses plying their trade, there were people coming and going that gave the place its own atmosphere, and there were the smells. Food smells, specifically. The thing about Byres Road was that this vibrancy gave it a weekend feel regardless of what night of the week it was. There were restaurants of almost every conceivable origin in the area. If Benny had to pick one, it would be Italian. There was no shortage in the number to choose from, but he had a favourite. The food was exceptional and the chef, first-class, but if he was being honest, it was as much emotion that drove his thinking as anything else. Before the tragic loss of his wife Emma, this had always been their place. Although it was not conscious thought, he was aware that on some subliminal level, eating there kept her close and that made him smile.

He walked up Byres Road towards the library, took the stairs that led up to the restaurant and was welcomed at the door with the same friendly face he had known for years.

"Ah, Mr Benny, what a surprise. Please, let me take your coat."

"Listen, I've been busy, and I haven't booked. Is that okay?"

"For you, always. Please, come with me."

He was shown to a table by the window which suited him fine as he could mind his own business and simply watch the world go by outside in the street. That would be a welcome distraction from the events of these recent weeks.

His friend brought him a menu, but Benny already had a good idea of what he wanted. It's not that he was a creature of habit, in fact it was the very opposite. When he and Emma used to visit Barcelona, they would always look for tapas. It was the variety of tastes and textures that appealed most.

When they went to Southern Italy for the first time, they discovered the Italians had their very own version of tapas. Stuzzichini. The first time they came to this restaurant, the man who was now very much his friend, explained that whilst the Stuzzichini was associated with the south, his cuisine was more Venetian and there they were called Cicchetti. Not exactly the same but close enough.

The choice seemed endless. He settled on three plates. A Collo Di Agnello – neck of lamb in a pea puree, Filetto – Scotch Beef medallions in foie gras, pan brioche, madeira sauce and truffle cream, and a Paccheri Frutti Di Mare – A tubed Neapolitan pasta with squid, king prawns, king scallops, mussels, clams and a shellfish sauce.

He knew it sounded like a ridiculous amount of food for one person, but he also knew from experience that they recognised he was dining on his own and as such, the plates would not be over filled. It was more about taste and less about quantity.

When he was finished, he wasn't disappointed. He never was. He settled up, paid his compliments to the chef and said his arrivederci's for the evening, promising to come back again soon.

Despite the lateness of his meal and the events of the day, he slept a full and deep sleep, waking at 07.45 am, feeling refreshed. First on the itinerary was a 6-mile run, a shower and get ready to call DS Mullen.

25

DS Mullen and her colleagues had worked late into the night, after which it had been suggested they come in a bit later in the morning, as DCS Cook wanted everyone rested and ready to go. It was going to be another busy one. With the house to herself, she was sitting in her lounge and was ready for her 10.00 am phone call. When Benny called, they exchanged a few pleasantries before coming to the matter at hand. The hostility and tensions from their earliest exchanges was no longer evident. They weren't friends, but it was closer to that than it was to being adversarial.

Benny explained to her how he had been trying to gather information about the Russians and had come across the name Peter Mann from a contact. He'd learned the man was a journalist, and after a further bit of digging it emerged that he was doing a spotlight piece into organised crime in Glasgow and was focussing on the Russians. They must have found out about this and according to Peter Mann, he was lifted off the street. It seemed logical to Benny that it was them who had him but the visit to South Street confirmed it. The handwritten note attached to the file from the desk in Artem's Bath Street office, was the first mention of South Street. He explained how he got someone to look into any possible connection between the two and he got a hit. The warehouse. He didn't go into detail about his fictitious courier business and how that was a cover to get him into the place. He skipped to the part about how he went there, found the place abandoned other than Peter Mann being held captive, released him and dropped him off at French Street with the bag of documentation.

"You know the rest from there."

"Well, I can tell you, the information from the bag you passed on to us, filled in a lot of gaps from the other lot that came from Mr Omelchenko's safe. That, and more besides. As a result of the paperwork from his safe, it's clear there are connections to other cases and things have grown exponentially, including the manpower to go with it. There is a considerable task force involved now, and I am very much at the heart of it, thanks to you. Your information has led to dozens of arrests already and it has allowed us to raise warrants authorising entry and search for various business premises, as well as homes and vehicles. This new stuff will only enhance that. I haven't personally carried out interviews yet, but I will today. I understand some of those arrested are already looking to do deals wherever possible and are giving up information as a result. There are a lot of people turning on one another."

Benny was thinking about his ultimate end game which was to get the Russians off his back once and for all. "That's good to hear. It all started with the kidnapped children. Is there anything that specifically relates to that?"

Jenny was more relaxed about discussing the case with him now and was less inclined to be on her guard during their exchanges. She knew that without him, they would still be scratching the surface. It's not that she didn't have confidence in her own ability or that of her colleagues, it's just that she was very aware it could have taken weeks or even months to get to where they are today.

"As a matter of fact, there is. There are several things linking them but there are two things specifically. One is the technician from our place. The one we identified as the leak. There are date and time stamped CCTV stills which we can tie directly back to him with 100% accuracy from his fingerprints. He has already given us information that could only have been obtained with inside knowledge and we have payments going into his bank account, but this ensures there is no ambiguity. Then we have a woman called Moira Tobin, who is now a person of interest to us. She is a supervisor for a cleaning firm that we can tie directly back to Mr Omelchenko, and least one other employee. It seems she is the physical link between him and the families of the four kidnapped children, as she has been inside all of their homes in recent times. There are copies of handwritten reports bearing her name and signature which should be easily identifiable as written by her, when matched up to paperwork that we will gather when she is brought in for questioning. It's very distinctive writing and forensic analysis should have no difficulty confirming the angle of the slants, the switch from cursive to printed, the flourishes and embellishments, and all the other things they take into consideration. I'm sure Omelchenko's solicitors will say it's circumstantial as he employs hundreds of people, but it's a good start."

She rounded off the conversation by saying she was confident the main players would all be in custody within the next 48-hours. Before they ended the call, Benny suggested it was probably safe to move away from the four times they had agreed to turn the burner phones on, now that the leak had been found and the guy was under arrest. He had her mobile number but for obvious reasons, wasn't going to give her his.

"If you're agreeable, let's keep the two burners for now, as a means of contacting each other should the need arise, but maybe bring it down to one 5-minute window each day. Would that suit you?"

"Yes, it would."

"As regards a time, does 02.00 pm work for you?

She said it did and they agreed to switch on again the following afternoon at 02.00 pm then the same time each day after that.

After removing the SIM card and battery from the burner, Benny started walking back to the flat from the spot on the walkway path that he used to make his calls. When he was back on the street, he took his other 'day-to-day' phone from his coat pocket and switched it on. When it powered up, it pinged once with a notification that he had a new voice message.

A quick look at the screen confirmed it was from a withheld number. Taking the stairs up to the flat two at a time, he was there in less than a minute. He put the phone onto speaker and retrieved the message while he took his coat and scarf off. It was Colin Campbell. Colin the money man.

The message was short and to the point.

"Good morning, It's Colin Campbell here. Can you call me back at your earliest convenience please? Many thanks."

Benny new it was both vague and professional, simultaneously, in the off chance that it was picked up by a third party. No names meant it could easily have been a wrong number that Mr Campbell had dialled. He deleted the voice message.

He didn't return the call straight away. He had to go out again and planned on calling Colin from the burner. Having seen the CCTV stills of himself on the black Kawasaki, he decided it was time for a change. He would take the subway to Ibrox on the city's southside where a short walk brought him to an out-of-the-way place, that was both a coffee-shop, and had six PC's that provided internet access on a pay-as-you-go basis. There were a hundred easier ways to get online and the chances of anyone following up on his browsing history were almost non-existent but detachment and staying under the radar were his priorities. The place had the level of anonymity that appealed to him. He was surprised that it still did business, now that almost everyone had online access through their smartphones.

Benny would search out another motorbike that met his requirements, and the only pre-requisite was that it was a private sale. He didn't want to put himself into the system that was inevitable if he used a dealership for his purchase. They would be obliged to undertake the necessary ID checks and satisfy the money laundering rules. He knew his other ID was more than adequate to withstand almost any level of scrutiny, but his thinking was, only be as exposed as you need to be. Any private sale was far less intrusive than the alternative.

He dressed accordingly in his easily forgettable attire. He had similar clothing to that he kept at the unit. The only thing that wasn't here was the large-framed specs with the clear non-prescription glass. The anorak and long-peak golf cap would be sufficient to cover his face.

The owners didn't refer to the place as an internet café, but that's how Benny saw it. When he arrived, there were two patrons using a PC each, and a middle-aged couple sitting at a table. The PC users were young and gave off a vibe that could easily flit between student or unemployed. There was nothing that suggested a regular, steady income, and Benny concluded that if there was an income anywhere in their world, they would have the latest smartphone with an 'all-you-can-eat' unlimited data plan, if the rest of their generation were anything to go by. They wouldn't be in a place like this.

Benny approached the lady at the counter, asked for a white regular coffee with no sugar, and pound coins for one of the PC's. The middle-aged couple paid him no more than a cursory glance which was borne out of curiosity more than anything else, then they seemed content to go back to their conversation which was centred around the young man at one of the PC's and his facial piercings. There wasn't the slightest attempt at discretion and the few other people in the place could hear them, including the young man. He was taking no notice whatsoever.

As he waited for the coffee to be poured, Benny mused on the reason for that. Maybe the young guy had spent years explaining his piercings to people and couldn't be bothered anymore, maybe he was engrossed in whatever he was browsing and filtered the conversation out, or maybe he considered the couple as ignoramuses and decided it wasn't worth dignifying by speaking up. Whatever the reason, he carried on typing and left them to it.

When he got his coffee and pound coins, he chose a PC that wasn't easily overlooked, and pulled up a chair. He looked for a place to set down the coffee and considered for a moment why they would even allow drinks to be placed in such close proximity to the keyboards and the drives. Surely it was an accident waiting to happen and could only end in trouble. Benny didn't actually want the coffee and merely bought it so as to fit in. He placed it at the side near the back, where there was virtually no chance of it being knocked over and started his online search. After forty-five minutes of trawling through relevant sites, he found what he was looking for. A silver BMW R1200 GS. It ticked off all of his requirements and the seller who lived in Dumbarton had included his mobile number in the ad.

Part of the internet café's service was the ability to print on a price-per-page basis. When he had what he needed, he printed it all off, closed the PC and paid the girl. As he waited for his change and the printed paperwork, he noticed the ignoramuses had topped up their teacups, or mugs to be more precise, and moved on to another equally offensive subject that he knew without doubt was none of their business either.

Leaving the café, he walked to the subway station, caught the next train on the inner circle line and got off two stations later at Kinning Park. Instead of going to the unit, he walked to the closed off street with the concrete bollards and sat on one of them. As expected, the place was deserted. Quickly assembling the phone, he made his first call to the man selling the BMW. There were no hitches. It hadn't been sold yet. The man said the bike and the necessary paperwork were ready to go and could be collected or dropped off depending on how far away the buyer lived. Benny went through the rest of the process. He haggled a little as he thought it would be expected. They settled on a price, and it was agreed that he would collect it today as the seller was on holiday and would be in all day. Benny asked if he would prefer cash, or a bank transfer and the seller said cash. That suited Benny a lot better than using the bank, but he didn't elaborate on it. He took the information he'd need to arrange insurance cover. They agreed a time and ended the call.

His next call was to Colin Campbell in London, and it didn't take as long as the call to Dumbarton. Colin told Benny he had made the arrangements they'd discussed previously and asked when he could come to London.

Benny said he'd be there on Friday morning.

His last call was to the insurance company to arrange a cover note for the bike. He was the last of a dying breed that still did this over the phone. Everyone else logged in using an app and did it themselves.

He went back to the unit and picked up everything he needed, including a holdall into which he put his helmet and leathers, locked up and left. The next stop was the safety deposit box to collect the money for his new bike, then it was a quick train journey to Glasgow Queen Street. After checking the times, he made his way to the low-level platform for the 14.07 train from Edinburgh Waverley that would be arriving at 15.30. The man on the phone told him it was a half hour journey, and he should get off at Dalreoch on the other side of the River Leven from the town centre. He said it would be walking distance from there. He was right on both counts. The journey from Queen Street took thirty-one minutes and he lived less than quarter of a mile away.

The handover went smoothly enough. As with his previous bike purchases, he used a fake name and address. He didn't use his complete, paid for legend, Ian Walker. That was designed specifically as whole new person that he might need to become someday. This was a watered-down version. It was adequate but wouldn't stand up to any real scrutiny. It was simply an at-arms-length fictitious person that would allow him to make various purchases that couldn't be traced back to him. The quality was decent enough as it came from the same people as the main one.

By 04.40 pm, Benny was part of the city-bound flow of traffic heading up the A82 on his newly acquired bike. If he was taking it home, it would be a straight run almost to his front door, but as it was, he was going back to the unit and would take the tunnel.

Ordinarily he would have sold the Kawasaki online but would have been careful not to use the same site that he used to buy the BMW. Certainly not a buy and sell on the same site, on the same day. Given that the police and the Russians knew about that bike though, he decided he would keep it in the unit for the time being. It's not like he needed the money.

He knew it was nigh on impossible that anyone would make a connection between the bike from the photos and the same make, model and colour being sold on the internet, especially with different sites, on different days, but why take the risk. Talking of not taking unnecessary risks, he knew he'd have to find a similar make and model and get a few sets of ringer plates made for the BMW.

It was just after 07.00 pm by the time Benny got the bike locked away and made his way home. He called his daughter and had a good chat with her. He said he would be in London on Friday to take care of some business and wondered if they were up for a visit. After explaining that he could stay over in the city on the Friday night and head down to Surrey on the Saturday, he suggested staying with them for the Saturday and Sunday, then heading back up the road on the Monday. She said that would be fantastic and they were already looking forward to it.

He made a further two calls. One was to Avanti West Coast to arrange a train ticket for Thursday, returning on Monday and he was happy to pay the extra for an upgrade to first class.

The other was to The Montcalm Royal Hotel in Finsbury Square, booking in for Thursday night and Friday night. Benny had stayed there a few times before and liked their rooftop brasserie, although it might be a bit cold for open-air dining at this time of the year.

Finsbury Square was ideally situated for his trip as Colin Campbell's office was two streets back from the main thoroughfare, Moorgate, which put it about halfway between the square and the river.

He had considered flying, but he wasn't in a rush, and he enjoyed being able to take in the scenery or sit back and read a book. It was a different pace, but one that appealed to him.

He'd sort out the onward travel to Surrey when he was in London. The family lived in the village of Chilworth, on the

Dorking Road. The house was walking distance from the station.

The pharmaceutical company his son-in-law Gary worked for was headquartered in London. Benny knew it was at least an hour's commute each way, every day and he never understood why they decided to move there. Of course, it was a beautiful house in a lovely part of the country, but he couldn't help thinking there were equally nice places a lot closer to the city. It's not like Gary had roots in Surrey. He'd never been there until they started house-hunting.

Still, they were happy and that was all that mattered.

26

Benny woke at 07.35 am. He very rarely needed to set an alarm, and this was a usual time for him to wake. It was Wednesday morning, and he had no big plans for the day. He would make a quick trip into town and pick up a few things for the visit. He was at an age where he had no idea what to get as gifts for the boys, but his daughter was able to point him in the right direction. The afternoon would be a visit to the gym for a good workout as he wouldn't be doing as much as he'd like to over the next few days. The hotel was well equipped, and he'd take advantage of the facilities, but he wouldn't do anything on the couple of days he was with the family, apart from maybe going for a run. Other than these things, all that was left to be done, was to pack.

Thursday morning was shaping up to be another fine, albeit cold, blue-skyed day as far as he could see through his bay window. He was as organised as he could be. He'd left a message for Jack to let him know he'd be away for a few days and wouldn't be at their usual Saturday get-together. He left out the part about Colin Campbell and just said he was seeing his family. As expected, Jack messaged back asking him to pass on his love and best wishes to all.

With his Corneliani Cashmere suit, Blake Mill shirts and Burberry Oxford Brogues packed away in readiness for his London meeting, the rest of his clothes were casual. Expensive, but casual. He had three pieces of luggage. First, there was a mid-sized hard-shell suitcase with wheels and an extendable handle. Next, there was a suit carrier that fastened securely on to the back of the case. Finally, there was a matching holdall, and all three were sitting by the door ready to be picked up on the way out. Anything else he needed was inside his pockets. He had his normal phone in his inside coat pocket and his burner phone in the holdall. As usual, both had the SIM and battery removed, and the normal phone would most likely remain like this for the whole weekend. It would only go on if he was stuck and needed to contact the family. The burner would go on each afternoon at 02.00 pm as planned. He didn't expect to hear from the Detective Sergeant, but he wanted to be prepared just in case.

He heard the taxi horn toot down in the street. It was right on time. He got his luggage, locked up and headed downstairs. The driver saw him approaching the car, opened the boot with the internal release switch, got out, made his way to the back of the car and lifted Benny's luggage in. The car had been pre-booked, and the driver knew the next stop was Glasgow Central Station. They made small talk on the way. The driver asked if Benny was off somewhere nice to which he replied, "Just heading down south to see the family." He didn't elaborate and the driver didn't pursue it any further.

When they arrived, the taxi pulled in just past the Blue Lagoon Fish and Chip shop on Gordon Street, parked with the engine running and both men got out. Benny got out his wallet while the driver retrieved the luggage. After paying him the fare plus a good tip, the driver said, "Have a good trip mate." Benny acknowledged him and walked up the slight incline to the station entrance carrying the holdall and pulling his case behind, as the driver got back in behind the wheel.

The station was in full flow with people coming and going. His first stop was one of the ticket machines. When he'd booked the ticket, the person on the phone had suggested he could go online, register for the app, log on and then generate an e-ticket, or an m-ticket as that would be a lot easier. It hadn't sounded a lot easier, and Benny said he'd rather just buy a good, old-fashioned ticket that he could pick up at the station. That was arranged with the appropriate instructions for collection explained. He should find a ticket machine, which would be located outside the ticket office. He should put in the credit card he used to purchase the ticket, then he should key in the 8-character reference he was provided with, and the ticket would be printed for him.

He wasn't entirely confident it would go smoothly but he needn't have been concerned. He found a machine, followed the procedure and had the printed tickets in his hand in a matter of minutes. These were securely put away in the inside pocket of his jacket. He'd left plenty time and still had almost an hour to wait before the train was due to depart. He bought a newspaper, made his way to a coffee shop and ordered a latte. After finding a table, he sat and browsed through the paper, not paying too much attention to anything in particular when he came to the story about the police investigation into the southside murders. It was no longer front-page worthy, but it still warranted almost a third of a page, a few pages in. The article didn't reveal anything more than he already knew and he quickly moved on.

From his seat he could see across the concourse to the arrival and departure display. The constantly changing display now showed the Glasgow to London Euston train but hadn't allocated a platform yet. Eventually, the platform was shown, and he made his way there with many others who he guessed were heading for the same train. The fact that most of them had luggage was a bit of a giveaway.

His seat in First-Class was pre-booked and he had no difficulty finding it. The carriage is laid out with single seats on one end of the aisle and double seats on the other. He had purposely booked one of the singles. All seats came with a guaranteed table. He was hoping the facing single seat on the opposite side of the table would not be booked and he would have the space to himself. He had opted for a seat that faced in the direction of travel, so he could take in the scenery. After stowing his luggage and settling in, he brought out the latest novel he was reading and placed it on the table in front of him. Eventually, all the passengers were aboard, and the train eased away from its stationary position to start its journey. The stated arrival time suggested it would take 4 hours and 29 minutes.

He was in luck. No one sat in the seat opposite.

They made good time, there were no issues at Euston, and he took a taxi across the city, checking in to his hotel room just before 10.00 pm. Everywhere was bustling. Thursday night in a place like London would always have a Friday or Saturday night feel to it.

By 08.45 am on Friday morning, Benny had already had a good workout, a swim and a healthy breakfast.

By 09.30 am, he was taking the three short steps from the hotel front doors down into Finsbury Square. Heading diagonally towards Moorgate and on into the Financial District, he was dressed in his tailored expensive suit and highly polished shoes, looking every bit like the many senior company executives who worked there. He fitted right in.

Benny had been to the building before and knew exactly where he was going. After taking the lift to the seventh floor, he was at Colin Campbell's office in plenty time for his 10.00 am appointment.

The young lady on reception offered him tea or coffee, which he politely declined. Instead of sitting in one of the two leather sofas, he walked to the window that looked out towards the old Bank of England Museum.

A few moments later, Colin came out and welcomed him into his office. The receptionist hadn't met Benny before and although there was a meeting scheduled in the diary, there was no name. When she saw how her boss greeted him, she could easily see the body language suggested he was greeting an old friend more than just another client. As if feeling the need to check, he asked Benny if he had been offered a tea or coffee. Benny said he had, but he was okay for now. Colin kept a tidy office. With no files or folders anywhere in sight, it was completely devoid of clutter. The furnishings and fittings looked expensive but there was nothing modern about the room. It all seemed to work though, and it looked appropriate for this type of business and this part of the city. Benny guessed most of 'modern' had moved from Moorgate to Canary Wharf where it was all minimalist with glass and brushed chrome. The highly polished ornate double pedestal desk had nothing on it apart from a leather desk diary, an expensive looking deep shine brown suede blotter, a Montblanc pen and one folder. It had taken Benny a few moments to work out what was different about the surface of the desk then he realised it was the fact there was no computer on it.

"I notice you don't have a computer here. How do you keep up with what's going on in the world, especially in your type of business? I'm sure the last time I was here you had a laptop."

Colin smiled and said, "I did, but I don't need it anymore. Let me show you this. I think you'll be impressed."

He opened one of the desk drawers and took out what looked like a remote control for a TV and an iPad style tablet. He turned his swivel chair towards one of the blank panelled walls, pointed the control and pressed a button. Like an old 60's spy movie, two of the Oak panels retracted to the left and right, respectively, revealing an ultra-modern curved screen monitor. Benny reckoned it was between 80 or 90 inches. A press of another button and the monitor flickered into life. As it did so, Colin turned to the tablet, logged in and started typing. What he was looking at in his device was being mirrored onto the big screen in real time. As he typed, Benny saw the letters appear on the monitor.

"The quality is exceptional. Watch this." He opened Google. As he tapped the screen of his tablet, Benny watched the words 'BBC News' appear in the search box. A few more clicks and some moving of the cursor, saw the streaming news coverage appear on the big monitor. The clarity of the picture and the quality of the sound was as good as anything Benny had at home. Better, in fact.

"It allows me to access the very latest information when I need it, whilst maintaining the traditionalist feel in the office. Many of our private clients are 'old money' and many others are not. This allows me to best serve both in a way that suits everyone."

"And what about me? Am I in the old-fashioned traditionalist camp with pen and paper, or am I in the modern camp with the latest gadgets?"

"You're half and half."

Benny smiled. He'd never thought of himself as half and half anything.

Colin paused the screen which caught the newsreader in a very unflattering pose, with her eyes closed and her mouth open. He removed the contents from the folder and spread them out on the desk. He picked up the remote, unpaused the screen and turned to the tablet. After a series of inputs, a digital file with a 5-digit number on it, appeared on the monitor where the newsreader had been.

Most of Colin Campbell's client's files had their name on them. There were, however, a few like Benny who required his discretion as much as his financial experience. For those clients, there were no names. Only numbers. Colin held the documentation securely and what he had in the folder were printed copies for Benny to take away with him.

Acting on Benny's instructions, Colin had opened a current/cheque account and a deposit/savings account, both with Banco Santander, using Benny's other persona, Ian Walker. It was straightforward as Ian Walker already had a bank account in the UK that he used regularly to pay standing orders etc. The reason Banco Santander was chosen was primarily because of their global reach. The bank was huge, with almost one and a half trillion euros under management, plus they were worldwide. From Europe to North America. From South America to Asia. The accounts were opened in Barcelona listing Ian Walker's status as a self-sufficient ex-pat. Colin's connection had secured a postal address in Barcelona, to ensure it would work.

Under the same name, Colin created investment accounts with three of the biggest fund managers in Europe, and he opened two credit cards. All of the accounts and cards were linked when they were set up, so it would be seamless for Benny to move money into or out of each. He pulled each document up on the screen, one at a time. As they went through them, Colin passed the paper version across the desk to Benny.

"There are only two other things left to be done here. First is the security. I have set these up with multi-factor authentication. I created the security information to meet the requirement myself. It's random. They all have money deposited and credited already. I've itemised that for you and you will see the credit balances on each. You can reimburse me for that later. The first thing I need you to do is log on to each and change the security settings to information that only you could know. Obviously, there is no need for me to know any of it as the accounts are now live. Change the security and it's 100% under your sole control. One of the documents in your folder is a step-by-step guide on how to do that."

"I understand and I'll sort that. You said there were two things?"

"Yes. The other is the transference of funds from your current arrangements, into these new holdings. As I'm sure you know, there are limits on what can be deposited or invested without attracting attention, and those limits are really low. The last thing you want is to deposit a sum of money and find that it's raised a flag somewhere. I have looked into setting you up – sorry – setting Ian Walker up as a small independent trader at the Diamond Bourse. I know you are still active in that market already so this wouldn't be a difficult step for you to take. Is it fair for me to say that your involvement to date has been mostly one way? That's to say, you are paying cash to buy stones, but you haven't sold many of them yet?"

"That's correct."

"When the time comes for you to start selling, that's when your problems will start. Whether you sell for cash and try to pay the money in, or have the buyer transfer the funds, it's the same thing. It still has to go into your accounts. If you are a registered and licensed diamond dealer then it makes it all legitimate. Obviously, you'll need to pay tax like any other business, but it frees you up to move substantial funds a lot easier, and you won't have to live entirely out of safety deposit boxes for the rest of your life. I'm still reasonably connected in the industry and can easily set you up in Hatton Garden or the Birmingham Jewellery Quarter. Nothing too grand, but enough to make it easy to move funds."

He went on to show Benny all the other documentation, explaining it as he went. He passed him the mail that had been forwarded from the Barcelona address. Some of it was unopened, some was open. It mostly related to the bank accounts, the investments and the credit cards. Some mail was from the Consell Municipal in respect of his Barcelona address. Colin said he'd taken the liberty of having someone open the envelopes with the cards so they could be activated in the Barcelona area.

"The statements for these will show a coffee purchase in Las Ramblas, a pack of socks from a shop in Maremagnum at Port Vell. There will be a €30 withdrawal from an ATM at Barcelona-Sants. They're only small things but necessary to get the cards in the system."

By the time the meeting was over, Benny had asked Colin to go ahead and set up the diamond dealing business in Ian Walker's name. Colin said he would. He gave Benny a copy of the invoice for the work undertaken, a breakdown of the money that was fronted by him to open the accounts and investments, and a note of his preferred account that the payment should be paid into, to settle the bill.

Benny asked if he would rather have cash, but Colin declined and said no thank you. He said he appreciated the offer, but in his world, it was six of one and half a dozen of the other.

When they were finished, Colin insisted on taking Benny for lunch, adding that it would be his treat.

As they walked the short distance to the restaurant, Benny couldn't help thinking that's how easy it was to go from Benny Fox, Master Thief, to Ian Walker, Diamond Dealer.

27

After thanking Colin for lunch, they left the restaurant, going their separate ways. Colin was heading back to his office to finish putting things in place as per his discussions with Benny.

Benny walked back in the direction of the hotel but veered off towards Finsbury Circus Gardens. It was 01.46 pm and he wanted to have the burner switched on in case DS Mullen called. Ten minutes later, he was sitting on one of the benches in the autumn sunshine, just off the perimeter walkway. He left the phone on until 02.05 but there was no call. That suited him okay. He was now focussed on enjoying time with his family and forgetting Glasgow and Russian thugs for a day or two at least.

The rest of Friday was pleasant enough, and Benny used the time in the way any regular tourist would. A bit of shopping and a bit of sightseeing.

On Saturday morning he checked out of the hotel. Stepping down into the square, he had his hand luggage strapped over his shoulder and his suit bag was secured to the case. Using the extended trolley handle and the built-in wheels, he easily pulled it behind him. He turned left and after short series of rights and lefts, he was at Liverpool Street Station. He thought how this end of the city, north of the river, had transformed beyond all recognition in recent years and on his short walk, Benny caught glimpses of a few of the now world-famous designs as he took in the architecturally designed landmarks. He could name a few. The Gherkin; The Cheesegrater; The Walkie-Talkie; The Heron.

He had already mapped out the train route and times before he left the hotel. Today's journey would take longer than usual as it was the weekend and the journey times varied depending on what time you were travelling and the number of changes. Today there were two. He took the underground to London Waterloo, where he picked up the Southern Western to Guildford, then he changed onto the Great Western from Guildford to Chilworth. Ten minutes out of Waterloo he switched on his mobile phone and sent a message to his daughter, Stacey. He had said on the phone when they spoke a couple of nights previous, that he would walk to her house from the station, but she insisted on picking him up.

In the message he had just sent, he said he would phone from Guildford a few minutes before his next train was due and that would give her ten minutes or so to leave the house and get to the station in time for him arriving.

It went to plan. As the train pulled into Chilworth Station which sat almost directly on top of a level crossing, he got his things and stepped off onto the platform. As he did, he saw Stacey standing at the corner of the building nearest the crossing barrier. As he walked to her, she motioned round the side of the building and said, "I'm just round here dad. I'm on double yellows and don't want to get booked. I'll get you at the car."

He walked round the corner of the red brick building and Stacey was standing by her Toyota RAV4 Hybrid. They hugged, loaded his things into the back, got in and set off. The house was only minutes away, but she said she had to make a stop in the village of Shalford first. Benny was happy to sit back and enjoy the drive. As they drove, the conversation was mostly about family and what had been happening since they had last seen each other, earlier in the year. Stacey said the boys were really excited about seeing him. Skype and Facetime was okay, but it wasn't the same.

Benny was adept at multi-tasking. He held a proper, meaningful conversation with his daughter as they drove, without missing a beat, but was able to take in everything around him at the same time. He was aware there were a lot more railway level-crossings and speed cameras on the road, than he was used to in West Central Scotland. He also noticed that a lot of the immediate Surrey countryside and villages gave off a Midsomer Murders vibe. Every now and then he would see a particularly big house which was walled and gated, and it made him think of Omelchenko's street in Strathblane.

When they arrived in Shalford, Stacey pulled up on the edge of the village green across from a Thai restaurant. She said she'd only be a few minutes, so Benny said he'd stay in the car. He watched as she disappeared round the corner at a coffee shop called the Snooty Fox. Even for the lateness in the year, the outside space was busy.

Five minutes later, Stacey was back at the car and a further fifteen minutes saw them at the house. It was 01.15 pm. She said Gary had taken the boys to their football training in Guildford and they'd be back around 03.00 pm. She said she was heading up to Waitrose to pick up a few things and asked if he wanted to come. He said he wouldn't, if that was okay and he could use the time to go for a run before everyone got back. That was of course a ruse as he had put in a good workout at the hotel gym, before leaving London. What he wanted was to phone DS Mullen at 02.00 pm.

He got settled into the spare bedroom, quickly unpacked and changed into his running gear. Stacey gave him a front-door key and the code to the house alarm before she set off for Guildford.

Minutes after she left, he locked the house up and secured the key into a zipped pocket. The only other thing in there were the parts of his burner phone. He headed off back in the direction of the train station. It was 01.48 pm. Five minutes later, he found a quiet spot, assembled the phone, and dialled DS Mullen. She answered on the second ring.

"Good afternoon, Detective Sergeant."

"Good afternoon, John."

"I was just calling to see if there were any developments in the investigation that you might be able to share with me."

"There are, and I am more than happy to confirm that it's mostly good news."

Not normally someone prone to being a 'glass half empty' kind of guy, Benny couldn't help but be drawn to the 'mostly' good news. He asked her to elaborate, which she did.

"Since we last spoke, things have moved at a blistering pace over at the Crime Campus in Gartcosh. Warrants have been issued; Searches have taken place on both residential and business premises; Numerous arrests have been made and currently, we have over thirty people detained pending their cases going over to the Sheriff court as early as Monday. It's most likely that the majority will see sentencing deferred and in most cases the Court will be asked to detain them in custody due to the nature and seriousness of the crimes. As you know, these are dangerous people. There are separate, parallel investigations. The woman I spoke of, Moira Tobin, has confirmed she supplied the information that led to the kidnapping of the four children. The paperwork from Bath Street led us to a Chartered Accountant Firm in the City. At this stage it looks like they are multi-locational and the Partner who manages the city office has also been managing the affairs of Yegor Omelchenko's other enterprises. Whether it's the firm as a whole or just him, is still being investigated."

She filled him in on the progress of all elements of the investigations and any connections, insofar as she could. The North Lanarkshire Scrap Metal company; The Southside murders; Cases of people-trafficking stretching back many years before the kidnappings; The disappearance of the man and woman who it's believed were directly tasked with overseeing the welfare of the children held captive; The connection with the Freeman Building, and finally Peter Mann.

"That brings me to the 'mostly' good news John. Right at the top of the tree, as you know, is Mr Omelchenko. Next to him is his second in command, a man we only know as Artem. It appears Artem favours a three-man team from their many footsoldiers. A driver and two heavies, all of whom are Russian. The five of them are missing. As things stand, we can't find them. It's our belief, based on the evidence and statements we have, Omelchenko may well be looking to leave the country, but we are sure the other four are still operating together as one unit. Border Policing Command have buttoned down all the airports, ferries and sea-ports."

Until now, Benny had listened on with great enthusiasm as it seemed clear to him that the whole operation was caving in on top of them. This last piece of information took the wind out of that particular sail.

"Don't get me wrong, I have no doubt it's only a matter of time until we have them all in custody."

"I'm sure you will Detective. It's the time between now and then that concerns me, and what happens in between."

Some small talk took place, he thanked her for filling him in on the investigation and at that, the call ended.

Benny sat where he was for another few minutes and thought about where this left things. He was a realist and could easily weigh up pluses and minuses without getting hung up on the emotions. He saw things both practically and pragmatically.

By the time he was finished, he concluded that he was in a much better position now, than he was previously, despite the last five still being at large. Before this, they had an army of personnel and an entire network of contacts at their disposal. That was gone. They did not know who they were looking for and as far as he could see, that had not changed. All he had to do was keep his head down and eventually the police would round them up. That, or they would leave the country, either of which suited him fine.

Feeling better, he set off on his run. He had been here before and had a good idea of where he was going. He turned south, heading for the village of Blackheath. It tickled him that someone with a sense of humour had taken the time to erect a home-made three-direction signpost at the village crossroads which pointed to This Way, That Way, and Somewhere Else. He turned right and headed west towards Wonersh Common. After he left the village, it was mostly a single-track road, but it wasn't busy. At the T-junction he took a right back towards Shalford where he had been earlier, and from there back to the house. By the time he arrived his spirits had lifted considerably. He always found running good for clearing the mind. Taking in the landscape and villages he had come through he could now see the attraction of the locale as somewhere to live and raise a family. He was reconsidering his earlier assertions as to why Gary would want to live here and commute every day.

Back at the house, everyone was home. The two boys made a big fuss of him, and it was clear to see he was loved, despite the distance between them.

Stacey said she would put his running gear through the wash while he showered and freshened up, which he appreciated. After he gave them all the gifts he had brought with him, they spent the afternoon catching up.

During the conversation Benny floated the idea of buying a house abroad that they could all use as a holiday home. He had given a lot of thought to this the previous afternoon in London, after he'd spoken with Colin.

He said he was torn between Florida, Barcelona or Majorca. Florida, because they spoke English as a first language and their way of life had many similarities, but the weather was a lot nicer than the UK. On the other hand, it was a long-haul flight whereas Barcelona or Majorca was only a few hours, even less for the family who would most likely fly out from Gatwick. Because of their age, the distance was no issue for the boys, and they were all for Florida. That was mostly due to Disney World and Universal Studios.

Like Benny, Stacey and Gary were more grounded and saw things from a different perspective than that of their children. Either way, the excitement at having their very own villa anywhere, was palpable.

"Of course, these are only suggestions. Realistically we can go anywhere. Give it some thought and let me know what you think."

They told Benny they would.

Everyone ate out on Saturday night and again on Sunday afternoon with Benny insisting he pick up the bill for both. Before he knew it, it was Monday and time for him to think about packing up and heading back to Glasgow. He said his goodbyes to Gary before he left for work, then to the boys before they went to school.

Stacey dropped him back at Chilworth station just after 01.00 pm, and he started his journey back. It wasn't quite the same journey in reverse, but it was close enough.

He arrived home at 10.15 pm. He put his things away in the bedroom, sorted what needed to go in the wash, made a coffee and checked the time again. 10.55 pm. He didn't want to call as he knew it was around bedtime in Surrey, but he messaged to say he had thoroughly enjoyed his few days there and that was him home safely. Stacey messaged back, sending her love and saying everyone enjoyed having him and that they were all still buzzing about the idea of a holiday home. He replied saying she could take that as read. 100%. All they had to decide was decide where.

In the morning Benny got himself ready and headed for Hillhead underground. He needed to go to the unit to pick something up.

He stepped out of Kinning Park station, turned right, under the overhead footpath and past the recycling bins. It was another fine autumnal day. Blue skies but cold enough to see your own breath. Scotland Street West was empty as he walked past the red sandstone tenement block on his left. The only noise was the perpetual sound of the motorway, over the rail and through the almost leafless trees on his right. Moving out through the bollards at the end of the street, he crossed over towards the industrial area. As he walked towards the yard gates, he saw something that stopped him dead in his tracks. Simultaneously, he felt the adrenaline rush and the quickening of his heartbeat. It was less to do with the people or the vehicle he saw and was everything to do with the colour.

It was red and it sat somewhere between arterial bright red and venous dark reddish-purple on the spectrum.

28

He saw the colour first, before anything else registered. He thought the car was a Ford. He couldn't have told you it was a Kuga. This aside, he knew beyond any doubt, it was the same car that was pulling in through the gates at the South Street warehouse, as he was throttling on the power on his way out with Peter Mann clinging to him, on the seat behind.

Benny moved away from the yard gates and carried on walking towards the nearest building. To anyone observing, it was one fluid movement and didn't immediately look like a man heading for the yard then changing his mind. When he got to the side of the building, he stopped and looked over to the unit. From where he was, he could see everything, but it would be almost impossible to see him.

The red car was parked in front of his unit, and he counted five men standing between both. He recognised one as the storage yard manager but didn't recognise any of the others. He could see the manager was talking to one of the four. That man looked like he was in charge. He had a polished, confident look about him. Like a Barrister or a CEO. Benny remembered the conversation he had with DS Mullen.

"Mr Omelchenko's General – his second in command – a man we only know as Artem. Artem favours a three-man team from their many footsoldiers. A driver and two heavies, all of whom are Russian."

Of the other three, two could definitely be described as 'heavies' in which case the last man would be the driver.

They were too far off to hear what was being said but it looked like they were enquiring about the unit. Enquiring about Benny. He could see his Squire Shackle padlock was still in place. He was confident they wouldn't try to force their way in, in broad daylight with the manager still on-site. He was also certain that would change when the manager left, and the place was empty.

Two thoughts dominated his thinking. Firstly, if his assumption was correct and it was the Russians, how did they find him and secondly, would they leave and give him the opportunity to get in for the BMW and get out again? He knew he could afford to leave everything else as he was meticulous, and nothing in the unit could be traced back to him. As the unit was not registered to him, that would be another dead end for them. Financially, he could easily walk away and leave everything. That would not faze him. It was just that it would be easier to grab a few things, get the bike and leave, rather than having to go through the process of buying whatever he needed from scratch.

In less than five minutes, he saw the body language changing and knew the conversation was coming to an end.

The manager moved away in the direction of his office. The one he thought of as the driver got in first, behind the wheel.

The two heavies got in the back and the one he thought of as the boss – Artem – got in the front passenger seat.

They sat for a few minutes then slowly, the red Ford rolled toward the gates. Benny knew they could only turn left or right at the gates. One direction, the side he was on, would bring them further into the industrial area. Turning the other way, away from him, would take them towards the main road and away from the estate. He thought they would choose the latter. To be safe however, he turned and started to walk along the street with his back to the gates. In the unlikely event they did come his way, he was certain they wouldn't pay him any notice at all. As it was, they headed for the main road.

Using the reflection of a transit van window that was parked just ahead of him, he was able to watch their departure without stopping and turning around.

As they disappeared round the corner, he turned round and stood for a moment. He had two choices. He could retreat to a safe place and wait to see if they came back, or he could start moving now, be at the unit door in less than one minute, have the place opened, the bike loaded with his backpack and laptop, lower the ramp and be riding out of the gates in less than three. Four minutes all in. He didn't hesitate a second longer. He sprinted for the gates.

It took three and a half minutes in total. Close enough. He had made the decision to lock the place behind him. His first thought had been to leave and not look back, but locking up could buy him some more time, if no one realised he had been in and away again.

He made his way deeper into the estate, found a safe, secluded place to stop and swapped his clothes for his leathers.

With everything stowed securely in the top box and the panniers Benny took a route out of the estate in the opposite direction from that the Russians had taken. He rode under the motorway on Seaward Street, took a left towards Gorbals and joined the rest of the traffic flow. He wasn't going anywhere in particular. Just as long as he put some distance between him and them.

As he had no way of knowing where they had come from or where they had gone, he thought it would be safer to leave the city altogether. He made his way to the M74 motorway and headed south. Exiting at junction 5, he rolled into Strathclyde Country Park. Following the road all the way through, almost as far as the exit at the opposite end, he noticed a car park on his right, by the water's edge. Pulling in, he saw there was a snack-van and he bought himself a coffee. Sitting at one of the many benches, he was thinking about what had just happened in the last thirty minutes or so. He kept coming back to the same question. How did they find him?

The reality was they didn't find him. They found their 'man in black' but they didn't find Benny Fox. They were following up on one of the few leads they had.

Twelve hours earlier, around the time he was messaging his daughter after arriving home, The Russians got a break. Artem had put the word out all over the city that he was looking for a motorbike. A Diablo Black Kawasaki Z1000SX to be specific. Someone had identified the make and model for him from the photographs. He had given up on anything coming back after the police raids had started until, out of the blue, his phone rang. It was a van driver who had a motorbike of his own and worked from a unit in the Kinning Park industrial area. He was a friend of a taxi driver who had obtained information for Artem before. He said he couldn't be certain, but he had seen a bike like that on more than one occasion. He said there were storage units near his work that specifically catered for bikes. He was certain about that, because he had used one of the units the previous winter, when his own bike came off the road until the Spring. He had a garage now and didn't need their services but thought it could be worth checking out.

Artem and his henchmen had arrived this morning, found the manager and told him what they were looking for. He was helpful enough up to a point. He said there was a bike matching the description in that particular unit, but he couldn't provide the owners details as that was a breach of privacy. Sensing there was a certain tension in the air, he lowered his voice, looked around and said if it was up to him, he'd give them what they needed but the actual records were held at head office along with a spare key for the padlock.

"It's one of the features of leasing our units. The leaseholder is the only one with a key on-site and that gives them access 24/7. I've seen a bike like the one you're talking about coming and going at different times, but I don't know the first thing about the man who rides it."

As Benny finished his coffee, his thoughts had drifted to his immediate surroundings, and he thought how this would have been a good place to come in the summer months. Between the grassed areas and the little beach, he could imagine it having a vibrancy to it. He was suddenly brought back into the moment. Of all the things that could have done that, it was a seagull. The cheeky beggar had landed on his bike as it eyed up the bins and the car park in general, looking for something to eat. As he stood up to chase it off, he realised there was something of an avian turf war going on between the gulls, the magpies and the crows.

Having formed some semblance of a plan, Benny got back on his bike and exited the park, heading for the city-bound motorway. He had two stops to make.

First was the Halfords Autocentre on the southside. He picked up two new nylon motorbike covers. The assistant said they had run out of silver and only had black left. That suited Benny fine. The next stop was the safety deposit box company, where he quickly arranged an additional box and used it to store the laptop. Along with the clothes he had changed out of, he kept his backpack. The backpack contained his black lycra unitard, mask, gloves and boots, and most of his tools and equipment which included his night vision gear. There had been no room for ropes etc, but he knew these could be replaced easily enough if need be.

When his laptop was safely locked away, he headed back in the direction of the unit. Having had time to think, he was now fully aware of what to expect and knowing every inch of the area, he was certain he would have the upper hand if the Russians were there. He hoped they would be. That was the point of going back. He hoped they would be staking the unit out waiting to see if he turned up to access it. They had no way of knowing he had already been in, less than two minutes after they had left.

The biggest benefit of Benny being on a bike rather than in a car was that he could easily roll between the bollards, taking him from one dead-end street into another. There were a lot of those in that area and he knew where every one of them were. Finding the perfect lay-up position, he rolled the bike between a van and an industrial sized recycling bin, so it was out of sight from any angle, unless you were standing directly in front of it, and he waited.

It didn't take long before he saw them. He had expected to see the blood-red Ford driving into the street, but they were already there. They had actually been there before he arrived one street over, and with the same idea as him, had parked their car in tight behind a Luton van. He could make out the two men in the front but couldn't see into the back. It was reasonable to assume the two heavies were there too.

Now it was simply a waiting game.

He thought about phoning DS Mullen and having them all arrested. That seemed the logical and sensible thing to do. There was only one problem with that.

It ran the risk of bringing up the reason why they were there in the first place. When they were being interviewed, it would only take one of them to mention his storage unit and suddenly there would be a forensic team going over it with the proverbial fine toothcomb. Whilst he was confident the Russians would find no trace back to him, he wasn't quite as confident when it came to the resources of Police Scotland.

It took almost an hour before they decided to give up. Benny had been sitting on the ground with his back against a wall. He had fashioned his coat into a makeshift cushion, and it provided a reasonable level of comfort. Not great, but it helped keep the cold out and was softer than the tarmacadam. When he saw the Ford start to move, he quickly got to his feet, got his coat on, and got on the bike.

He followed at a considerable distance, ensuring to keep at least three cars or more between him and them. Even from that distance, he could clearly see there were four men in the car.

Good fortune was with Benny as they took the on-ramp to the M74 motorway. It meant he could sit a long way back safe in the knowledge that the big BMW had the muscle to accelerate hard at the first indication of them coming off again.

He watched as they made to exit the motorway at the Daldowie Crematorium junction.

Maintaining a safe distance, he followed as they came up the slip road, took a left then left again heading in the direction of Mount Vernon.

They slowed down on the Hamilton Road, and he watched as the car indicated and pulled into the driveway of a detached house near the train station. Even though much of the foliage had gone from the surrounding trees and bushes, what was left still afforded the house a reasonable degree of privacy. He didn't want to push his luck by getting any closer. He planned on coming back later. Around 03.45 am seemed like a good time.

Satisfied that the four Russians had gone into the house, he started back to the unit in Kinning Park and made it in good time while sticking to the speed limits. With the speed and agility his bike had over their Ford, he knew that he would have at least five minutes over them even if they'd decided to leave Mount Vernon when he did and drive straight there, which he was sure they wouldn't do. That made no sense at all. He was also sure that there had hadn't been a fifth person who would've been left behind to monitor the place. He would be alone, and five minutes would be more than enough. He was certain they would come back and force the padlock after the yard office had closed for the night. He intended to ensure there would be nothing for them to find except a filing cabinet, a table, a chair, a lamp and a three-seater sofa. Not that there was much else, but anything that there was, would be removed. That included the black Kawasaki.

As he was riding through the estate towards the unit, something caught his eye and gave him an idea. He pulled the bike to an abrupt stop. There was a City Council bin on the pavement, and it looked like it was recently emptied. There was a full black bin liner sitting next to it and the bin itself looked empty. He couldn't be sure, but he figured the bins may be emptied by one person on foot, and the bags collected by another person in a vehicle. He had a quick look around and saw he had the street to himself. He walked over, picked up the bag of rubbish, and carried it back to the bike. He got on, wedging the bag between his back and the top box, and rode round to the unit. Parking across the road, he crossed over into the yard. Quickly letting himself in, he dropped the bag on to the floor by the sofa and got the Kawasaki out.

Stepping back inside, he ripped open the rubbish bag and tipped it onto the sofa and the floor around it, spreading the contents liberally. It created a considerable mess but in reality, it could be swept up in minutes. The smell was a different story and would take a bit of effort to remove.

He locked up, got on the Kawasaki and rode it a couple of streets away to the end of Middlesex Street where there were residential flats, got it on its stand and pulled one of the newly acquired black nylon covers over it. Between the industrial traffic and the residential traffic, he knew the bike could stay there for weeks, if need be, without attracting a second glance from anyone. Such was city life where people could go through their lives and not know who 90% of their neighbours were. Not that that mattered. The bike wouldn't be there for weeks. It would be away in less than 24 hours.

The other things from the unit were in the panniers and top box. There was nothing of any real value. The small radio; the kettle; the mug; the Lee Childs novel.

He had no doubt the Russians would break into the place. That would mean the inevitable involvement of the police when the unit owners discovered the break-in. The details the owners held for Benny were fictitious and would be a dead end for the police or anyone else involved, but he knew he had slept on the sofa many times and the idea of the rubbish from the bin bag was to contaminate any DNA that he might have left behind. Of course, a break-in to the unit with some rubbish scattered around would never register on the radar of the Specialist Crimes Division, but as soon as anyone mentioned Black Kawasaki, he knew the police would put two and two together and dispatching a forensic unit was not inconceivable.

With all manner of detritus spilt from the bag, from food to waste packaging to used paper hankies and everything else in between, it would be almost impossible for forensics to collect anything meaningful. It would be like a well-used petri dish

Benny hurried back over the road to the BMW, got on it and left Kinning Park for the last time. He would contact Jack and arrange for someone who could be relied on to collect the Kawasaki and have it destroyed.

29

Benny rode the BMW back towards his home but parked up on the other side of the River Kelvin in the same spot that he had parked before. As it was at a junction between three different roads, it was busy with parked cars and as such, was anonymous. He got his things out of the panniers and top box and placed his helmet and gloves in before locking them and pulling the second nylon cover over and securing it in place. He cut down through the park, crossed the bridge and emerged in his own street a few minutes later.

After a quick ascent to the flat, he locked the door behind him and called Jack. He arranged to meet him at the café for some breakfast in the morning. It would be the first he had seen him since his return from Surrey.

He organised the things he had to, had a light meal and went to bed, setting his alarm for 02.15 am.

Despite everything that had gone on, sleep came easily enough, and he didn't stir until the alarm went off. A quick look out the window told him it was dry but cold. As long as there was no rain, ice or snow, he was okay.

Within thirty minutes, he was riding along Great Western Road towards the M8 motorway. Another twenty minutes saw him parking his bike in a railway access track that ran parallel to one of the two walkways into Mount Vernon station. He quickly changed into his black lycra and fastened the backpack on. Having put on the night vision head gear, he made his way through the trees into the garden of the nearest house. The garden was substantial and provided plenty of cover. The target house where he had seen the red Ford turn in, was three houses away. He got there easily enough and without incident. There were no dogs and as he'd stayed tight to the boundaries, away from open ground, there were no security lights.

When he got to the house, he saw the car in the drive. This was what he had come for. Having seen the Russians at the back of the Freeman Building with assault rifles slung over their shoulders, then having heard of the murders during their turf war with the Asians, he had no intention of going anywhere near the house.

He produced a pen and sheet of paper that he had brought with him and wrote down two numbers. One was the car registration number. He had anticipated that the number plate may have been changed for a ringer like he did with his bikes, so he was looking for a second number. He noticed that the car had a sizeable split through the plastic moulding in the area between the driver's side front fog light, the grille and the main headlight unit. It had clearly been hit with some force.

The other number he was looking for was the Vehicle Identification Number – the VIN – and he was hoping it hadn't been removed. He looked inside the windscreen in the bottom left-hand corner.

It was still there.

After writing it down, he checked it two more times. At 17 characters long made up of numbers and capital letters, he knew he could easily make a mistake, especially in the dark.

Satisfied he had what he came for he was turning to leave when a movement caught his eye. He froze, not moving a muscle. It was involuntary but he held his breath. Moving only his eyes in the direction of the movement, he breathed a sigh of relief when he saw, of all things, a fox, less than ten feet to his left. It momentarily flashed through his mind that there would be the makings of a joke in there somewhere.

"Did you hear the one about the two foxes in a garden in Glasgow at four o'clock in the morning…."

As Benny turned to move back through the gardens, the startled fox shot off into the undergrowth.

He was soon back at the bike, in his leathers and riding out of the track on to the main road. It was one of his favourite times of the day, and he always appreciated riding on the empty roads. More so in the summer months, but even in the Autumn, it was a pleasure as long as it was dry. He took a different route back home for no reason other than to enjoy the ride.

In less than an hour, the bike was secured back under the cover, and he was back in his bed.

As with previous visits, he was at the café five or ten minutes before his friend. When Jack arrived, they soon got caught up and enjoyed a big breakfast. Eventually they got down to the subject of the Kawasaki parked up in Kinning Park. Benny gave Jack the keys and its location. Jack said he knew the ideal person who would sort it, discreetly.

"He has a 7.5 tonne box lorry with a tail-lift. I trust him completely Benny, but I'll go with him in case he needs a hand. It can go to the scrap yard and through the crusher or it can get stripped down into spare parts. It's entirely up to you but either way, there will be nothing recognisable left by tonight."

"I know it's a waste, but I'd be happier if it went through the crusher Jack. That way there's finality. No loose ends."

"That's what will happen, then. You're the boss."

They finished up with Jack saying he would call later to let Benny know everything was done, then Benny settled up the bill and they went off in different directions.

At 01.55 pm, He was in his usual place as he made his call to DS Mullen. Not entirely sure whether she would answer or not, he was pleased when she did. They made some small talk then Benny came to the point.

"I have something for you."

"That's good because I have something for you too. You can go first."

He asked if she had a pen to hand. She said she did.

"Okay, write this down." He gave her an address, a car description with the registration number, and a VIN for the same vehicle."

"So, who does this relate to?"

"That relates to Artem, the driver and the two heavies. It's the house the four of them are currently living in and the car they are currently driving. I don't know how long they will be there, but you might want to round them up sooner rather than later."

The immediate silence told him she was taken aback.

"How on earth do you get this stuff? No, in fact don't answer that. I don't want to know."

"You're quite right Detective. Plausible deniability. It's always safer. You said you had something for me?"

"I do. Two things actually. I just learned today that Mr Omelchenko was arrested trying to board a British Airways flight from Glasgow International bound for Chicago, USA via London. I spoke with my boss and as far as we can determine, he and his family were ultimately heading for Alaska. Apparently, it has one of the world's biggest concentrations of Russians outside Ukraine and Kazakhstan. That is a major result. I'm sad to say I am less enthusiastic about the other piece of news. John Munro, the stepfather of one of the four kidnapped children, is in intensive care. He was the victim of a hit and run and is undergoing surgery as we speak. The doctors say its touch and go and there are no certainties, but they're quietly optimistic he'll come through it. We're not clear at this stage if it's directly linked to the case but we're not ruling it out. He was the only person who wasn't prepared to pay the ransom demand and he contacted us. That's what started the whole investigation."

"Jesus." It was actually a thought, but the word came out loud.

"What? What is it?"

"The hit and run. The car that those details I just gave you came from had a big split on the front driver's side. I assumed something had hit it with a lot of force. Maybe it's the other way about and the car hit something. Or someone."

"Listen John, I need to go and deal with this information right now. Have your phone on later and I'll call you at 06.00 pm with an update."

She was gone before Benny realised it. He was deep in his thoughts with this latest information she had just given him. Omelchenko being arrested was a big step forward.

If DS Mullen and her people could round up Artem and his crew, the worst of Benny's problems would be behind him. He was no longer concerned about the storage unit. If they broke into the place, which he assumed they would have by now, they couldn't know if he had used it or not. There was nothing of any value left in it. Certainly nothing that could point to him. If things went to plan with the police, today could see the end of the whole affair.

By 06.15 pm, only four hours later, this is what Benny Fox knew.

As yet, things had not gone to plan. DS Mullen had just confirmed to him that the property in Mount Vernon was now under surveillance but as yet, the remaining four Russians were still at large. The surveillance operation was under the operational command of a senior Specialist Crime officer named Jim Murdoch. DCI Murdoch confirmed that Specialist Firearms Officers were on standby awaiting instruction.

The Ford Kuga was identified as being registered to a Haulage, Freight and Courier business on the Air Link Industrial Estate, out by the airport. As far as Police Scotland could determine, it was another legitimate business owned by Yegor Omelchenko. Early interviews with bona fide employees confirmed that he and the other four Russians who were still at large had been in and out of the place on a regular basis over the last week.

The car registration number had been entered into the system and would be flagged up if it passed through any of the ANPR – Automatic Number Plate Recognition – cameras operated by Traffic Scotland.

She said the hospital confirmed John Munro's condition had improved slightly by this afternoon. He was still a million miles away from being okay, but he was moving in the right direction.

Jack had called to say the Kawasaki had been dealt with and it was going to cost Benny £900 for that. "I stayed right to the end to make absolutely sure it was done. It's £400 for the guy with the truck and £500 for the two Irishmen that own the scrap yard," said Jack.

Benny thought it was more than reasonable for the discretion and the tying off of one more thing. Something else he could put out of his mind.

He continued to boot up his burner at 02.00 pm daily, but for the next three days there was nothing. On the fourth day, his phone rang.

"We got them, John."

DS Mullen didn't have to elaborate. Benny knew exactly who 'they' were, and a feeling of relief washed over him.

She carried on, "They never did return to Mount Vernon. Maybe they knew about the surveillance but then, I think they would have ditched the car if they knew. The car - that's how we got them. They came up on an ANPR camera at Baillieston Interchange. They had enough sense to change the number plates for ringers, but we had anticipated that and had the foresight to load every number for that make, model and colour on to the system. After an unmarked car from Road Policing had caught up to them, following unobserved, it was easy to coordinate, and they were all eventually arrested without any trouble. An initial search of the vehicle revealed a small but significant arsenal of weapons and ammunition. The people at Gartcosh are going over the car as we speak, paying close attention to the front offside damage and the weapons are with a ballistics team. We're confident we will find a match to other crimes. It looks like they were still driving around as a strategic four-man unit carrying out Yegor Omelchenko's bidding, despite everyone else having been rounded up."

Benny thanked her for letting him know and ended the call.

Life can be cruel and can swing from high to low in a heartbeat. In Benny's case it was more than a heartbeat. It was just over four hours. After the news he had received from DS Mullen, he left his burner phone intact. He saw no reason to dismantle it. It rang at 6.23 pm, and he knew it could only be one person.

"DS Mullen, this is unexpected. Is everything okay?" He knew before he asked, that everything wasn't okay.

"I'm sorry John but I've just learned that the GEOAmey vehicle moving the four Russians has been in a crash and one of them has escaped. What I know so far is that they were being transported between police custody suites and the vehicle they were in, was in a collision with a Scania concrete mixer truck. Road policing is still working on whether the crash was deliberate or not, but early indications are that it wasn't planned and was just a crash. The wrong place at the wrong time. The Scania hit them full-on, on the driver's side and the transport vehicle ended up on its side with a buckled chassis and one of the back doors twisted open. Not wide, but wide enough to squeeze through. Two of the escort personnel were able to secure the vehicle but only after the Russian was gone. The others have been taken to the hospital to check on their condition as a precaution, but they are all in handcuffs. There is also a line of enquiry into why there wasn't a police escort with the vehicle, given their profile. I can't imagine you being at any significant risk from this, but I wanted to let you know. I'll call again as and when I have anything else that I think you should know."

Benny thanked her and ended the call. Like the detective, he didn't think he was in any immediate danger but at the same time, he couldn't be entirely sure he wasn't. He reckoned there was no way the Russian could know who he was and right now he had far more important things on his own mind, like evading capture and staying out of prison. Knowing there was nothing he could do but hope the police would catch him sooner rather than later, he thought about getting changed and going for a long run later, to clear his head. Sitting around dwelling on things would achieve nothing.

In the space of 35 minutes, his life was about to take a turn for the second time. There was a knock at his door which in itself, was very unusual. It was a buzzer entry at street level, and he almost never got visitors. As Benny stepped forward to the peephole and looked through, he instantly recognised the face of the man standing on the other side of the door. For a split second, he was rooted to the spot and didn't know what to do.

It was only when the door knocked a second time, he was brought back into the moment. He didn't feel there was any threat from the man on the other side of the door. He just couldn't understand what he was doing here. He would find out soon enough. He undid the chain, and the security bolt and opened the door.

"Hello John, or should I say Benny?"

"Mr Stack, this is very unexpected. Please, come in. Benny let Donald Stack in, closed the door and put the chain back on. He didn't engage the bolt.

Taking a seat, they sat opposite each other. Benny spoke first. "I must say, seeing you at the door knocked me for six. If I may, how did you find me? Not so much my address, but how did you find me?"

"With a bit of difficulty to be honest, but in the end when you have the telecoms technology that a firm like mine has, no-one can get completely off-grid unless they're prepared to leave civilisation behind. With what I can only assume was removing and replacing batteries and SIM cards on a continual basis, you were a lot harder to find than most. Initially I obtained details of the key police officers in the enquiry. I had someone who works for me, whom I trust implicitly, gather their phone details and had all of their phone traffic monitored. Calls and texts. Everything in and out. One of the officers, a Detective Sergeant Mullen received a text from an unknown number asking her to call him using a second phone. The message was from a 'JJ'. She had been in my home and was asking about a John Johnstone as part of her enquiries. It wasn't much of a leap from there, and what I already knew, to make the connections. I now had a number for JJ. For you. Within minutes it was called from a second number which I now know to be the Detective Sergeant's, and I've monitored both phones ever since."

The night he dropped Peter Mann off at the police Gateway building. Despite all of his precautions, that was all it took. One lapse in judgement.

As if reading his mind Donald Stack said, "Don't misunderstand me. At least half a dozen different laws were broken in doing what I did, and without the technology I have, this would be incredibly difficult for anyone else to do. After that, there was a bit of 'round the houses'. Another number you reached out to from that phone was a 'Jack Buchanan', who called you on what I now know was your personal phone. After that, getting your address was easy. As for getting to your front door, one of your neighbours held the downstairs door open to let me in as she was going out. I have a trusting face."

"That explains how you found me. What I don't understand, is why? Why would you go to the trouble of sourcing the communications between the police officers in the investigation?"

Donald Stack seemed to ponder this for a few moments then asked, "Are you a family man Benny?" Rather than looking at Benny, he seemed to be looking at something only he could see on Benny's floor, and simply voicing his thoughts rather than speaking to him specifically.

Before Benny had a chance to answer, Donald kept speaking. "I believe you are. I thought long and hard about the trouble you had gone to when you lifted my son and those other children out of that place and travelled the distance that you did, through those streets. Kyle told me you carried that little girl the whole way. I thought of the gesture when you blew her a kiss just before I drove off. I thought of how you put yourself in harm's way without any real thought for your own well-being. That was compassion on a level that could only come from someone who is a father."

Benny wasn't quite following the point he was making but said nothing and let him continue.

He looked at Benny and said, "I'm asking if you're a father but it's rhetorical really. What I'm saying is, your love knows no bounds when it comes to your children. If you are a father, then I know you'll know that. I was trying to make my peace with the fact that I hadn't done enough to keep these people from coming into our home. That was bad. The fact they lifted Kyle right out of his bed while I slept. That was worse. It would take time, but I would get past it. Then Kyle told me how one of these men hit him so hard, he wet himself. He's eight years old Benny and he told me the pain was worse than anything he has ever experienced in his life – but it wasn't as bad as wetting himself. He said he couldn't stop crying. That's something I'll never get past."

Benny was sure he could see the other man's eyes glistening as he spoke.

"I decided right there and then, I will find this man, and I will kill him."

Benny knew he wasn't speaking figuratively. He said, "That's understandable, and yes, I am a father, and I know exactly what you're talking about. So, what brought you here?"

I know you're only half an hour off the phone with DS Mullen and she told you one of them has escaped while being transported. What she didn't tell you was, it was the mongrel bastard that lifted his hand to my son. She couldn't tell you because she doesn't know that. No one does, except us. I'm still monitoring calls and I was in my office here in the city when she called you."

"So, what do you want with me? Is it something I can help you with? I will of course help in any way I can."

Benny knew his own problems would be solved if the police caught the Russian first but if they didn't, his problems would still be solved if Donald Stack caught him before them. That aside, he thought of the children and knew he would help, regardless of his own situation.

"Thank you, Benny. I appreciate that more than you'll know. These Russians are well connected across this city, but they're not any more connected than I am. There isn't much I don't know about them already. From Mr Omelchenko right down through his stinking organisation. Most people will give up whatever you need, for money. It's amazing how much more they will give up for revenge. This specific handful of Russians have crossed many people over the years and those people have been waiting for the chance to get their own back. It turns out the three people who took my son were a driver and two others. I have no interest in the driver. One of the other two took Kyle's slippers from his bedroom and put them on his feet. So long as he goes to prison, I have no interest in him either. It's the third man. Pavlo Volkova. He hurt my boy and I am very much interested in him. It turns out he is the one who escaped today and that's the reason I am here. I need to know where he would be most likely to go, and I hoped you might be able to shed some light on that given the dealings you have had with these people."

Nothing immediately sprang to mind, and Benny would need to give it some thought. Almost as an aside he asked, "The prison transport van. Was that you?"

"No."

After asking Donald if he wanted a tea or coffee, he went to the kitchen and put the kettle on. By the time he had sorted two cups and brought them back to the living room, he had an idea. Given what Donald Stack had told him about having all of his communications, there was no point in trying to be subtle. He lifted his own phone and called Jack.

"Benny, how are you?"

"I'm fine Jack, thanks. I was wondering if you could do me a favour."

"Of course. Anything. What is it?"

"Could you contact Peter Mann for me on the quiet and ask him something without going into any detail? Ask him if his spotlight into the Russians threw up anywhere that one of them could go to ground if they were stuck. Somewhere that the police were unlikely to know about."

"Sure, I will. Give me ten minutes and I'll call you back." It took less than five minutes and Benny's phone rang.

"If you have a pen handy, I'll give you an address. It's a house in Newton Mearns and belongs to a lady and her husband who were friends with a lot of people in the Russian Cultural Centre. According to Peter, it's a tight knit community, and they would have people from Glasgow and Edinburgh around in a social context on a fairly regular basis. He reckons they wouldn't necessarily know about the criminal activity, but it might be a good place to start."

Benny gave the address to Donald Stack and asked if he wanted him to come with him.

"No thank you Benny. You've been more than helpful and again, I'm in your debt. As regards the transcripts of calls and messages etc, be rest assured these will all be destroyed and there will be no trace."

As Donald got up to leave, Benny said he would keep his eyes and ears open and if he got any new information, he would get in touch with Donald. Donald nodded, thanked him again, shook hands and left.

Benny only ever had one more dealing with Donald Stack. The Newton Mearns lead must have worked out okay. He switched on the burner phone two days later and there was a text message from an unknown number. It simply read "The mongrel has been put down and is no more. Take care."

30

Benny's life got back to some semblance of normal as Autumn moved towards Winter. It was never going to be like flicking an on/off switch, but as the ensuing days became weeks, each one came and went without incidence, and he no longer felt the need to be on his guard 24 hours a day.

He only spoke with DS Mullen one more time and she confirmed their enquiries into the search for the Man in Black were being scaled back, as the Russian case was being wound up. She said they never did find the escaped prisoner but reiterated that she was certain he was in no danger as the Russian had most likely found a way to flee the country. He knew he was in no danger, but not for the reasons she believed. He followed the outcome of the situation in the media as it unfolded. All the players who needed to be in jail, were. Despite his wealth, it couldn't keep Yegor Omelchenko out of prison. His other dealings were still being investigated in Europe as well as the UK, and it was reasonable to expect further charges to be brought against him as time went on. He wouldn't see outside for many years to come.

As for Benny Fox, he had already decided his days, or nights to be more specific, of burglary were finished. Destroying every trace of that life with Jack's help, from the phones to the clothing to the lycra to the BMW bike didn't trouble him. He wasn't that emotional. He never saw the money he had paid for it all as an issue either. There was one thing that did trouble him. It troubled him immensely, but he knew it was for the best. He put his flat up for sale. Not just his flat. His and his wife Emma's flat. He battled with that psychologically but in the end, it was his friend Jack that helped him decide.

"It's bricks and mortar Benny. That's all. It's not the place, it's what happened in the place that matters and that will never leave you. As long as there's Stacey and the boys, as long as there's you. Christ, as long as there's me, then it'll be in your mind and in your heart forever, and that's the only thing that matters." Benny knew he was right.

Telling his friend, he was leaving Scotland wasn't as difficult as it might otherwise have been. He explained he would be buying a place in the Mediterranean and Jack would have his very own room, where he was welcome any time, for as long as he liked. Knowing him as Jack did, he would have bet everything he had, that Benny would be back living in Glasgow by the following summer. He kept that thought to himself.

Benny had thought of the four children and hoped the parents, with the very best of intentions, wouldn't take an incredibly bad situation and make it worse. He knew without doubt that young children like these four were naturally resilient creatures and more often than not, they would move on through their lives without dwelling on the traumatic events of the past. It was when parents continually reminded children that they were now somehow different as a result of their experiences, that things got worse. He could easily envisage a lifetime of counselling and therapy ahead on that road, and desperately hoped it would never come to that.

By Christmas, he had sold up and moved out of Glasgow, going to stay with his family in Surrey for a while. By the middle of March he bought a big house on the coast in Majorca and spent more time there than he did in Surrey. Jack had already been three times in as many months. He said he was developing a taste for Rioja in place of Chateauneuf du Pape. The family went out to see him at least once a month in addition to school holidays, and he was back in the UK on a regular basis as his new business venture went from strength to strength. He juggled the plates between being Ian Walker and being Benny Fox.

Given the obvious and significant problems it posed living two lives, not least of which was keeping it from his daughter, he knew that in the fullness of time, Ian Walker would gradually disappear and there would only be Benny Fox. His friend in London, Colin Campbell, would see to that, creating Trusts and Offshore companies, transferring holdings and ownership. The more legitimate his businesses became, the easier the transition was becoming.

It was a normal weekday morning at the villa. Mariana and her son Miguel had turned up at their usual time. Benny employed them both. Mariana took care of the house and Miguel sorted the garden, the pool and did any heavy lifting, not that there was ever much of that. As employers went, Benny was one of the best. He even gave them keys for the Land Rover Defender 90 SWB to come and go as they pleased. In the beginning Mariana had insisted they take the bus. Benny had insisted she let Miguel drive and take the car. There was a second car in case he needed to get around. And a motorbike. It had panniers and a top box but the only things that went in them was fresh produce, bread and seafood from the market. Lycra unitards, balaclava masks and Night Vision Goggles were nowhere to be seen.

As they were busying themselves with their work, a taxi pulled into the drive. It was Senor Jack whom they both knew well by now. He hadn't told Benny he was coming, and it would be a pleasant surprise. He had picked up steak sausage, 'tattie' scones, black pudding, and sliced haggis from Rodger Butchers on Byrcs Road and brought them with him. He knew Benny always ate healthy, but he wasn't averse to a taste of home from time to time. From the villa you could see all the way along the beach. Mariana asked Jack to sit outside by the pool and she brought him chilled fresh squeezed orange juice and coffee. She asked him to watch for Senor Benny coming back from his run and let her know so she could put the grill on for their breakfast. She took one look at the black pudding and the haggis and shook her head.

When he got to the house Benny was delighted to see Jack. He gave him a big hug despite being drenched with sweat and in dire need of a shower. Jack didn't seem to mind. As he was going through the house to get cleaned up, Benny could smell the breakfast cooking and knew exactly where it had come from. After breakfast and some catch-up chit-chat, Jack got changed into his swimming shorts and headed for the pool. Still sitting under the parasol, Benny picked up the Herald newspaper that Jack had brought with him. As he browsed the pages, a story caught his eye about a Detective 'Inspector' Jenny Mullen.

He thought to himself, "So, you got promoted Detective Sergeant. Good for you."

Leafing through the rest of the paper it differed from other times and took on a strange dynamic. As he read the words in each of the articles, he didn't just see the images in his mind as he normally would. This time they seemed to evoke familiar smells too. It felt incredibly powerful to him. Reading a piece about the next generation of 'Green' buses for the city, he was drawn back to the smell of diesel from the older ones. Even further back to the Corporation Daimler double deckers of his childhood. Another piece made him think of the smell of the brewery that used to permeate most of the city at certain times. Then there was an article about the Necropolis and the scents of grass and greenery came to mind. Freshly cut grass. These conjured images of the city and other smells started coming in waves. The subway; The open fire in the Chip; Restaurants and food outlets; The butchers; Bernard Corrigan's fish market behind The Scotia Bar on Stockwell Street.

The nostalgic trip down memory lane was interrupted by Jack. "Are you alright there, fella? You look like you are miles away."

"I was actually. I was just thinking about home and wondering if maybe I should buy a wee flat there. Nothing fancy, just somewhere to come back to every now and then."

As Jack pushed himself away from the pool's edge to swim to the other end, he beamed a huge smile and said, "Not even the summer yet. I can read you like a book Mr Fox."

ACKNOWLEDGEMENTS

I'd like to thank the following people and extend my appreciation for their input, suggestions and support in the writing and production of Right Place, Wrong Time.

My daughter Karyn. As always, your honest feedback and suggestions ensured I didn't stray too far off course.

Scott Easton. For your expertise in all things motorbike.

Colin Hyslop Photography – @ColinHyslopPhotography. The Glasgow 'night-time' imagery on the cover provides a real visual perception of what is going on inside the book. Thanks Colin.

Sharon Boult. For your encouragement and input from the very beginning, right throught to the book title. Your continuous support means the world.

Danny at Farrell Electrical for your knowledge and experience in the technicalities of domestic electrical circuits. This allowed me to create the perfect escape for Benny Fox.

Thanks to Alexa Whitten at The Book Refinery Ltd for the continued support and guidance. It's been a pleasure Alexa and I look forward to working with you again soon.

ABOUT THE AUTHOR

Tom Ward has been an avid reader since he was a teenager. His favourite books were always Crime Fiction / Thrillers, although it wasn't constrained to that genre. Supernatural fiction included Stephen King, Dean Koontz and James Herbert. He was content with anything that fired up the imagination.

Born and raised in Hamilton, he moved to Falkirk more than thirty years ago where he has lived ever since. Having spent almost thirty-five years working in Financial Services, writing started as a hobby a few years ago, and was a welcome distraction from day-to-day life. The more he wrote, the more focussed and absorbed he became and what began as a hobby, was now very much a part of weekends, evenings and holidays. That time and effort has been rewarded with two novels now published, *Easy Money* and *Right Place Wrong Time*, with a third novel under way.

ALSO BY TOM WARD

EASY MONEY

It began with a witnessed transaction on an isolated country road. It's 5.00 am, and as far as he is concerned, Joe Russell has the world to himself. There isn't another living soul for miles.

Except there is.

It's a blind drop drugs exchange. £1.2 million for 64 kilos of street-grade cut heroin that's destined to spectacularly fall apart. He steals all of it.

A series of seemingly unrelated stories that converge in one explosive finale. From Money Laundering to drug trafficking between Helmand province and the streets of Edinburgh. From a cold, callous and calculating thug called Maxi Hall, to the biggest surveillance operation in the history of Police Scotland. It will change people's lives forever in ways they couldn't imagine in their wildest dreams… or their worst nightmares.

BOOK 3 [TO BE TITLED]

A metal box buried behind a headstone in a graveyard in Central Scotland over twenty years ago.

Another metal box dug up from an allotment in South Wales only yesterday.

Over 400 miles apart, seemingly unrelated, but when they were opened, the contents of each box was identical. Contents that appeared random, unconnected and meant nothing to anyone.

But they weren't.

They weren't random. They weren't unconnected and they very much meant something to one man. The man who had put them there and knew exactly what the connection between them was.

A story that will span the last twenty years. A time during which fame and fortune flourished for a chosen few. A time when some celebrities rose from obscurity to became household names. A time that saw political careers rise from lowly positions to the ultimate seats of power in Westminster.

One thing connected them all. One man held the key and was about to let his pet psychopath off the leash.